The ramshackle River Queen Hotel is home to vagabonds, gamblers, and heathens—and now, to new widow Rose Peterson. The rundown Gold Rush establishment is the only thing her late husband, Emmet, left her. Despite its raucous saloon and ladies of the evening, Rose can see the hotel's potential. Her late husband's family claim that sheltered Rose isn't capable of running the Sacramento inn herself. But she is determined to make a new life for herself and her young daughter, even if it means flying in the face of custom and propriety. She feels as if she hasn't a friend in the world.

Except, perhaps, one. Decatur "Deke" Fleming, a tall, lanky Australian who once served as Emmet's farmhand. Pride prevents Deke from revealing his moneyed past; conscience keeps him from confessing his feelings for the still grieving widow. But when Rose is tempted by wealthy civic leader and hotel owner Mason Talbot, Deke may be the only person who can save her—and the one man capable of reviving her bruised and battered heart . . .

Visit us at www.kensingtonbooks.com

Books by Shirley Kennedy

Women of the West Series
Wagon Train Cinderella
Wagon Train Sisters
Gold Rush Bride

In Old California Series
River Queen Rose

River Queen Rose

In Old California

Shirley Kennedy

LYRICAL PRESS
Kensington Publishing Corp.
www.kensingtonbooks.com

Lyrical Press books are published by
Kensington Publishing Corp. 119 West 40th Street New York, NY 10018

First Electronic Edition: December 2017
eISBN-13: 978-1-5161-0438-3
eISBN-10: 1-5161-0438-2

First Print Edition: MDecember 2017
ISBN-13: 978-1-5161-0441-3
ISBN-10: 1-5161-0441-2

Printed in the United States of America

I dedicate this book to my daughter, Lindy, who has always been "a mother's delight" in every possible way.

Foreword

Although this book is a work of fiction, many of the incidents are based on fact. During the Gold Rush, there really was an area along Sacramento's waterfront where rowdy, rip-roaring saloons never closed. Where fortunes could be made or lost over the turn of a card. Where steamboats occasionally exploded and monstrous floods covered the entire Sacramento valley.

Chapter 1

In the foothills of the Sierra Nevada Mountains, September, 1854

Rose Peterson shivered in her underwear as she stood in the freezing cold creek. She flinched as she splashed cold water on herself. She'd gone days without a bath and gladly endured the shock of it just to get clean. She turned to her sister-in-law who stood in her chemise beside her. "Just one more day. Think of it! One more day and we'll be there."

Drucilla returned her familiar mocking smile. "Just one more day? Thanks for telling me, Rose. I hadn't noticed."

"I'll wager you hadn't." Rose accompanied her words with a scoop of creek water splashed over her sister-in-law's head.

Drucilla splashed her back. "Are you excited about seeing Emmet again?"

"Of course I am." Rose hoped she sounded convincing. Strange, how she didn't feel the least excited, even though she hadn't seen her husband for over two years. She wasn't the only wife who'd been deserted when word of the Gold Rush reached Illinois. Like thousands of others, Emmet rushed to California. Unlike most of the thousands, after finding a little gold, he concluded there were other ways to make money without breaking his back in a freezing cold stream. He bought a hotel in Sacramento and a small farm outside of town. Everyone rejoiced when he finally sent a letter asking his family to join him.

"I'm clean enough," Drucilla announced. "Let's get out of this freezing water."

Rose readily agreed. She was getting goose bumps from the cold. She ran a hand over her thick, golden-bronze hair that hung halfway to her waist. What a relief to have it clean again. She laughed to herself. Before they left Illinois, she'd taken great pride in her appearance. Perhaps that pride involved a bit of vanity, but when she looked in her mirror, she couldn't help but be pleased at her tall, slim figure, her even-featured face that everyone said was pretty, and her long, thick hair that she loved to wear hanging loose or sometimes swept in a bun atop her head. Those days were long gone. After spending five miserable months in a wagon train with her in-laws, she didn't much care what she looked like, nor did anyone else. Her main interest now was keeping her daughter safe and staying alive.

As they climbed from the water, Drucilla called, "Just think, the next time I take a bath, it will be in a real tub with real hot water."

"I can't even imagine it." Her teeth chattering, Rose quickly pulled her dress over her head. There were lots of things she couldn't imagine. Like sleeping in a real bed. Like eating at a real table.

Like being a wife to Emmet again.

Since they were married, they'd lived with his family, so she'd never had to worry about cooking his meals or washing his clothes. Coralee, his mother, did all that. Thin and wiry, a never-stopping bundle of energy, she treated her daughter-in-law as nothing more than a willing helper. The one area that didn't belong to Coralee was the bedroom. On the long trek west, Rose hardly gave it a thought, but now, with their destination less than a day away, she was remembering those many less-than-thrilling nights when Emmet insisted they "make love." He misspoke. Love had little to do with his near nightly performance: a quick kiss—climb on—a few hard-breathing grunts—final big grunt—roll off, and it was over. How very tiresome. In fact, Emmet and his wooden personality were tiresome. He was a good husband in many ways, but not in the bedroom, not like…

Anthony. Like a sinful pleasure, thoughts of that long-ago night crept uninvited into her head. She quelled them quickly, as she always did, telling herself it never happened, that she could never have behaved in such a wanton, disgraceful manner.

The truth was, she'd enjoyed these last two years when she slept alone and didn't have to deal with Emmet's attentions, but she'd better face the fact that those enjoyable days were nearly over. She recognized her wifely duties and would never dream of complaining. After all, Emmet wasn't a bad man, a bit quick-tempered, perhaps, but in all other ways, he'd been kind to her. He was surely a good provider, and when Lucy came along, he got tears in his eyes when he saw his new daughter for the first time. Indeed, he couldn't have been a better, more loving father. So, of course, she'd be glad to see him again. Not thrilled, maybe, but happy enough, and really, what more could she expect in life than the role Fate had assigned her as a wife and mother?

Or so she kept telling herself.

Sometimes a hunger rose from deep within her for something more in her life. The trouble was, she didn't know what. At the age of twenty-six, she sometimes got the feeling that life was passing her by and what had she accomplished? Lucy, of course. Watching her little girl grow was an ongoing, joyful miracle, but couldn't she have something more?

Well, of course not. After all, she was a woman, so what more could she expect? She should count her blessings and forget such foolishness.

* * * *

The Petersons were part of a train of fifty-five wagons, now parked in a circle far down the western slope of the Sierra Nevada Mountains. Returning to the campsite, Rose sensed the excitement all around her. California! After months of grueling travel, they'd reached the Golden Land. Fortunes would be made. Life would be good in this sun-drenched state that brimmed with opportunities. She searched for Lucy. Of them all, her five-year-old daughter had fared the best on their wearisome journey. She never complained about the monotonous beans-bacon-and-biscuits diet. After a long day on the trail, when the adults moaned about sore muscles and aching feet, Lucy was running around with other children on the train, bright and happy with endless energy.

Rose spotted her daughter playing at the wagon next to her own. As she drew close, she sensed something different. Something, but what? Somehow her little girl with the bright eyes and long, blond curls didn't look the same. Oh, no, her hair! This morning, Rose had swept it back from Lucy's forehead and fastened it into two braids. Now it hung loose, and someone had cut low-hanging bangs so long they nearly touched her brows.

Lucy skipped up to her, blue eyes sparkling. "Mommy, how do you like my hair?"

"Why, I…I…"

"Grandma cut my bangs. She said I'll look my best when I see Daddy again."

The nerve! To conceal her rage, which surely must show on her face, Rose bent low, as if to closer inspect her daughter's new hairstyle. How dare Coralee cut it without even asking! That was a mother's job and nobody else's, not even a doting grandmother's. But too late now. Above all, she mustn't make Lucy feel bad. With an effort, she forced her lips into a smile and raised up. "You look very pretty, sweetheart. Daddy will think so, too."

As Lucy ran off, Rose took a deep breath to compose herself. This sort of thing had happened before, and she shouldn't have been surprised. No use complaining. Emmet always took his parents' side. She'd long since realized she wasn't first in his heart, not like a wife was supposed to be. Even when he sent the letter telling them to come, he'd addressed it to Ben and Coralee, not to her. She and Lucy were a mere mention at the bottom of the list. She admired his fierce loyalty to his family, but there were times when her resentment ran deep, especially the times when she pleaded for a home of their own, and he turned a deaf ear.

But she always tried to count her blessings. Thank goodness she got along well with the Petersons. Their trip west, spending five months cramped in two wagons, could have been a nightmare, but it wasn't. Ben and Coralee were strict but fair. They adored little Lucy, and she adored them. Thirty-year-old Drucilla, her sister-in-law, was the ongoing despair of her parents, but Rose got along with her just fine. Often they rode together, Rose on Star, her chestnut mare, and Drucilla on her beloved buckskin gelding, Arion, whom she'd named after a Greek god. As for Raymond, her strange brother-in-law, what could she say? He certainly wasn't her favorite, not with his silly jokes and childish behavior, but he had a generous heart and not a mean bone in his body.

When Rose led Lucy back to the wagon, they were met by a beaming Coralee who asked, "Doesn't she look darling in bangs?"

Rose forced a smile. "Yes, indeed, she looks adorable." No use complaining. Although Coralee had a heart of gold, she blundered through life with absolutely no conception of how her actions might affect others. At least she adored Lucy, her one and only grandchild. In her own mind, she was only being a good grandmother. The thought would never have occurred to her that she was wrongly invading a mother's territory. That settled it. Rose felt a new sense of purpose as she made up her mind. Ever since they were married, she'd pleaded with Emmet for her own home away from her in-laws. Now she'd demand it. She would not be a submissive daughter-in-law any longer. As soon as they reached Sacramento, she would inform him she wanted a home of her own. High time he cut the apron strings, and he'd better not say no.

* * * *

The next morning, in a high state of excitement, they packed up for the last day of their journey. As usual, Rose's father-in-law took complete charge of everything. A tall, broad-shouldered man with a full head of snow-white hair, Ben had such a domineering nature that as always, they scurried around to do his bidding. They started out in their usual fashion, Ben driving the first wagon, Coralee and Drucilla beside him. Raymond drove the second wagon, Rose and Lucy sharing the seat. As the train wound its way down the ever-more-gentle western slope, Rose gave thanks that tomorrow she wouldn't have to sit beside her brother-in-law all day, listening to his silly conversation and raucous, unnecessary laughter. Raymond might be twenty-eight years old, but he'd yet to find a purpose in life, although to hear him talk, you'd think he was on his way to becoming a millionaire. "Soon's we get there, I'm heading back up the hill," he'd just declared. "I'm going to find me some big gold nuggets and get richer than anyone."

"That's fine, Raymond." She'd long since learned the best way to handle her brother-in-law was to humor him. He always had big plans that went nowhere. He and his brother, Emmet, looked alike, both with a large build, but there the resemblance ended. Whereas Raymond was a fool with no ambition, hard-driving Emmet never had an idle day in his life. He took life far too seriously, but maybe the past two years had loosened him up a bit, at least she hoped so.

Besides all that, Lucy loved her father and could hardly wait to see him again.

By noon the train had left the last of the foothills behind and was rolling along the flat surface of the northern San Joaquin Valley. They began to pass farms where fields of vegetables and cotton lay ready for harvest. Finally they reached the outskirts of Sacramento, and the train stopped for the last time. Rose and her family said goodbye to their fellow travelers. From now on, they'd go their separate ways.

Rose's heart beat faster as they headed through town. Real streets! Real houses with front and back yards! Following Emmet's careful directions, the two wagons came to the edge of town and traveled two miles farther on a country road. They started looking for a small sign on a fence that said Peterson Farm. "There it is," Ben called. "Ahead to the right."

The two wagons turned off the road, down a long driveway that led to a large, two-story farmhouse with a wide front porch that wrapped around three sides. A large barn stood in the yard behind, along with a stable and corral, tank house, and what looked like a large chicken coop. As the two wagons pulled to a stop, Raymond let out a whoop, stood, and waved his hat. "Hey, Emmet! We're here!"

All smiles, everyone climbed from the wagons. Holding Lucy's hand, Rose looked toward the front door. Emmet would be coming out any second now, big smile on his face, delighted they'd finally arrived. "We're going to see Daddy?" Lucy asked.

Rose swept her up in her arms. "Yes, we're home, sweetheart. We won't have to live in a wagon anymore."

They waited. The front door remained closed. "Do you suppose he's not home?" Ben asked. He started up the porch steps. "Maybe he's sleeping."

Coralee followed him. "Emmet would never sleep in the middle of the day."

They had almost reached the front door when they heard someone calling. Two people came around the corner of the house. One was a tall man around fifty with a neat beard who looked like a farmer in his button-down shirt, soft, felt hat, and twill pants held up with suspenders. The other, a small, white-haired lady with a hunched-over walk, spectacles, and a deeply wrinkled face, could well be his mother, or maybe his grandmother. As they approached, the man called, "Are you the Petersons?"

Ben answered with a nod. "This is Emmet Peterson's farm, isn't it?"

Close up, Rose could see the man had a strange look on his face. He was not smiling as he extended his hand to Ben. "Hello, sir, I expect you're Emmet's father. I'm Tom Murphy, his neighbor from next door." He glanced toward his companion. "This is Dulcee Bidwell, my mother." He cast an affectionate glance her way. "She looks fragile, but you don't want to mess with her."

"Yes, I'm Ben Peterson." Ben shook his hand. "Pleased to meet you." Not one to mince words, he asked, "Where is Emmet?"

Tom Murphy's brows drew together in an agonized expression, as if he had something terrible to say and dreaded saying it. What was wrong? Rose got a sick feeling in her stomach, watching the man struggle for words.

Her father-in-law broke the heavy silence. "Out with it, sir. If you have something to say, then say it."

Dulcee Bidwell jabbed her son with an elbow. "Wait, Tom." She nodded toward Lucy and addressed Ben. "I believe I'll take the little girl inside. Do you mind?"

Ben shot an inquiring look at Rose. Sick at heart, she nodded. She was beginning to guess what Murphy was going to say.

They watched in silence as the old lady led Lucy into the house. When they were gone, Murphy gave a decisive nod, as if recognizing he had an unpleasant task to perform and no way out of it. His gaze swept over them, eyes full of sympathy. "I can't tell you how excited Emmet was, waiting for his family to arrive. That's all he talked about. But now? We were all shocked. Such a tragedy. I'm sure sorry to have to tell you this, but we buried him this morning."

* * * *

Afterward, Rose had only a vague memory of those terrible moments after they learned her husband was dead. Drucilla breaking into rare tears. Coralee's piercing scream and near collapse, and Ben and Raymond holding her up. Rose couldn't remember how she acted, other than she stood frozen in shock, staring in stunned disbelief.

Ben was the first to speak. "Tell us what happened."

"There's something you must see." Murphy turned, motioning them to follow. Along with the rest of her stricken family, Rose trailed him around the side of the porch where a row of tall Eucalyptus trees shaded the house. A grave lay under one of the trees. Plainly, it was newly dug with its mound of dirt on top, strewn with fresh bouquets of flowers. Rose drew close. On a small, roughly constructed cross at the head, someone had neatly printed, EMMET PETERSON.

In stunned silence, the family gathered around the grave as the neighbor continued to speak. "A fine man if ever there was one. If we'd known you were coming so soon, we would have waited, but we didn't know, so we held the service this morning. Quite a few came. Neighbors. People from town. Reverend Walters was in charge. You can rest assured, Emmet got as fine a sendoff as his friends could give him."

Ben's face had turned a sickly white. His arm around Coralee, who was quietly sobbing, he asked, "My God, what happened? Far as I know, my son was in good health."

Murphy shook his head. "He didn't get sick, Mr. Peterson. Health had nothing to do with it."

"Was it an accident?"

"No."

"Then...?" Ben could hardly get the words out. "You mean he was murdered?"

"Not exactly. You could say he was and he wasn't."

Through gritted teeth, Ben exploded, "For God's sake! Tell us what happened."

Murphy heaved a regretful sigh. "I wish it had been his health, a stroke maybe, or his heart. Or some kind of accident, but the truth is, Emmet was killed in a duel with a fellow named Mason Talbot. He's a big man in these parts. Owns a brewery as well as the Egyptian Hotel. He keeps a collection of paintings there and fancies himself an art connoisseur. The thing is, I reckon you can't call him a murderer, being as Emmet started the whole thing. He's the one who did the challenging."

Ben's jaw dropped open. "Emmet never held a sword in his hand in his life."

"Oh, it wasn't swords, Mr. Peterson. It was dueling pistols. I don't know if he ever held a gun in his hand either, but a bullet to the head is what killed him."

Chapter 2

My husband is dead. Rose kept repeating the words, but they had yet to sink in. Thank goodness, that nice lady had taken Lucy into the house so she hadn't witnessed the family's outpouring of grief when they heard the news. Of course her daughter must be told, but she'd find a way to break the news as gently as possible. The family didn't stay long at the grave. Coralee would have collapsed if Ben wasn't holding her up. Drucilla had turned white and looked as if she might faint at any moment. Both should be lying down. Being the men of the family, Ben and Raymond struggled to show a brave front, but clearly they, too, were shocked and torn with grief.

As they headed back to the house, Tom Murphy gave them some useful advice. "Emmet had a cook named Bridgett who already took off. You're going to need a new one. Then you've got the farm to think of. There's the chickens to take care of, stock to feed and the like, but at least the hired help is still here. Deke Fleming. Comes from Australia. He's crippled, so he can't do much, but he's a good man. Like as not, you'll find him in the barn."

Rose was about to follow her family into the house when she noticed the two wagons and their teams of oxen left neglected in the driveway. Ordinarily the men saw to the animals, but this wasn't an ordinary day, so at the moment, the poor beasts stood thirsty, hungry, and forgotten after long hours on the road. She wasn't sure she knew what to do, but one thing she did know—she couldn't let the animals suffer. "I'll be right in," she called. She grabbed the reins of one of the teams. Tears kept filling her eyes as she led the four oxen, still hitched to the wagon, toward the large barn in the back. Once she stumbled, so blinded with tears she hadn't seen where she was going. All right, no more crying; not now anyway. This chore had to be done right now so she could get back to Lucy. She couldn't unyoke the oxen by herself, or at least she'd never tried, but hadn't

Mr. Murphy mentioned the hired man from Australia? Surely he could help. When she reached the barn, she halted the team and was about to go inside when a man appeared in the doorway. Tall, lean, and sinewy, he had straight brown hair that nearly reached his shoulders. He was dressed in a workman's clothes. "Are you the hired man?" she called.

"That I am," he answered in a friendly voice. His face lit in recognition. "Blimey, you must be the family."

"We just arrived. We had no idea." More tears welled. With an effort, she forced them back. "Emmet told you we were coming?"

The man came closer, slowly because he was hobbling on crutches. "It was all he talked about. He could hardly wait."

He's crippled. She dropped her gaze. His right pant leg was split to the knee, a cast visible beneath. But staring was impolite. She quickly looked up. "I'm Rose Peterson, his wife. This is all so sudden, and I…" A lump rose in her throat and she couldn't go on.

"It was sudden, all right. I'm Decatur Fleming. Call me Deke." He regarded her with warm, grey eyes. "Looks like you got the bad news."

"Mr. Murphy just told us. I can't quite believe it yet."

"Of course you can't." His voice held an infinitely compassionate tone. "Everyone's shocked. Emmet Peterson was fair dinkum. Shouldn't have happened. Do you want to sit down? Can I get you some water?"

"No, no. I'm fine, thank you." Strange, the way he talked. *Fair dinkum?* What did that mean? She'd never heard an Australian accent before. It was thick, although she could easily understand him. He had a nice face, too craggy to be handsome, but somehow appealing with its generous mouth and square jaw. He must have been in the sun a lot, what with that bronzed skin and those tiny crinkles at the corners of his eyes. Age couldn't have caused them because he didn't appear to be past thirty or so. She gave Maggie, the nearest ox, a pat on the head. "There's this team and another in the front that need to be unhitched. I was hoping you could help me, but I didn't realize…" She glanced at his cast again. "I'll get my brother-in-law to help."

"I'll do it."

"Of course." She'd caught the quick glint of resentment in his eyes and realized her mistake. Men had their pride, and here she'd just insinuated he wasn't capable of helping her. "I'd appreciate it, Mr. Fleming…Deke." How he could lift those heavy yokes off the oxen while on crutches, she couldn't imagine, but she wouldn't argue.

His mouth curved into a crooked little grin. "Don't worry. Stand by. You can put them in the corral when I get them unhitched."

At least he wasn't so prideful he couldn't admit he needed a bit of help. She watched as he threw one crutch aside, hobbled over to the four oxen, and proceeded to lift the yokes off with little difficulty. Amazing what he could do while standing on one foot. Of course, his exceptional strength didn't hurt. She couldn't help noticing how the muscles in his arms rippled beneath his shirt sleeves when he lifted the yokes off the animals' necks. Soon as they were unyoked, she led each pair to the corral and penned them inside. She brought the second wagon around to the barn, and they did the same. At least the chore kept her busy for a while. Tending to the animals left her little time to think, but when all the oxen were penned, watered, and fed, thoughts of the horrible events of the day came rushing back. "I'd better go inside now." Her voice was shaking. There was nothing she could do about it, and she was beyond caring. "I thank you very much for your help, Deke."

"Any time, Mrs. Peterson. He was a good man. I'm going to miss him."

She hadn't thought about it until now, but he must also be grieving. And he must know more about what happened. "Mr. Murphy said my husband was killed in a duel. How is that possible?"

"That's a good question. Duels are illegal in this county." He frowned with concern. "It's a long story that maybe you'd best wait to hear 'til later."

He was right. At the moment, all she wanted was to get in the house and find Lucy before somebody else told her the news. "Yes, it can wait. Good day, Deke. Thanks for your help."

The shadow of a smile crossed his face. "If you need someone to talk to, I live in the barn"—he jerked a thumb over his shoulder—"any way I can help, I'd be glad to."

"I'll keep that in mind." Maybe she would. Deke might be just the hired help, but there was something about him—maybe his sincerity and the compassion in his eyes—that made her think she'd seek him out again.

* * * *

Deke Fleming watched after the retreating figure of Rose Peterson until she'd rounded the house and was out of sight. The poor woman had just lost her husband, yet she'd shown a lot of strength and hadn't fallen apart. She'd put the animals first—apparently no one else in the family had—and he admired that. He also admired the tall, straight way she carried herself and how her thick, shiny hair, sort of a gold-bronze color, hung loose around her shoulders.

He looked down at the cast on his leg and gave a cynical laugh. *Oh, sure, Deke, that wasn't pity you saw in her eyes. She's already crazy about you.*

He'd lived his whole life in the Australian outback. He hadn't known a lot of women, but those he had met were nothing quite like the newly widowed Mrs. Peterson.

* * * *

Rose found Raymond sitting on the porch, head in his hands. He looked up when he heard her coming up the steps, and she saw he'd been crying. "I can't believe it," he said in a bewildered whisper. "Emmet was… Emmet was…" He wrung his hands. "What are we going to do?"

She bent and took his hand. "Emmet was a wonderful brother to you, and you must always remember that." Indeed, her husband had always treated his younger brother with the greatest of kindness, despite all his faults. "I know how you feel. This is so hard for all of us. Was it only hours ago we'd started our last day on the road, everyone cheery and joyful? Now look at us." She patted Raymond on the shoulder. "We'll talk later. Right now, I must find Lucy."

Heartsick, she left Raymond and hurried inside. She glanced around. At another time, she would have been eager to see the whole house, but now all she wanted was to find her daughter. After a quick search, she found Lucy sitting at the kitchen table, a slice of bread covered with butter and jam in front of her. Tom Murphy's mother stood at the sink. "I hope you don't mind, Mrs. Peterson," she said in her raspy voice. "Lucy said she was hungry, so I fed her." She gave an indignant sniff. "Couldn't find much. Looks like Bridgett made off with all the food. I never liked that woman."

"Of course I don't mind. That was very kind of you." Rose stepped to the sink and spoke softly. "Does she know?"

The old lady shook her head. "Thought you'd want to tell her," she whispered back. "You'd better do it soon, though. She knows something's wrong." She flicked her gaze upward. "Emmet's ma is in a state, and his pa has got her lying down. The sister's lying down, too. I'll be going now."

"You don't have to leave, Mrs. Bidwell."

"Call me Dulcee. Everyone does. It's best I go. If you need to talk to someone, I'm right next door, the house with the big red barn." Her faded eyes filled not only with compassion but keen understanding. "I reckon sooner or later, you'll need someone to talk to, so come over any time. I fix a fine cup of tea, if I do say so."

After she left, Rose sat at the table, across from Lucy. Dulcee was right. The uneasy expression on her daughter's face signaled her sense that something was wrong. Rose hunted for the right words, but whatever they were, they eluded her. Best to tell her straight out and not worry about perfection. "I have something very sad to tell you, sweetheart."

"Is it about Daddy?"

"Yes. You see…" Her voice caught, but she must control it. This was no time to break down. "You won't be seeing Daddy for a while. He's in heaven now."

"You mean he's dead?" A tear slid down her little girl's cheek.

"Yes, he's dead, and I'm so sorry. This is a terrible time for all of us, but you must be strong. I must be strong." She couldn't help it. Tears blinded her eyes and choked her voice.

Without another word, Lucy slid from her chair, came around the table, and put her arms around her. "We'll be all right, Mommy. Please, you shouldn't cry. It doesn't do any good to cry."

Rose hugged her tight. What a brave little girl, and she was right. She didn't need the wisdom of a five-year-old to tell her tears were useless. She didn't know what sorrows the future held, but from this moment on, she was done with them.

For the rest of the day, Rose found plenty to do. First off, she found a tiny bedroom off the kitchen that no doubt had belonged to Bridgett, the infamous cook. She put Lucy down for her nap on the single bed. That was only temporary. Later they'd decide which upstairs bedroom would be hers and Lucy's. Now was her chance to see the house. Downstairs, she walked from the kitchen into the dining room and then the parlor. How spacious the rooms were, and nicely furnished, too. On the second floor, everyone was lying down. Tiptoeing, she found three large bedrooms and what looked like a sun room. How sad Emmet wasn't here to see how impressed she was. If all had gone as expected, she'd be celebrating right now, reunited with her husband, joyful that this beautiful home far exceeded her expectations. But she had no time to dwell on what might have been. Tom Murphy had warned about the cook running off. Ordinarily, that wouldn't have mattered because Coralee did the cooking and was always in complete control of the kitchen. Not today, though. Her mother-in-law was in no shape to cook and neither, it appeared, was Drucilla. Despite their grief, they'd all still be hungry.

She would cook the dinner herself. Back in the kitchen, she searched the cupboards and icebox and found them practically bare. While she was mulling over what she could possibly serve, her sister-in-law appeared.

Ordinarily, she looked the picture of health, but now her pale cheeks reflected her grief. "Drucilla, you should be lying down."

"Nonsense. I might as well grieve standing up as lying down. I'll help with dinner."

Rose knew better than to argue. To say Drucilla had a mind of her own was an understatement. To say she was the despair of her mother was also an understatement. Nearly six feet tall, she'd reached the age of thirty with nary a suitor in sight. As Coralee had pointed out perhaps a million times, she possessed a pretty face and nice figure, and if she "applied herself," she would surely find a suitable husband despite her height.

"Suitable husband, my foot," would come her daughter's reply. "I've better things to do with my time than sit around simpering over some vapid fool who's shorter than I am."

Rose understood. Indeed, her sister-in-law was not one ever to sit around. An avid reader, she devoured books on all subjects, not only books of fiction, but scholarly tomes on mathematics, history, and the classics. She spoke several languages fluently, especially French, which she spoke like a native. The dream of her lifetime was to travel to France where she could study the famous chateaux of the Loire Valley. "An event not likely ever to happen," she would remark with a typical disdainful sniff.

Drucilla looked in the cupboards. "They're bare. What are we supposed to eat?"

A knock came at the back door. When Rose answered, she found Deke standing on the stoop. Despite the crutches, he was holding a bag of what looked like greens in one hand, a newly butchered chicken dangling from the other. "Please come in," she said.

He shook his head. "Bridgett ran off with everything she could get her hands on. I figured you couldn't give dinner a fair go without food in the cupboard."

"Why thank you, Deke. How very thoughtful." A *fair go*? Another strange term, but she found it rather charming.

Balancing on one crutch, he held up the bag. "Here's some string beans. Emmet had a garden back of the barn, so I just picked these." He switched his balance to the other crutch and held up the chicken. "It's fresh. Do you know how to clean it? Not meaning any disrespect, but there's some ladies who'd fair faint away before they plucked the first feather."

She smiled. "I've cleaned many a chicken, so no worries there." And so she had. All the time she'd lived with the Petersons, it was she who was assigned the thankless task of plucking and cleaning the chickens. Before that, she'd done the same. Her parents, both gone now, had owned the Birchwood Inn on the outskirts of Cairo, Illinois. Ever since she could remember, she'd helped with everything from making beds and scrubbing floors to working in the kitchen, and that included the task of cleaning whatever fowl was being served for dinner. She'd done it so often, she never thought twice. Some might think it was an onerous task, but to her it wasn't unpleasant at all. She took the string beans and chicken. "You're sure you won't come in?"

"No, but I'll be back with some milk for the little girl, soon's I milk the cow."

"But how can you do all that when you—?" *Uh-oh.* There went that glint of resentment in his eyes. Again, she'd said the wrong thing. "I didn't mean…"

He smiled. "Don't worry about it."

She watched as he hobbled off. At least his leg was in a cast, so maybe he wouldn't always be that way. Still, her heart went out to the poor man. She'd like to know how he broke it, but he obviously had his pride, so she'd better not ask.

* * * *

Hobbling back to the barn, Deke could feel her eyes drilling into his back. *Damn.* He'd seen some disagreeable sights in his life, but nothing worse than the pity in that woman's eyes. What a pathetic sight she must think he was. A near-helpless cripple. Half a man. Damn these crutches. Damn the boat that sank, and damn Mitch, whose life he'd saved. No, not right. Mitch was a fine fellow whose life deserved to be spared. Only Fate was to blame. Fickle Fate, that traitorous harlot he should never have trusted in the first place. So calm down. Go milk old Bessie, a cow after his own heart. No sympathy there. Every time he milked her, she turned her head and gave him a look that said she'd give him a good kick if she had the chance.

* * * *

That night, thanks to Deke, Rose was pleased with the way dinner turned out. Drucilla had found a few potatoes in the cupboard, so the fried chicken, fresh string beans, and mashed potatoes made up a real feast, especially good after the monotonous diet they'd endured for five months on the trail. The whole family gathered at the table in the dining room. Even Coralee had come down, more quiet than Rose had ever seen her, her strained face still white from shock. Raymond looked lost. Ben seemed greyer somehow. Before today, he'd always stood straight as a rail, but now he was walking with a slow step, his shoulders hunched over. At first the family ate in gloomy silence, but soon they began to speculate on what had happened to Emmet. He fought a duel? Unbelievable. Whoever heard of such a thing? And who was Mason Talbot, the man who had killed him? Ben clenched his jaw in righteous indignation. Tomorrow he would go into town. Talk to the sheriff. Find out why the man who killed his son hadn't been arrested. Toward the end of the meal, Ben stood up, pushed his chair back, and walked to the cook's room that opened directly off the kitchen, the room where Lucy had taken her nap. After a quick look inside, he gave a nod of satisfaction and came back to the table. "Here's what we'll do about the bedrooms," he announced. "Upstairs, Coralee and I will of course have the largest room. Raymond gets the middle, and Drucilla, you get the one on the end."

A numbness started down Rose's spine. "What about Lucy and me? Where are we going to sleep?"

The slightly annoyed look her father-in-law sent her clearly indicated she should already know. "In that room off the kitchen, of course. It's small but adequate."

Coralee spoke up. "That will work out perfectly since we won't be hiring another cook anytime soon. Think how handy this will be for you, Rose. You'll be working in the kitchen a lot, and this way you'll be real close."

The servant's room? Is that how she stood? What a slap in the face to be told she was the least important member of the family. She had to admit there were only so many bedrooms upstairs, but why hadn't Ben put Raymond in the tiny room off the kitchen? His precious son didn't give a fig where he slept as long as he could joke around and get his three meals a day. So galling! She burned with resentment and longed to speak up, but this was hardly the time for a big, ugly scene. She swallowed hard and managed to put an agreeable expression on her face. "I guess it will have to do."

The second the words left her mouth, she felt sick inside. So this was how her life would be from now on. Emmet's family would always be kind, but her place was at the bottom of the heap, the eternal chicken plucker, scrubber of floors, kitchen helper, all of it of under the direction of bossy Coralee.

Chapter 3

That night, Rose had a hard time sleeping in a bed barely wide enough for one, let alone two. Lucy's constant shifting in itself would have kept her awake, but she probably wouldn't have slept much anyway, what with the awful events of yesterday stabbing at her heart. She had thought she'd be cooking breakfast in the morning, but not long after the sun rose, she heard noises in the kitchen. She hurriedly dressed, stepped out of her tiny room, and found Coralee busily engaged in preparations for breakfast. She might have known her energetic mother-in-law wouldn't be down for long. Her face looked pale and haggard, but she moved with her usual quick efficiency.

"Good morning, Rose." Coralee nodded toward a bowlful of eggs. "See what the hired man brought? Have you met him? His name's Deke. He talks funny, but he seems nice enough. I want you to go out to the wagons and bring in a bag of flour." She shook her head with indignation. "I'd like to get my hands on that cook who ran off with the food. I'd surely give her a piece of my mind."

"So would I." Rose was pleased to see that despite her sorrow, Coralee was already back to her usual bossiness. Rose herself couldn't shake off her own gloomy mood. For one thing, she couldn't help her twinge of resentment when her mother-in-law didn't ask but told her to get the flour. Funny, she hadn't minded so much being ordered around before, but now she did. Maybe that was because she'd always assumed that someday soon she'd have a home of her own and be her own boss. Now she looked into an empty future in which she'd always have someone ordering her around. Of course, she could always get married again, but what was the point? Why marry a man she didn't love? She'd be trading one kitchen for another, and throw in those miserable nights when she had to do *that* before she went to sleep. Even her one marriage had been foolish, but at the time, what choice did she have? When her mother fell ill from a stomach tumor, and her father's heart began to fail, they begged her to marry Emmet. "For our peace of mind," they said, so they'd know she'd have someone to care for her after they'd gone. She liked Emmet well enough. He was an old family friend, so of course she complied.

Maybe she'd fall in love again. Wildly, completely in love, but the chance she'd find another Anthony was next to none. And why would she want to? *Anthony Parks*. Even now, she got a flutter in her stomach just thinking about the irresistible first mate of the steamboat *New Orleans*, who spent an occasional night at the Birchwood Inn. What a romantic figure he cut in his uniform. From the start, his teasing eyes and roguish smile easily captured her sixteen-year-old heart. And when he invited her to his room that night... *Oh God, how wonderful*. Never had she felt that way again, certainly not with clumsy, uncaring Emmet. After that glorious night, Anthony promised he'd come back, but as the days went by, and he never returned, she finally realized he never would. Concealing her broken heart was the hardest thing she ever did, but of course she had to. Her parents must never find out. Thank heavens, they never did. She reached to touch the gold locket at her throat, as she had done countless times before. Anthony had given it to her. A lock of his golden hair lay coiled inside. "Wear this so you won't forget me." He'd pressed it into her hand, his eyes alight with love and future promises.

But enough. Anthony was a long time ago and maybe someday she'd stop thinking about him. Right now breakfast came first, and she'd better go get the flour.

Outside, as she approached the wagons, she saw Deke in the chicken yard. Clucking chickens surrounded him as he reached in a canvas bag and cast seed in a wide swath. "Good morning," he called, a pleasant smile on his face.

"Good morning, and thanks for the eggs."

"How are you feeling?"

Ha! Ordinarily, she'd answer fine, but she didn't have the heart to lie. "Not so good."

"Do you have a minute?"

"Of course." She waited while he finished feeding the chickens. When he left the coop, carefully closing the gate behind him, he led her to the two-story tank house that sat close by and opened the door to the lower floor. Several large barrels, all fitted with lids, filled the small room inside.

As she followed, he called, "Did you ever run your hands through a barrel of chicken feed?"

"Never. We always bought our chickens at the market."

Deke leaned his crutches against the wall. He removed a lid, reached deep in the barrel with both hands, and scooped them upwards. "Give it a try. I guarantee running your mitts through a barrel of chicken feed will cure whatever ails you. Clears your head." He gave her a teasing smile. "Brightens your day."

"Really?" She plunged both hands into the barrel and slowly brought them out, instantly loving the velvety feel of the seed running through her fingers. How delightful. She'd never felt anything quite like it. "I believe you're right." She dipped them again. "The perfect cure for what ails me." Actually she did feel better, although it wasn't the feel of the chicken feed that lifted her spirits as much as it was Deke, his friendly smile and the playful humor in his eyes.

"Come try it any time. The door's not locked." Deke took up his crutches again.

She couldn't resist asking, "You won't always need those crutches, will you?"

His face went grim. For one revealing moment, a raw bitterness glittered in his grey eyes. "I hope to God I won't."

Up to now, she'd considered Deke to be a lot like Raymond, pleasant and likeable but without much depth. She'd been mistaken. There was more to him than she'd thought. What was Deke like beneath all that amiability? She'd like to ask more questions, but common sense told her she'd better not. She said goodbye and thanked him, got the bag of flour from the wagon, and returned to the house.

After breakfast, everyone gathered at Emmet's grave for what Ben called their own private family service. Bible in hand, Ben read from the scriptures. After that, each family member spoke up with some fond remembrance. At the end, they bowed their heads as Ben said a final prayer. They were headed back to the house when a smart-looking curricle pulled by two matched greys came rolling at a brisk pace down the driveway. A middle-aged, nicely dressed gentleman with bushy white eyebrows and a neatly trimmed goatee pulled the carriage to a halt with a flourish. His gaze swept over them until he spotted Ben. "Are you Mr. Ben Peterson, Emmet's father?"

"That I am, sir," Ben responded. "And who might you be?"

The man alighted from the carriage, bowed, and with a grand gesture swept off his brushed beaver top hat. "Archer Field, at your service. I was your son's solicitor. May I offer my condolences?" He shook his head regretfully. "Such a tragedy. It should never have happened. This is your family, Mr. Peterson?"

Ben nodded and introduced everyone. When he was done, he asked, "Perhaps you can help us, Mr. Field. We arrived only yesterday. We know my son was killed in what they said was a duel but have yet to learn the circumstances of his death."

The solicitor nodded with understanding. "I'd be happy to give you what few details I possess. May I come in? There are certain matters I wish to discuss."

Like everyone else, Rose was curious as she and the family trailed Ben back to the house. Matters to discuss? What was that about? After they'd settled in the parlor, and the solicitor was offered tea, which he graciously refused, Ben asked, "Can you tell us what happened? We have only the sketchiest account as to why my son is dead."

"I'll tell you as much as I know. Mason Talbot is one of Sacramento's most prestigious citizens, well known with a spotless reputation. He's one of the lucky ones who found gold early on and owns the Majestic Mine up near Hangtown. He lives in Sacramento now—owns the Egyptian Hotel as well as a brewery. Last Saturday night, he paid a visit to the River Queen, which of course you know was Emmet's hotel. Mr. Talbot was playing at one of the faro tables when an altercation ensued."

"Faro?" Ben sat back in surprise. "Emmet never mentioned there was gambling in his hotel. Are you sure?"

A smile ruffled the solicitor's mouth. "Quite sure. Sacramento swarms with miners, especially on a Saturday night when they come down from the diggings with their pockets full. You'd be hard put to find any hotel around Front Street that doesn't provide liquor, games of chance, and... ahem, other activities. As I was saying, Mr. Talbot was upset because he suspected the dealer, a man of dubious character by the name of Ned Barrow, was cheating. Which"—he arched a cynical eyebrow—"he probably was. That's when Emmet stepped in. Instead of soothing the waters, however, he made matters worse by defending his employee. Talbot grew extremely angry. He informed your son that among other things, he was no better than a thief. From what I understand, he made other scurrilous accusations as well. Emmet, who as you know was a bit hot-headed, got red in the face and highly insulted. That's when he challenged Talbot to a duel."

"It's not possible." Coralee shook her head in disbelief. "My son would never do such a thing."

Sitting next to his wife on the horsehair couch, Ben gently took her hand. "That's not so, my dear. As you well know, Emmet had a problem with his temper all his life."

Rose silently agreed. Although her husband had always been a kind man, occasionally his temper got the better of him, and he started yelling. Nothing physical, though, and his fits of outrage never lasted long.

The solicitor brushed an unseen piece of lint from his paisley silk vest. "That's all I can tell you. I wasn't present at the duel itself, and for good reason. For one thing, duels are a highly illegal activity. Even attending a duel is against the law. For another, I had no interest in seeing two men using weapons to settle their differences. The height of foolishness, if you ask me. At one point, Emmet asked me to be his second, but I refused."

Rose spoke up. "What do you mean by a 'second'?"

Mr. Field wrinkled his nose with distaste. "A duel is a lot more than two men trying to kill each other. There's protocol to be observed. From what I understand, a second is generally a friend who's chosen by the aggrieved party to conduct the rules and protocol of the duel. He attempts to resolve the dispute upon terms acceptable to both parties. Should this fail, he arranges and oversees the process of the encounter. Be that as it may, it was a bad business all the way around, and I wanted no part of it."

"So who was Emmet's second?" Ben asked.

"Last I heard, he'd asked an Australian by the name of Decatur Fleming. I believe he worked for Emmet. Why he'd hire an Australian, I don't know. Most of them are convicts, a scurrilous lot, the bunch of them, and not to be trusted. If he's still working here, Mr. Peterson, I'd get rid of him."

So Deke was a convict? And Emmet's second in his fatal duel? Rose hoped she managed to keep her shock from showing on her face as Ben nodded, looking as if he agreed, and continued on. "So what else can you tell me?"

"That's about all. As I said, I did not attend the duel, so I can't give you any details, other than Mason Talbot shot and killed Emmet Peterson."

Ben took a moment to consider the solicitor's words. With what appeared to be a decided effort, he took a deep breath and continued on. "You said you had certain matters to discuss, sir?"

Archer Field looked relieved, as if he welcomed the change of subject. "I'm a sensitive man, Mr. Peterson. I have no wish to intrude on this family's grief. However, a client of mine has made an offer, and I'm duty bound to present it."

"And what offer is that?"

"Being your deceased son's closest male relative, you have inherited the River Queen. My client would like to buy it and will pay you twenty-one thousand dollars. That's a price which frankly I advised him was outlandishly high, but he insists. I give you my word, you'll never find a better offer than this one."

"And who is making this offer?"

"Mr. Mason Talbot."

Amid shocked gasps, Ben asked, "The man who killed my son?"

"The very one." If he'd been asked the time of day, the solicitor couldn't have appeared less concerned. "I'm aware how you must feel, but I must be blunt. Talbot wasn't the aggressor in this…uh, most unfortunate situation. Emmet was the aggressor. It was he who made the challenge. You can talk to the sheriff if you like, but it's highly unlikely Talbot will even be investigated, let alone arrested. The fact is, duels may be illegal, but if a man of integrity is challenged to one, he must accept. It's a matter of honor. To tell the truth, no one blames Mr. Talbot." He rose from his seat. "I shall intrude no further. Think about it, Mr. Peterson. You can easily find my office on J Street. Come in any time. We'll discuss the offer and see if we can come to terms."

After the solicitor left, everyone was full of questions, but Ben remained grim and silent. Rose had no idea whether or not her father-in-law was considering Talbot's offer until he announced he would go to town this very afternoon. Not only were provisions needed, he wanted to see the hotel.

"Don't you dare leave us home," Coralee told him. "We'll all go. Does this mean you might sell?"

"I leave all options open."

* * * *

Although Emmet had left a two-passenger buggy and a large, four-wheeled coach sitting in the stable, that afternoon, Ben and Raymond hitched the oxen to one of their wagons. They'd be hauling back a large amount of groceries and supplies and needed the room. Sitting in the wagon, Rose looked for Deke as they left the yard but saw no sign of him. Had he really been Emmet's second for the duel? If so, why hadn't he mentioned it? Ever since Archer Field's hostile remarks about Australians, she'd been wondering what Ben would do. Somehow she couldn't believe a congenial, easygoing man like Deke could be a criminal, but if Ben thought so, the hired man would be gone in an instant. She hoped not but must wait and see.

Once in town, Ben told the family their first stop would be the River Queen. After asking directions of a passerby, he found it was located near the Sacramento River on J Street. Driving along Front Street, they were met by a growing crowd consisting mostly of gamblers and revelers, some of them obviously none too sober. Hotels and saloons crowded every block, doors invitingly open, loud music blasting from within. Some saloons were nothing more than large tents. Others seemed of a flimsy construction, only one story high. Only a few were more solidly built of brick and more than one story. When Ben turned up J Street and pulled the wagon to a halt in front of the River Queen, Rose saw it was one of the better built hotels: three stories high, made of brick, with a large statue of a gold miner guarding the entrance. Just then, the double doors swung open and two men engaged in fisticuffs came tumbling through. A small crowd followed, egging them on with raucous voices laced with curses. "You all stay here," Ben told the family.

"Can't we go in?" asked Rose. "I'm dying to see Emmet's hotel."

Ben's jaw tightened. "Certainly not. From what I see so far, it's not a fit place for ladies." He glanced at Raymond. "Nor you either, son. You're to stay here and guard your family."

As they sat waiting in the wagon, Coralee turned to Drucilla and gestured toward the crowd of miners milling about the street. "Look at all those men. I'd wager many of them are single. Seems to me you might meet one who tickles your fancy."

Drucilla heaved the same when-will-she-stop-trying sigh Rose had heard a thousand times before. "Please, Ma, I don't want my fancy tickled. Leave it alone." She exchanged an eyebrows-raised expression with her sister-in-law, her chief confidante who always understood. Rose did understand, more than anyone in the family, but privately wished Drucilla might be a bit more flexible.

A few minutes later, a grim-faced Ben returned. Without a word, he climbed in the wagon and took the reins. "Well?" Coralee asked. "Where are we going now?"

Ben snapped the reins. "To Archer Field's office. I've decided to sell. I want no part of this den of iniquity Emmet called his hotel."

In the well-furnished office of Archer Field, only a block from Front Street, the entire Peterson family sat across from the solicitor's desk. Rose, Drucilla, and Coralee hadn't wanted to come. They'd caught tantalizing glimpses of the many shops lining Front Street and were anxious to take a look. Who cared if Ben sold the hotel? Legal affairs didn't concern them. Ben had insisted, though, so they sat listening with halfhearted interest while Mr. Field explained the details of the transaction. "Mr. Talbot has offered twenty-one thousand dollars for the property. An extremely generous offer. That includes the building itself, the stable in back, and all amenities."

"I accept the offer." Ben's stern voice reflected his resolve. "I don't hold with gambling and want no part of it. As to what else goes on there, I'm appalled that Emmet—" He bit his lip in chagrin. "When can I sign the papers?"

The solicitor allowed himself a fleeting smile of satisfaction. "I'll have them drawn up immediately. They should be ready tomorrow."

They all got up to leave. Rose could hardly wait to get out of there. Maybe a bit of shopping would cheer her up. She especially wanted to find a dressmaker and order some new dresses. They were about out the door when the solicitor called, "By the way, Mr. Peterson, one more thing."

Ben turned back. "Yes?"

"You must bring Mrs. Peterson along. I'll have special papers for her to sign."

Ben frowned in puzzlement. "My wife? Why should she be involved?"

"Not your wife, your daughter-in-law. After I spoke to you, it was brought to my attention that the 1849 California Constitution Convention gives a wife the right to own property separate from her husband. That means the hotel and farm are her property, technically speaking, of course." Mr. Field chuckled. "Next we know, they'll be asking for the right to vote. It's all nonsense, but the law is the law, no matter how misguided, so make sure Mrs. Rose Peterson accompanies you tomorrow."

Ben smiled and shook his head. "Such insanity." Without consulting Rose, or even looking in her direction, he continued, "She'll be here. I want this unfortunate business over and done with."

Outside the solicitor's office, Raymond spoke up. "There's something I don't understand. Did that solicitor say the farm and hotel belong to Rose now?"

Ben smiled indulgently. "Women aren't allowed to own property. You should know that."

Coralee threw a disapproving look at her son. "Really, Raymond, whoever heard of such a thing?"

Raymond hated to get involved in any kind of argument. He announced he wanted to go look at horses and would meet them later.

As they climbed in the wagon, Coralee pressed her lips in a disapproving line. "Wives owning their own property? What were these Californians thinking of? Did you ever hear anything so outlandish?" She turned to where Rose and Drucilla were settling themselves in the back. "Don't bother your head about it, Rose. Ben will take care of everything. And you can rest assured you'll always have a home with us. In fact…" With a delicate shrug she added, "It's much too soon to even think of such a thing, but someday, when you think of marrying again, you might consider not having to change your name."

"Why is that?" Rose asked.

"Just fancy, if you married Raymond, you could remain Mrs. Peterson and live with us forever and ever." Coralee turned back again.

Drucilla covered her mouth to hide her laughter and jabbed an elbow into Rose's side. "Just think," she whispered, "you could be Mrs. Raymond Peterson. Aren't you thrilled?"

Rose jabbed her back and softly hissed, "That's not funny."

Drucilla kept laughing, and Rose could hardly blame her. Much as Drucilla loved her brother, she was well aware of his shortcomings.

* * * *

At first, Archer Field's offhand reminder to Ben that Rose must sign the papers didn't sink in. She was far too busy at the dressmakers, where she, Coralee, and Drucilla ordered new gowns. How wonderful to have something new after wearing the same patched, faded dresses day after day for months. Such an exciting event put everything else out of her head. Not until they'd finished their shopping and were headed home did its significance strike like a bolt from the blue. Not in her wildest dreams had she thought she rightfully owned the hotel. And the farm, too? How utterly astounding. Funny, how Ben and Coralee hadn't shown the least concern. They took for granted that their dutiful daughter-in-law would sign the papers without a murmur. She couldn't blame them. When she married Emmet, she was well aware everything she owned now automatically belonged to him, but that was the way it was in this world and always had been. She was only a woman, after all, and women had no rights and lived their lives under their husbands' direction.

Only now… Dear Lord! Did she really own the hotel?

"Is something wrong, Rose?" Drucilla had noticed how quiet she'd been.

"Nothing's wrong. I…was thinking about Emmet."

Drucilla gave a sarcastic sniff. "Of course you were."

Her shrewd sister-in-law could always see right through her. Not the rest of the family, though. She shouldn't tell lies, but if they knew what was going on in her head, they'd be dumbfounded. But this was ridiculous. What was she thinking of? Of course she'd accompany Ben to Mr. Field's office tomorrow and sign the papers, like she was supposed to. Any thoughts to the contrary, she would firmly, and most definitely, put out of her mind.

Chapter 4

After they reached the farm, Rose spent the next few hours helping put provisions away, and then helping Coralee with dinner. Darkness had fallen by the time she put Lucy to bed and decided to go for a stroll. She'd tried to keep so busy she'd have no time to think about Archer Field's startling revelation, but despite her vow to the contrary, she couldn't get it off her mind. She headed for the barn, hoping Deke would be there. When she arrived, she found a saddled sorrel quarter horse tied outside, the saddlebags full. Was it Deke's? She stepped inside the barn and found him sitting on a bale of hay cleaning a pistol. His face lit when he saw her. "Rose! Come sit down. I hoped I'd see you before I left."

She sat on a bale of hay across from him, spreading her skirt decorously around her. "That's your horse out there?"

"Yes, that's Sidney."

"You're leaving? I didn't know."

Deke's mouth twisted into a wry grin. "Seems your father-in-law thinks I'm a criminal."

With a stab of disappointment, she asked, "Ben dismissed you? That's so unfair."

"I don't blame him." Unconcerned, he continued cleaning the pistol. "We Australians are none too popular around here. Thieves and murderers, the lot of us."

"Not you. I don't believe it."

"Not me."

"I could talk to him."

"Don't bother." He cast a quick gaze at the crutches resting beside him. "Despite what you think, I can take care of myself. Always have, always will."

She'd be wise not to pursue the subject. "Before you go, I need to ask—were you my husband's second at the duel?"

Deke's head jerked back. "Who told you that? Blimey, no. He asked me, but I turned him down. What's more stupid than a duel? I wanted no part of it. In the end, he got another of his employees, Jake Grunion, to be his second. I was there, though. He wanted me to drive him, so I did. Now I wish I hadn't."

Rose's heart wrenched. Until now, Emmet's death hadn't seemed real, but here was someone who'd actually been there, seen him die. Getting the words out was painful. "One thing I've been wondering. Was he killed instantly or did he...well, linger?"

"Instantly. No pain at all."

She smiled in relief. "Thank you for that. I wouldn't have wanted—"

"I understand. You can rest easy. He didn't suffer."

Thank goodness. Time to get away from such a depressing subject. Besides, she really wanted to talk to him about something else. "You'd never believe what I found out today..."

In great detail, she described the family's visit to Mr. Field's office and how Ben had readily assumed the farm and hotel now belonged to him. "Then, just as we were leaving, Mr. Field mentioned that because of the new California Constitution, I'm the one who owns the farm and hotel, and I've got to sign some papers in order to turn them over to Ben."

Deke chuckled. "I'd wager that father-in-law of yours must have been surprised. How did he take it?"

"He wasn't the least concerned, and neither was Coralee. They expect I'll do as I'm told. They couldn't imagine I'd do otherwise."

"Would you?"

"Of course not. For one thing, Emmet's family has been good to me. For another, I wouldn't have the nerve. I can't even imagine what their reaction would be if I told them I wasn't going to sign the papers."

"But you've been thinking about it, haven't you?"

Deke gave her such a piercingly wise gaze that for a moment she had to look away. "Of course I've thought of it. You wouldn't know it to look at me, but I happen to know how to run a hotel." She told him about the Birchwood Inn in Illinois, and how, when her parents were so ill, she'd practically run it by herself. "Of course, the River Queen is much larger, and there's more going on."

Grinning, he replied, "You could say that, being as the River Queen is one of the biggest and most notorious saloons on the riverfront." He grew serious. "I think you'd like to give it a go, even though you deny it."

"I'd love it, and I know what I'm talking about. At the inn, the work was hard. There were always things going wrong that I had to fix, but the good part was, I was in charge. I made the decisions, and at the end of each day, when the guests were content and I'd made a profit, I had this... this...wonderful feeling of accomplishment."

"Well then, seems to me you'd better think twice before you give up what's rightfully yours. You wouldn't be the first female owner of a hotel in this town. A woman named Fanny Wentworth owns the Silver Star. She's quite a gal."

Rose briefly wondered what he meant by "quite a gal" but didn't ask. "I might like the idea of running my own hotel, but I can't imagine actually standing up to my in-laws and saying, 'I'm not going to sign.' My blood runs cold at the thought. I'd never have the courage."

"You wouldn't? It all depends on how you define courage. What do you think it is?"

She sat thinking a moment. "Courage is a lot of things. For a man, it's like bravely marching off to war, or running into a burning building to save someone. For me, it's different. I'm a woman, and women aren't expected to do heroic things. Women are pretty much expected to do what they're told, so for me courage means staying in my place, no matter what, and not complaining, no matter how resentful I might feel. That takes courage, too. It's not easy to be humble and do as I'm told when inside I want way more in this life than I'm supposed to have."

"Blimey." For a time he sat silent, lines of concentration deepening along his brow. "In a way, you're right. There are different kinds of courage, like for me it's acting like I don't care my leg is broke when inside..."

The look of pain that crossed his face disappeared in an instant, but she hadn't missed it. "How did you break it?"

"I'll tell you sometime. Let's get back to courage." He clasped his hands together and leaned forward, his grey eyes intense upon her. "Here's what I think. Being a woman has nothing to do with it. If the law says you own the hotel and the farm, then so you do, and those in-laws of yours can go take a flying leap. You're quiet, but you're strong. Smart, too. I haven't known you long, but I'd wager whatever you set your mind to, you could do it. The worst of it is, if you don't speak out and claim what's rightfully yours, there will come a time when you'll regret it, only then it will be too late and you'll spend the rest of your life wishing you'd spoken up when you had the chance."

She'd been caught off guard by the intensity in his voice and couldn't think how to answer. Nobody had ever talked to her like that before. "I must say, you're honest enough."

"That's my advice. Take it or leave it." He stood, shoved his pistol in a holster, and took up his crutches. "I'm done here. Come along. You can hold my crutches while I get on my horse."

Pleased that he'd actually asked for help, she followed him outside and dutifully held his crutches, noticing how gracefully he swung into the saddle despite the cumbersome cast. She handed him the crutches, which he tied over one of the saddlebags. "Where are you going?"

A thoughtful smile curved his mouth. "I'll know when I get there." With a sudden downward swoop, he kissed her on the cheek. "Mind what I said. You're made of stronger stuff than you think you are, Rose Peterson. It was nice knowing you." With two fingers he touched the broad brim of his hat. "Very nice."

Rose watched Deke Fleming nudge Sidney and ride away. He sat his horse well, as if he'd spent lots of time in the saddle. Such broad shoulders. A shame about the crutches. Today he'd opened up enough to let her see how much he hated that cast on his leg. She touched the spot on her cheek where he'd kissed her. Was it her imagination, or was it still warm? Ah, well, he was gone now, and she'd never see him again. He'd given her something to think about, though. What he said made a lot of sense, and she would have liked to talk to him more about it. Not that she'd change her mind.

* * * *

As Deke rode away, he gave a quick shake of his head, his habit when the world closed in around him and his spirits got down. That's when he'd think of home. He had only to shut his eyes to be back at Amalie Station, in the heart of the outback, where he'd lived all his life on the most beautiful, most unforgiving land on this earth. His beloved Amalie—a place of silence and beauty where the fish-filled streams ran crystal clear and the water birds hovered above; where the beautiful Flinders Range with its ever-changing colors loomed in the distance; where he could herd a thousand bleating sheep for days and never see another soul, only wallabies, kangaroos, lizards, and the like; where he could sleep on the ground by an open fire, stars twinkling above, and consider himself the luckiest man on earth.

Rose made him laugh when she asked if he was a convict. He'd honestly told her he wasn't. What he hadn't said was that his father was. At the age of fifteen, Jonathan David Fleming was caught committing the heinous crime of stealing two rabbits off a pushcart in the Brixton district of London. At his trial, he told the judge he'd stolen the rabbits because his family was starving, but his explanation fell on deaf ears. He was convicted, and because the cost of the rabbits was over five shillings, the judge sentenced him to hang. Not until he stood on the gallows, noose around his neck, was he given a choice: either hang or be sent to Australia on a convict ship.

Only in the last years of his life did Deke's father talk about those months on a convict ship where he was chained below deck the entire time, beaten and nearly starved. Where nothing lay ahead except the dismal prospect of serving time in one of Australia's notoriously brutal prisons. But he survived the journey, and when he arrived in New South Wales, he got the luckiest break of his life. He never served a day of his sentence in prison. Labor was so scarce he was immediately sent to work on a sheep station near Adelaide. Soon awarded his freedom, he married Amalie, a girl he'd met while they were imprisoned on the ship, and was granted some land of his own. He named it Amalie Station, and that was where Deke was born and grew up.

After his father died, Deke took over the small sheep station. Over the years, he expanded, bought adjacent land. His property got so big that he could get on his horse at one border of Amalie Station, ride three days, and still be on his own land.

The profits rolled in. He started thinking maybe he'd build onto the homestead and get a few luxuries like a pump in the kitchen and rugs on the floor. And maybe he'd start looking for a wife, although on the rare times he got to Willowbrook, the town closest to Amalie, he didn't see anyone special that he liked, so there wasn't a hurry about that. Then the Australian market for wool started slumping badly. His profits dropped, along about the time word came about the California Gold Rush. When his friend, Mitch Carter, who owned the nearest station to Amalie, said he'd bought his passage on the next boat to San Francisco, he urged Deke to come along. "The trouble with you, Deke, is you're sheep-rich but bored," Mitch told him. "What you need is an adventure." Deke got to thinking he should go. And why not? He was healthy, fit, and strong. His trusted manager could run Amalie Station just fine without him. His friend Mitch was a sober, deeply religious man whom Deke highly respected. So maybe he'd have a go at it, catch the same ship as Mitch. They would sail to California, make their way to the gold fields, and find enough gold to make their fortunes. Even if they didn't find those giant-sized nuggets everyone talked about, so what? He'd have had himself a fine adventure. Would that be so bad? What did he have to lose?

Deke bought his passage to California. He'd go to what they called "the diggings," take a look, and if he didn't like what he saw, then he'd bloody well go home.

On a bright, sunny afternoon in June, eighty-one days out of Sidney, Australia, Deke and Mitch stood on the deck of the bark *Elizabeth Archer* along with a bunch of other gold-hunting Australians and cheered as the ship sailed through the Golden Gate into San Francisco Bay. Ahead, they saw a forest of masts, all from ships that had been abandoned, the crews having taken off for the gold fields. To the east, Deke saw what looked like a long, low bank of white clouds. He soon learned they weren't clouds at all but the snow-covered Sierra Nevada Mountains, 150 miles away. "Looks like we're not there yet," he said. "It'll take a while."

Mitch shook his head. "Not so. From what I hear, we can sail across the bay and up a river that will take us all the way to Sacramento, so it shouldn't be a problem."

His friend couldn't have been more wrong. In Deke's worst nightmare, he could not have imagined how big a problem his journey to the gold fields would turn out to be. Both having arrived in California with substantial funds, he and Mitch purchased a longboat taken from an abandoned ship. They were joined by five fellow Australians they'd met on the *Elizabeth Archer*, each having offered to pay for their passage. After asking directions and checking maps, they started out, aiming their longboat across San Francisco Bay. Because of their ample provisions and the weight of seven men, the boat rode low in the water, but they crossed the northern part of San Francisco Bay to the Strait of Benicia without incident and spent a convivial night in a hotel in the town of Benicia. All the next day, they sailed and rowed east across Suisun Bay toward the mouth of the Sacramento River. With hopes and excitement running high, Deke enjoyed the journey. They laughed and joked a lot, and there was much speculation about what they'd do with all the gold they were going to find. Deke remembered that day well. It was the last day he was a whole man, fit and confident that if he had to, he could take on the world.

When night fell and the tide ebbed, they were still several miles from the river, so they decided to drop anchor until dawn. They bundled themselves against the cold wind and slept as best they could. A few hours later, Deke suddenly awoke to find the boat listing sharply and cold water rushing in. He didn't know until later that the anchor had gotten stuck in the mud of the bay floor. As the water rose with the tide, the boat tipped completely over. He felt himself being flung into the water just as the edge of the boat smashed down on his leg. At the time, he hardly noticed. Others were screaming. He himself was a strong swimmer, so when Mitch started desperately yelling, "I can't swim," and flailing his arms, he grabbed hold of his friend's coat collar and held him up. What next? He could hang on to the overturned boat, but they were already shaking from the cold, and he knew they'd never last long in the freezing water. Tugging Mitch behind him, he began a one-armed paddle toward what he hoped was shore. Along the way, exhaustion overcame him and he thought he couldn't go on unless he let Mitch go. But no, he couldn't do that. Mitch was his friend, and he'd either get him to shore or they'd go down together in the icy, unforgiving waters of Suisun Bay.

Soaking wet and freezing, Deke, Mitch, and two other survivors somehow made it to land. An icy, bitter wind cut into them as they crawled up a bank and lay exhausted on the muddy ground. It was then Deke's right leg let him know it was broken, sending out such an agonizing wave of pain, he had to grit his teeth to keep from crying out. He tried to walk and couldn't. In silent agony, he made it through the rest of the night, and when the sun came up, he saw how the raw end of a broken shin bone was sticking through the skin of his right leg.

Deke couldn't walk. Thank God, he'd kept his money in a waterproof belt around his waist, but like his companions, everything else he owned had been lost in the bay. It was a sorry-looking lot that managed to hail a passing whaleboat. By then, Deke could do nothing, other than grit his teeth to stifle his cries of pain while his companions carried him onto the whaleboat and laid him on the deck as carefully as they could. Even so, the least bit of jostling brought spasms of agony, a couple of times so bad he passed out. When they reached the town of Stockton, they looked for a doctor but were told they must travel on to Sacramento to find the nearest one available. So they found another boat, hauled Deke up the Sacramento River, the most agonizing ride of his life, and finally reached the office of Dr. Horace Andrews, a kindly, white-haired man whose medical school diploma on the wall gave Deke confidence that he knew what he was doing.

"It's a bad break," Dr. Andrews said. "I'm going to set your leg and put it in a cast. I'll use something new called plaster of Paris. You'll be my first patient to have it."

With his mates holding him down, Deke had his leg set. Even though the doctor gave him a dose of laudanum, the pain was so bad he mercifully passed out. When he came to, he had a huge heavy cast on his leg. The doctor gave him some crutches. "Here's so you can get around."

"How long?"

"At least six weeks. Then come back and we'll see."

"What if I don't wait six weeks before I get off the crutches?"

Dr. Andrews looked him in the eye. "If you walk on that leg a day before I say you can, you'll likely be crippled the rest of your life."

After an unhappy parting accompanied by profuse apologies and expressions of regret, his friends went on without him. After all, he couldn't expect them to stay when they were keen on getting to the diggings. Hiding his profound disappointment, he smiled, told them he'd be fine, and watched as they rode off toward the mountains. So now what would he do? Or more like it, what could he do? One thing he knew: He'd been busy all his life and couldn't just sit around waiting for the leg to heal.

Lucky for him, one day in the River Queen Saloon, he met a man named Emmet Peterson who loudly complained how he desperately needed a farmhand, but nearly every able-bodied man in town had taken off for the gold fields. Deke saw his opportunity. Would he take a hardworking Australian who, despite the crutches, could still give a good day's work? Emmet said he would, and that's why Decatur Fleming, owner of a thirty-four-thousand-square-kilometer sheep station in the heart of the outback, became the humble farmhand on a twenty-acre farm on the outskirts of Sacramento.

Now what would he do? Stay in Sacramento, he supposed. Rent a room. Find something to keep him occupied until the cast came off. Maybe he'd see Rose Peterson again. He would like that. He didn't like that he'd had to lie to her, but what else could he do? What good would come from her knowing her husband suffered greatly for hours before he died?

And that wasn't all he hadn't told her. *Mason Talbot.* He clenched his jaw. If the Petersons knew what Mason had done? But they didn't know, and damned if he'd be the one to tell them. Best let sleeping dogs lie.

So he'd stay in Sacramento, at least until Dr. Andrews took the cast off. Nearly five miserable, frustrating weeks he'd waited. Now he had just over a week to go before Rose Peterson saw him walk like a man again, and he'd make sure she did. It would be the longest week of his life.

Chapter 5

Rose didn't sleep well that night. She was having a hard time suppressing her resentment that her father-in-law considered her opinion so unimportant he hadn't even asked if she wished to sign those papers. She would, though. She couldn't imagine not signing and had definitely made up her mind.

In the morning, she helped with breakfast as usual. In contrast to that first day when the cupboards were bare, an abundance of food filled every shelf, nook, and cranny in the kitchen. Not only had the family bought their own provisions, neighbors from all around brought offerings of everything from oranges, walnuts, and all kinds of vegetables to slabs of beef and a salmon freshly caught from the Sacramento River. Coralee was so grateful she nearly cried. "It's not the food so much as it is these people care, even though they don't know us. I felt like a stranger, but now I'm beginning to feel like this is home."

They would go to the solicitor's office in the afternoon. As the hour drew closer, a heaviness centered in Rose's chest. She would sign the papers, even though she couldn't get Deke's words out of her head. She'd live to regret it, he said, and she knew she would. Even so, like she'd told Deke, she'd never find the courage to stand up to the family, especially Ben. She cringed at the thought of defying the man who ruled his family with an iron hand.

Toward noon, when no one was in the kitchen except Rose, Dulcee Bidwell from the farm next door arrived with a freshly baked apple pie. "Today's my baking day," she said. "Tom picked the apples this morning." Rose invited her to stay for a cup of coffee, and soon they were sitting at the kitchen table, chatting away. Dulcee was easy to talk to. Like a lot of elderly people, she was frank in a funny kind of way. Commiserating with Rose's loss, she remarked, "I had three husbands myself. The first two died. The third walked out on me and five children and disappeared. I'd wager he's dead, too, by now."

Rose frowned in sympathy. "That's terribly sad. I can't imagine the grief you've gone through."

"Piffle." The old lady sniffed and took a sip of coffee. "I didn't love any of 'em. I married Murphy, my first husband, because I had to. Tom's father." Her eyes twinkled. She brought a finger to her lips. "Shh. To this day Tom thinks he was a seven-month baby, but he wasn't."

Rose couldn't think how to reply. Best to move on. "What happened to Murphy?"

"He was chopping down a tree one day and was dumb enough to be standing in the wrong place when it fell. So there I was, a widow with a young'un, and everyone telling me I should get married again because I was only a woman and how could I make it on my own? So I married Ebenezer, who was the first man I could find who had a clean shirt and no dirt under his fingernails. Five years later, he up and drowned in the Mississippi River. By now I was a widow with four young'uns, so what did I do? You guessed it. Got married again." Her expression softened. "Don't get me wrong, they weren't all bad. It's just, I never had the kind of love of my life that a girl dreams of. No knight in shining armor, like in the fairy tales." She cocked an eyebrow. "What about you, missy? Did you love him?"

"Love who?"

"Your husband, of course, unless you had a lover on the side. Don't let me shock you. It's my age. I can say anything I want and get away with it because everyone thinks my brain has withered and I can't help it. Well, it hasn't."

"I can see that. As for loving my husband, I...I..."

Dulcee peered over her spectacles. "I thought not. Emmet was a fine man, but at best you could call him sturdy and dependable. At worst, he was a bore, excuse me for saying so. A volcano could erupt in his front yard, and he wouldn't bother to look. I had more interesting conversations with a tree stump than with Emmet Peterson."

After a stunned moment, Rose burst into laughter. She looked around to make sure they were still alone. "You're right. I never loved him. I married him mostly because my parents wanted me to."

"Thought so." Dulcee tipped her head. "You're young and you're pretty. Did you know there's fifty men to every woman around here? You won't have any problem finding another husband, if that's what you want. Maybe the next one won't be such a stump."

Rose hadn't thought about it yet, but Dulcee's suggestion made her lift her chin and stoutly declare, "I can tell you right now I'll never marry again unless it's to someone I truly love." She touched the locket at her throat. "I was in love once—weak-in-the-knees in love. It didn't work out. He broke my heart, but even so, I swear I'll never bed a man I'm not crazy about." She sat back in her chair, surprised at herself. She'd never spoken this frankly, but then never had she talked to someone so understanding and sympathetic as Dulcee Bidwell, who brought out the best in her—or was it the worst?

Dulcee's wrinkled face grew pensive. "I hope you stick with what you said. If I had it to do over again, I wouldn't be the wishy-washy woman that I was. I'd stick up for myself. I'd be like a man and not listen to everyone telling me what I ought to do. I'd have the courage to speak up, say what I wanted to say, and the consequences be damned."

Rose nodded in agreement. "Sometimes that's hard to do. For years I've lived with my in-laws, always looking forward to that wonderful day I would have a home of my own. Now I'm stuck. Not that Ben and Coralee aren't wonderful people but..." She gave a wordless shrug.

"You've sure as heck got yourself a dilemma." Dulcee got a knowing look in her eye. "You're not stuck. Nobody's tying you down. You can do anything you want. Have faith in yourself and you'll figure out what's best to do."

"I'm not so sure."

"It's up to you, missy. Don't underestimate yourself. Now let's have some of that pie."

The conversation switched to other, more inconsequential things, but long after her elderly neighbor left, Rose couldn't stop thinking about what she'd said. *Have faith in yourself and you'll figure out what's best to do.*

But would she? Did she have the courage?

* * * *

In the afternoon, Ben hitched up the coach. Rose gave Lucy a hug. "I'm going into town for a while, sweetheart, but Aunt Drucilla will be here, and Uncle Raymond, too."

Always full of questions, Lucy inquired, "Why are you going?"

"Grandpa and Grandma and I are going to the lawyer's office to sign some papers." She always tried to be honest. "It seems the farm and hotel legally belong to me, so I must sign them over to your grandpa."

Lucy frowned in confusion. "But if they're yours, why don't you keep them?"

"It's a long story, and I'll explain later."

Why indeed? Rose wondered as she and her in-laws drove into town. She hoped Lucy would forget to ask again.

At the law office, Mr. Field greeted them with a smile, announcing the papers were ready for their signature. After they were seated in front of his large, mahogany desk, he remarked, "I'm expecting Mr. Talbot any moment. He will, of course, be bringing you the check for twenty-one thousand as agreed."

So they were going to meet Emmet's killer? Rose sensed both Ben and Coralee flinch as they sat beside her. She, too, got a tightness in her stomach. Ben spoke up. "See here, I didn't think I'd be meeting the man who killed my son."

"I understand how you feel." The solicitor's voice oozed with sympathy and understanding. "But once you meet him, you'll see—"

"That's all right, Archer. Let me explain."

The deep, silky voice came from behind them. Rose turned in her seat. One of the most handsome men she'd ever seen stood in the doorway. Tall and broad-shouldered, he had a thick crop of wavy blond hair, firm mouth, and square-cut jaw. His well-tailored trousers and frock coat, silk cravat and brocade vest made her suddenly conscious of the patched and faded dress she was wearing. What a shame the new dresses she'd ordered weren't ready. He held an ivory tipped cane and top hat in his large, perfectly manicured hands. With a purposeful stride, he crossed the room, put down the hat and cane, and turned to face them. "Good afternoon. My name is Mason Talbot." His gaze focused on Ben. "You must be Mr. Peterson. Yes, I'm the man who engaged in a duel with your son, and I want you to know the day doesn't go by that I…" His mouth set in a grim line. "If there was any way I could have avoided it, I would have done so."

Ben stood up. Dressed in his plain black Sunday suit, he was no match for the elegantly dressed hotel owner, yet Rose knew he wouldn't be intimidated by Talbot's powerful presence. "Tell me why you killed my son," he said, his voice taut with suppressed anger.

Talbot didn't appear the least surprised by Ben's reaction. "The duel was Emmet's idea, not mine. He did the challenging. I tried reasoning with him, but he wouldn't listen. When I finally realized I actually might have to go through with it, I appointed Rudy Avery, one of my employees, as my second. I sent Rudy to talk Emmet out of it, but he wouldn't listen, was hell-bent on going through with it. What could I do? Despite my misgivings, I was honor bound to accept Emmet's challenge, insane though it was."

Mason's deep blue eyes gazed into Ben's. "I'm not presumptuous enough to ask for your forgiveness, sir, but I hope for your understanding."

A long, tension-charged silence followed. Rose held her breath. Would Ben accept the apology? Punch Mason Talbot in the nose? Storm out? Viewing her father-in-law's stone-like face, she had no idea what would happen.

At last Ben opened his mouth to speak. "Let's get down to business, shall we?" He sat again.

Rose breathed a sigh of relief as Mason Talbot flashed a congenial smile. "I'm pleased to see you've accepted my offer to buy the River Queen. I assure you, it's a generous one, the least I could do."

The solicitor also smiled. Ruffling a pile of papers on his desk, he addressed Talbot. "You brought the check?"

Talbot patted his right breast pocket. "Just drawn up at Wells Fargo."

With a smile of satisfaction, Mr. Field dipped a pen in a bottle of ink and held it out to Rose. "I have some papers for you to sign, Mrs. Peterson. If you'll step to my desk?"

She started to rise but couldn't unbend. It was if she was glued to the chair. Deke's frank advice rang through her head. *If the law says you own the hotel and the farm, then so you do, and those in-laws of yours can go take a flying leap.* No! She must get out this chair and sign. Again she tried to rise, but her legs refused to move. Dulcee's wise words crowded Deke's. *If I had it to do over again...I'd have the courage to speak up, say what I wanted to say, and the consequences be damned.*

Seconds went by. *Get up!* There was still time. If she got up this instant, they'd never know she had the least objection, but if she waited any longer...

Her knees still refused to unbend. Heads began to turn. Coralee, who sat next to her, gave her a nudge. "Mr. Field wants you to sign the papers, dear. You need to go to his desk."

Ben bent forward and peered around Coralee. "Get up there, Rose. I want this thing signed and done with."

Too late. The time had passed that she could continue her role as the passive, obedient daughter-in-law. *By God, I'm not going to do it.* She breathed deep and steadied herself. Even though her heart was pounding, she willed her voice not to shake when she spoke. Instead of the stark fear she expected, a flood of relief ran through her. With far more ease than she expected, she stood and addressed the puzzled solicitor who still held the pen in his outstretched hand. "Are the hotel and farm truly mine, Mr. Field?"

"If you were legally married to Emmet Peterson, they are."

"Then I don't choose to sign." She turned to Mason Talbot. "I'm sorry you've gone to this trouble for nothing, sir, but the property is mine and

I'm not selling." With a firm lift of her chin, she turned to Ben and Coralee. "Until this moment, I planned to go through with it and sign. Now I find I cannot. I hope you understand. It's just…honestly, why should I? If the property is mine, then so it is. You can rest assured, you'll always have a home on Emmet's farm however long you choose to live there. As for the hotel, I don't want to sell because I want to run it myself. Can you possibly understand?" She braced herself for Ben's wrath. Like Emmet, he had a temper which mostly he managed to control. She'd witnessed a few occasions when he'd lost it, though. His scalding fury had been so frightening, everyone ran for cover.

To her surprise, Ben hardly looked at her. With an easy smile, he turned to the solicitor. "You must forgive my daughter-in-law, Mr. Field. She has just lost her husband, so naturally she's not thinking clearly." He threw Rose a quick glance loaded with sympathy. "We'd best get her home and put her to bed."

"And I'll get her a nice glass of warm milk." Coralee stood up and patted Rose on the shoulder. "There, there. It's going to be all right."

Rose was so dumbfounded she couldn't speak. She'd been prepared for her in-laws' wrath but not this. "I don't need a glass of warm milk, and I don't need to go to bed. I meant what I said."

"Well, of course, you do," said Coralee. "Whatever you say."

Go to bed? Warm milk? How outrageous. She had to get out of there. Head held high, she marched from the office of Archer Field, out the front door, and into the teeming traffic on J Street. She started walking, hardly noticing where she was going. She'd been braced for their anger, not their sympathy. How dare they treat her that way? As she continued on, the street became more crowded. She passed a long row of hotels, all with saloons with swinging doors and tinny music pouring through. Men in rough miners' clothes seemed to be constantly shoving in and out. They seemed a rough lot, smelling of whiskey and tobacco, jostling and shouting curses. A man in a scraggly beard and dirty clothes pointed at her. "Look there! Ain't she sweet?"

Dear God, she needed to get out of here. The man came staggering after her. She was about to run when…was someone calling her name? She stopped and turned. Deke was approaching on Sidney. As he rode up to her, he frowned down and asked, "Rose, what are you doing here by yourself? Get on." He reached out his arm. She hesitated. Surely he didn't have the strength to pull her up. "Take it," he commanded. So all right then. If he thought he could do it, who was she to argue? She grasped his hand. In an instant, he swung her up and behind him in one effortless motion. Before she knew it, she was seated with arms around his waist, and Sidney was moving up the street at a brisk pace. "Thanks," she called.

"Blimey, girl!"

Deke said no more until he pulled Sidney to a stop in front of a long wooden building open in the front. "Welcome to the restaurant where all the miners come." He dismounted and asked, "Need help getting down?"

"I can manage." She'd ridden horses all her life and swung off with ease.

He retrieved his crutches. Soon they were seated at one of the rough-planked tables, cups of coffee in front of them. "We're lucky it's not dinnertime," he said. "This place is a madhouse then." He cocked his head. "Now tell me, what were you doing on J Street by yourself? Not a good idea, you know, going for a stroll on one of the rowdiest streets in town."

"I'd rather not discuss it."

"Then we won't," he replied easily.

She bit her lip. He'd just rescued her. Besides that, the poor man was crippled. She could at least be polite and give him an honest answer. "Sorry. I'm a bit upset, but it's not your fault. Do you remember what we talked about? That I own the hotel and the farm?" She told him what had occurred in the solicitor's office. When she mentioned Mason Talbot, his face clouded.

"That scum."

"You think so? I found him to be quite obliging, and congenial as well."

Deke remained silent.

"Don't misunderstand me. It's not that I don't care, but Mr. Talbot seemed quite apologetic about the duel and what happened."

"Mason Talbot apologetic?" Deke got a strange look on his face, as if he wanted to say more, then thought better of it. "Just go on."

"Nobody took me seriously. My in-laws thought I needed to drink warm milk and lie down. So now what do I do?"

"Sounds like you've already done it. What do you care if they don't believe you? You didn't sign the papers and that's what counts. Good for you. You own a hotel, and that's that."

She took a moment to ponder. "You're right. I'm the new owner of the River Queen. It's just now sinking in."

"Have you seen it yet?"

"Only on the outside. When Ben saw it, he decided it was much too rowdy for delicate females like myself."

"You've got to see it. I'll take you."

"Of course I want to see it." She regarded Deke with new eyes. Such a nice man, and not bad looking at all. She liked the way deep dimples appeared in his bronzed cheeks whenever he smiled. So far, the conversation had been all about her, and that wasn't right. "How are *you* doing, Deke? Do you know where you're going yet?" Without thinking, she flicked a glance at the crutches resting beside him. "What can you do?"

"I won't be panning for gold anytime soon. There are other ways to make a living, though. I've got some ideas."

"So you'll be staying in Sacramento?" He nodded. "That's wonderful. I'm glad to hear it." And she was, surprisingly so. Deke was easy to talk to, besides being helpful. "What are your ideas? Will you tell me one?"

"Ice."

"Ice?" How curious. She wanted to find out more, but a guarded expression had spread over his face, and she'd better not.

"Let's leave it at that," he said.

She wouldn't dream of pursuing the subject. "When we get to the River Queen, I'll say I'm Emmet's wife and nothing more. I don't want them to know I plan to run the place until I talk to Mr. Field. I want to make sure whatever needs to be signed is signed, and everything's legal."

"Quite right. Finish your coffee and we'll go take a look."

Chapter 6

There were two front entrances to the River Queen Hotel & Saloon. A wide-open doorway with swinging doors led to the saloon. Rose chose the smaller door that lay to the right. Inside she found a shabby-looking lobby with mismatched furniture that looked as if it could use a good dusting. No carpet, just a rough wooden floor that looked as if it hadn't been swept for days. Such negligence would never have occurred at the Birchwood Inn.

A small man with thinning hair stood behind the counter. "Looking for a room?" he called.

Deke behind her, Rose walked to the counter. "I'm Mrs. Emmet Peterson, and I came to look around."

"Do tell!" The little man scurried around the counter and shook her hand. "I'm Howie Sanders, chief room clerk. So sorry about your husband. What can I do for you? Just name it. Anything. Anything at all."

"Nothing, thank you. I'll not take up your time." She didn't care for the little clerk's fawning attitude and hoped he would just leave her alone.

Howie pointed to the stairs. "All the rooms are on the second floor." He pointed toward an archway. "The saloon's through there, although"—he frowned with concern—"a lady like you might not want—"

"Don't worry about it." She turned to Deke. "Shall we?" They walked through the archway into the vast gambling hall where they were met with a huge swell of noise coming from a mixture of men's boisterous voices, glasses clinking, corks popping, and who knew what else? The room itself was huge, at least ninety by fifty feet with a ceiling at least sixteen feet high. Large gas-lit, brass chandeliers provided plenty of light. Men dressed in miners' clothes crowded around various games of chance. Deke nodded toward a crowded table. "That's faro. Over there's monte and poker. See that wheel? That's roulette."

A mahogany bar ran almost the entire length of one side of the room. Several large paintings hung from the wall above, interspersed between four huge, long mirrors. Rose looked closer. *Oh, dear.* The paintings all featured women with ample figures in various stages of undress. One was completely nude, reclining with her arm over her head and a come-hither smile on her face. Definitely the indecorous ladies would have to go. The floor was absolutely nauseating. Around the numerous brass spittoons, it was stained with the evidence of the miners' poor aim. The spittoons would also have to go, along with those paintings.

The few women she saw were dressed in fancy gowns cut so low much of their cleavage was showing. No decently dressed women in the place, as far as she could see. At least Deke made her feel secure as he followed her around on his crutches. Lots of people knew him. A woman in a red satin gown with too much rouge on her cheeks came over to where they were standing. She reeked of cheap perfume. Slapping Deke on the back, she declared, "Well, if it ain't the Australian! Haven't see you in a coon's age."

Deke turned to Rose. "Meet Tillie LaTour. She works here. Tillie, this is Rose Peterson, Emmet's wife. She's the new owner of the River Queen."

If Tillie was surprised, she didn't let on. Her brazen expression disappeared as she directed her gaze toward Rose. "Sorry about your husband. If he hadn't been so hot tempered, he wouldn't have got himself shot. Are you going to run the place?"

"I'm not sure." At the moment, Rose wasn't sure about anything, she was so startled by the bluntness of this woman.

Tillie gave her a friendly pat on the arm. "Look, honey, if you need any help, and you probably will, you can find me on the third floor. I'm in charge of the girls up there." She addressed Deke. "Has she met Jake yet?" When he shook his head, she rolled her eyes. "I'd like to see the look on Jake's face when he finds out his boss is a woman. Good luck, Mrs. Peterson." She blew Deke a kiss and was gone.

Rose watched after her, "What does she do here?"

"She's a hostess and a dancer, as well as"—his lips twitched with amusement—"she pretty much told you what else she did. Her girls entertain select gentlemen on the third floor. For a price, of course."

"I see." Rose struggled to hide her surprise. According to Emmet's letters, he was running a perfectly respectable hotel. Never had he mentioned gambling, drinking, prostitution. He'd led his family to believe all guests were in bed and asleep by nine, and nothing stronger than tea was served in the decorous dining room. Mustn't let Deke think she was so naïve she hadn't known. He seemed to be well acquainted with Tillie. Was he one of those "selected gentlemen" her girls entertained on the third floor? Somehow she didn't think so. He'd have a hard time getting up there on crutches, but more than that, he didn't seem the type of man who'd pay for a woman's favors. She could be wrong, though. Now, more than ever, she was realizing her experience with men had been limited at best.

She looked more closely at the long, mahogany bar crowded with men. Something strange occurred to her. Where were the women? Not the painted, gaudily dressed ones, but ordinary women like herself.

Deke took her arm. "There's a restaurant. Do you want to see it?"

"Of course." They peeked into the one-and-only restaurant. It didn't look like much with its dirty floor and long, rough plank tables without any tablecloths. She'd be checking on that later. They were leaving the restaurant when a man in his forties with well-oiled, slicked back hair and bright red suspenders walked up to Rose and eyed her boldly. "You're Emmet's wife?" When she nodded, he stuck out his hand. "I'm Jake Grunion. Pleased to meet you. I run the joint."

She didn't care for the discourteous tone of his voice, but always polite, she shook his hand. "I'm pleased to meet you, Mr. Grunion. So you worked for my husband?" Jake nodded. "Then I'm assuming you have an office somewhere."

"In the back, but I don't expect a lady like you to trouble herself. This hotel runs smooth as glass, so you don't have to worry."

His polite words didn't fool her, especially when she caught the flash of insolence in his eyes. She smiled and in her most pleasant voice replied, "Of course, you're right, Mr. Grunion, but even so, I might wish to visit your office." She touched her hand to her heart. "In memory of my dear, departed husband, I want to feel closer to him—see where he worked, meet his friends and employees. Surely you understand."

Grunion's mouth pulled into a thin-lipped smile. "Er...of course. Emmet Peterson's widow is welcome to visit my office any time." With a quick bow, he drifted away.

Deke gave her a nudge. "Dear, departed husband? What was that all about?"

"You know very well what it's about. What an awful man."

"They don't come any sleazier than Jake Grunion."

"Then why would Emmet hire such a man?"

Deke shrugged. "He had his reasons. Have you seen enough? Do you want to get out of here?"

"Let's go. I need some fresh air."

Once outside, they walked to where Deke had secured Sidney. He untied the reins and gave her a quizzical look. "Now that you've seen the place, what do you think?"

Her first visit to the River Queen Hotel & Saloon had been an eye-opening experience. With its raucous noise, indecent portraits, revolting spittoons, tobacco-stained floors, and the awful stench of tobacco, beer, and unwashed bodies, it wasn't at all what she expected. Worst of all was meeting Jake Grunion, so unpleasant she hadn't had time to think. Now outside, she took a breath of clean air, stepped back, and gazed at her hotel. The tallest building around, its solid brick structure had an air of permanence about it, not like many of the flimsy structures that lined the street. Just reading the large sign across the front, THE RIVER QUEEN HOTEL & CASINO, caused a ripple of pride to run through her.

"The River Queen is mine and I'm keeping it, Deke. Right now it's a disgrace. What was my husband thinking? There's much to be fixed, but I'm full of plans already. Just wait until I get my hands on that restaurant. It'll take money, but I think Emmet left me some. If not, I'll get it somehow."

Deke broke into a grin. "Good for you. You're a smart woman, and you made a wise decision. What next? Where do you want to go?"

"I want to go home, Deke. I need to get back to Lucy. And also"—a flicker of apprehension coursed through her—"I must talk to Ben and Coralee. They think I've lost my mind. I must convince them I know what I'm doing."

She held Deke's crutches as he mounted his horse. He was reaching down to grasp her hand when a smart-looking phaeton drawn by two matched white horses drew up beside them. Mason Talbot sat on the high seat, reins in hand. He smiled down at her. "Ah, there you are, Mrs. Peterson. Your mother- and father-in-law were worried after your...shall we say, hasty departure."

She drew herself up. "No need for concern, sir. I'm fine."

So far, Mason hadn't acknowledged Deke's existence or even looked in his direction. Focused entirely on Rose, he inquired, "May I give you a ride?"

Rose flicked a quick look at Deke. "Thank you, but I have one."

Mason appeared not to hear. "I've been talking with Mr. Field. He has much to discuss with you. Did you know Emmet had accounts of considerable size at Wells Fargo?" With alacrity, Mason sprang from the carriage and offered his hand. "I'll tell you more on the way home."

How could she refuse when she was dying to know what the solicitor had said? Framing an explanation and apology she looked up at Deke, but before she could speak, he brought two fingers to the brim of his hat, murmured a quick, "Good day, Mrs. Peterson," touched his heels to Sidney's flank and rode away.

* * * *

Curse the anchor that caught. Curse the boat that overturned and broke his leg, and curse the doctor who told him if he took one step before the cast was off, he'd be crippled the rest of his life. Ordinarily Deke took whatever Fate had in store for him in his stride, but riding back to the cheap room he'd rented, his frustration hit new heights. Damn these crutches! Just now, he'd felt like a helpless fool, having to hobble along after her, and she, so considerate and concerned, would get that look of pity on her face that made him want to puke. Then, even worse, he could hardly believe what he was seeing when Mason Talbot drove up in that fancy phaeton of his, and she, little fool, gazed up at him all delighted, like she'd seen a man so handsome, so poised and sure of himself every single woman in town must be panting after him. Good God! Little did she know. *Rose.* Whenever he thought of her—which was much too often—he pictured her with her hair down, like it was that day they met, all silky thick and golden bronze, hanging loose around her shoulders. Last night, after he went to bed, he imagined what it would be like to run his hands through those silky strands, pull her warm body close... What was he thinking? Better stop day dreaming. Now that she'd met the rich and irresistible owner of the Egyptian Hotel, she wouldn't be giving this cripple the time of day. But wait. One more week, Dr. Andrews said. *One more week, Mrs. Rose Peterson, and then we'll see how taken you are with the likes of Mason Talbot.*

* * * *

Rose looked down at her faded, patched dress and heartily wished she were wearing something elegant that befitted Mason Talbot's fine carriage. Even so, he'd handed her into his carriage as if she were a queen. As he picked up the reins and pulled away, he threw her a delighted, side-long glance. "I'm glad I found you, Mrs. Peterson. Your in-laws were worried. I must say, you gave them quite a surprise."

"Then you're not angry?"

"Why I should I be?"

"You went to all that trouble to draw up the check, and Lord knows what else, only to be disappointed."

Mason chuckled. "Not at all. There are too many namby-pamby women in this world. I rather enjoyed seeing a young woman stand up for herself. A rare sight, if I may say so."

How kind of him. What a relief that he understood. "I'm concerned about my in-laws. I expected they'd be shocked and horrified, but instead they couldn't believe I was serious."

"I wouldn't worry, especially since you've assured them they'll always have a home. Although of course"—Mason slanted a cautionary glance— "are you sure you've made the right decision? I assume you've seen the hotel. Now that you have, are you sure you can handle—?"

"Quite sure." She wanted him to understand she wasn't one of those namby-pamby women he talked about. "My parents owned a hotel, and I helped run it. I must admit, the River Queen is far different from the Birchwood Inn of Cairo, Illinois, but I like a good challenge and I'm absolutely not going to sell."

He chuckled again, seeming to delight in her words. "Call me Mason. When we arrive at the farm, would you like me to come in? Perhaps I could soothe a few wounded feelings, make your case, so to speak. Also, I'd like to further explain about the duel. Not that I expect your in-laws' forgiveness, but perhaps I can help them understand."

"Would you? I think that's a fine idea and much appreciated."

As Mason drove her home, Rose got a knot in her stomach that grew increasingly tighter the closer they got to the farm. She kept picturing that moment when she would walk through the door and find Ben and Coralee waiting to confront her. Surely they must have realized by now she meant what she said. At the very least, they'd be angry. She would do her best to make them understand. Having Mason Talbot by her side eased her anxiety considerably. How comforting to have a distinguished man like him to help her explain. "Do call me Rose."

"Rose, then." Mason flicked the reins with a flourish and threw her a confident smile.

At the farmhouse, Rose, followed by Mason, found Ben and Coralee in the kitchen. She was greeted with glacial stares. Lucy had been put to bed. Raymond and Drucilla had retired for the night. Her heart pounding, Rose opened her mouth to speak, but before she could say a word, Mason greeted them politely and remarked, "Sorry to bother you, but could we go to the parlor and talk? If it wouldn't inconvenience you, of course. I have much to say, and I believe Rose does, too."

After a long hesitation, Ben gave them a frosty nod and they all traipsed into the parlor. With a sinking heart, Rose noted no refreshments had been offered, an ominous indication of her usually hospitable mother-in-law's hostility. When Rose and Mason were seated, they faced Ben and Coralee who sat stern-faced and ramrod straight on the horsehair sofa across. Mason was first to break the icy silence. "Rose wants to talk to you, but first…" He cleared his throat. "I have already told you how it came about that I engaged in a duel with your son. As for the duel itself… It's hard for me to talk about such an unfortunate event, but I want to explain what happened."

Ben raised his palm. "What's the point? My son is dead. Nothing you might say will bring him back."

"If you don't wish me to go on, then of course I won't. I suppose in a way I'm being selfish. I admire and respect the both of you and don't want you ever to think I murdered your son in cold blood. I want you to understand such was not the case."

Ben was about to answer, but Coralee silenced him with a quick jab to his ribs. "Let the man speak. I want to know exactly why my son is lying dead in his grave."

Mason ignored the enmity in Coralee's voice. In a calm, level tone he continued, "That day, as was usual, I worked long hours at my brewery. Darkness had fallen when I left. I had dinner, and then stopped by the River Queen. It was my way of relaxing—getting away from my own hotel—playing a few hands of faro before I went home. On that night, the only table open was run by Ned Barrow, a dealer I didn't like because I suspected him of cheating. I always made a point to avoid him, but that evening I had no choice. I cautioned myself to be extra vigilant, and before long, sure enough, I caught him dealing marked cards. That's when I realized the whole table was gaffed. Excuse me—that means set up to cheat. The corner of each card was shaved so slightly that unless you were looking for it, you'd never notice. I must admit, I allowed my temper to get a bit out of hand. I demanded to speak to Emmet, whom I knew fairly well. When he came to the table, I didn't mince words. I accused his dealer of cheating and implied Emmet knew. He did not take it well, and I—"

"What!" Ben's eyes widened in anger. "My son was an honest man, Mr. Talbot. I never knew him to so much as touch a card, let alone cheat."

Mason cast him a look of sympathy. "It's the insanity of the Gold Rush, sir. Greed and avarice have caused many a man to do things he'd never do at home. Sorry to cause you further grief. I'm only telling it like it is. If you like, I'll stop right there."

"Continue on. I want to hear it all."

"We continued to argue. I didn't back down and was adamant that the faro table was gaffed. Emmet called me a liar. He became extremely agitated. Kept insisting I was wrong. By then, I was beginning to realize the argument was going nowhere. I was about to back off when Emmet completely lost his head and challenged me to a duel."

Coralee spoke up. "But nobody fights duels anymore. Emmet would never do such an idiotic thing."

"I'm only stating the facts. If you want, I can produce plenty of witnesses. Your son had murder in his eye when he told me he'd send his second to my office in the morning so we could settle on the arrangements."

"What do you mean by 'arrangements'?" Ben asked.

"Illegal or not, there are accepted guidelines for affairs of honor. For instance, in most cases the challenged party is given the choice of weapons. The seconds decide all the details, such as the number of shots permitted, how many paces they must take before they turn and fire. They take care to ensure the ground chosen gives no unfair advantage to either party. They arrange for a doctor to be on hand, which, in our case, there was. Duels are often formal affairs, so the seconds agree on the dress code. They also decide whether or not refreshments will be served."

"At a duel?" Ben's jaw dropped open. "Refreshments? Good God!"

"I can assure you, no refreshments were served at our duel. Only a handful of witnesses were present, including our seconds. All who were there realized the gravity of the occasion. As I said, we did have a doctor present, although unfortunately, when the time came, nothing could have been done…"

Mason appeared to think better of what he was about to say and continued on. "That night, I left the River Queen and went home. Next morning, I hardly gave the whole sordid affair a thought. I figured by then Emmet would have come to his senses, but I was wrong. Along about ten o'clock, here came Jake Grunion, whom Emmet had appointed as his second. Jake demanded I select the time, place, and weapon. 'Swords or pistols?' he asked. I was astounded. I'm not one of those swashbuckling swordsman from *The Three Musketeers*. What choice did I have but pistols?"

Rose couldn't keep silent. "Why chose anything all? Why didn't you simply tell him you refused to engage in a duel? The whole affair is incredible. It appears my husband was at fault, but I still don't understand why you didn't just say no."

"I'm not a coward, Mrs. Peterson. As I said, it's a matter of honor." Mason gave her a rueful smile. "Men are like that, fools that we are. You women wouldn't understand because you're smarter, and far more practical."

Ben leaned forward intently. "My son was not a stupid man, Mr. Talbot. It's beyond me to understand why he'd do such an outrageous thing."

"It's not so much that Emmet wanted to kill me as he wanted to restore his so-called tarnished reputation by demonstrating a willingness to risk his life for it."

After Ben thought a moment, he seemed satisfied with Mason's answer. "Please continue on."

Mason described the duel itself: pistols at dawn in a secluded spot along the Sacramento River. They each brought their second. Jake Grunion for Emmet and Rudy Avery for Mason. "As I said, tradition decrees the seconds are to negotiate, sometimes down to the last moment, and hopefully come to an agreement that would save the honor of both participants without resorting to bullets. They did their best, but Emmet was obstinate. Couldn't be dissuaded. And so…" Mason spread his hands. "I'm so deeply sorry, but to be honest, if I had it to do over, man of honor that I am, I wouldn't change a thing."

For a time Ben sat silent. Finally he gave a brief nod. "Thank you for explaining, Mr. Talbot. I can't say that my wife and I can forgive you, but you've helped me better understand." His gaze shifted to Rose. "We need to talk."

He was angry. She could tell from the harshness in his voice. "Anything you have to say, I don't mind if Mr. Talbot hears. I love you both, and I'm sorry I upset you this morning. It's just that when I learned the farm and hotel were mine—"

"They are *not* yours." Ben stood up, his whole body shaking with anger. "After you left, I talked further with that idiot solicitor. He made a mistake. Emmet acquired those properties with the profits of his gold discoveries. You had nothing to do with it. Therefore, I am the closest male relative, and the property goes to me. We're to meet in Field's office tomorrow morning. Whether you sign the papers or not, it's only a formality." He addressed Mason. "Can you be there, Mr. Talbot? I want to get this entire affair over and done with."

"Yes, of course."

"Fine." Ben turned to Coralee. "Come, we're going to bed."

Numb inside, Rose watched her in-laws leave the parlor without another word. This was horrible, worse than she ever imagined. She turned to Mason. "I never dreamed they'd turn on me like that."

Mason took her hand. "How upsetting this must be for you. Believe me, I'll help in any way I can. I'll be at Field's office in the morning. We shall get this affair settled and avoid further conflict." With a chivalrous bow, he took up her hand and kissed it. "Good night, my dear. This is all for the best. You're a beautiful woman, much too beautiful to be troubling yourself with such mundane matters as running a hotel. Good night. Don't bother showing me to the door."

Alone in the kitchen, Rose made her dinner from some bread and a piece of leftover fried chicken, but her in-laws' hostility had caused her to lose her appetite and she could hardly eat. What had she been thinking of? Like Mason pointed out, how could she, a mere woman, handle her own affairs? How could she possibly have thought she could defy her in-laws and win? She would apologize—beg their forgiveness and promise she'd never again be foolish enough to claim she owned her own property.

She tidied the kitchen, lit a candle, and stepped into the tiny bedroom that was now hers and Lucy's. Such an awful room, miserably small with its battered chest-of-drawers, tiny high-up window, and narrow bed. She found Lucy sound asleep, gave her a kiss, and slid her little body over a few inches so she'd have room for herself, although they'd still be cramped together. Again, she couldn't help thinking how unfair it was that Drucilla and Raymond had more room than they needed upstairs, especially Raymond, who never gave a thought to neatness and wouldn't care if he lived in a pigpen. She shouldn't be petty, though. It was just...

Would this be her life from now on? If she stayed with Ben and Coralee, she'd always be last on the list, no better than a servant, actually. Her only escape was to marry. She'd certainly have no problem finding a husband, considering, as Dulcee had pointed out, around here there were fifty men to every woman. But so what? One loveless marriage was enough, and she'd never do it again. Of course, there was always the possibility she might find a man she could love. Mason Talbot, for instance. She could tell from the way he looked at her that he liked her. She liked him well enough, but as yet he hadn't caused her to heart to flutter. She certainly didn't ache for his touch, not like she had Anthony. Of course, given time? Maybe she could learn to love him. She certainly ought to, being that he was rich, handsome, and charming besides. The only other man she was acquainted with was Deke. She smiled, remembering how he'd shown her how to run her hands through the barrel of chicken feed. What a silly thing to do, but even so, he'd raised her spirits that night. She liked him a lot, but could she ever fall in love with him? Even if she did, the poor man was down and out. He could hardly take care of himself, let alone take on a wife.

So Ben owned the hotel after all. What a blow. Only hours ago, she'd been thrilled at the thought the River Queen belonged to her. How she would have loved to make it into a first class hotel, the dream of a lifetime.

How sad that now she could only contemplate what might have been. But wait, she'd thought of something.

With a sudden urgency, she slipped from the covers and reached under her bed where she kept her valise and dragged it out. By flickering candlelight, she sat cross-legged on the floor and drew out a large envelope that contained a few documents and a packet of letters tied together with a bit of blue ribbon. She read everything through, including all documents and letters. When she was done, she clasped her hands together and whispered, "Yes!"

Chapter 7

Sitting behind his desk, Archer Field furrowed his brow in puzzlement as he stroked his well-trimmed goatee. His gaze rested on Rose. "Would you repeat that, Mrs. Peterson? I didn't quite grasp your meaning."

Rose sat facing the solicitor, the envelope clutched tight in her hands. To her right sat Mason Talbot. To her left, Ben and Coralee sat stiff and stony-faced. The three had driven into town together amidst a miserable astrosphere of hostile silence. In a steady voice, Rose replied, "I'm happy to repeat it, Mr. Field. The River Queen is mine, and I can prove it."

"How so? Can you explain?" The solicitor leaned back in his chair and tapped his fingers together.

Rose pulled some papers from the envelope and held the top one up. "This is my marriage license, showing that I was legally married to Emmet Peterson on August 20, 1847." She laid it on her lap and held up the next. "This is my parents' will. Since I was the only child, and they had no other male heirs, clearly their property was left entirely to me, and that included the Birchwood Inn in Cairo, Illinois."

Mr. Field nodded agreeably. "So?"

Rose held up the third document. "Shortly after my parents died, and directly before I was married, I sold the Birchwood Inn for twenty-five thousand dollars. Here's the bill of sale. As you may know, in the State of Illinois when a woman marries, all her assets belong to her husband, so naturally, when I married Emmet, the money from the sale of the inn went to him."

Ben turned and glared at her. "That's absolutely right. So what are we doing here? This is a waste of time."

"Hold on." Rose pulled the last paper from the envelope. Not a document this time but a letter. Strange, how her hand was steady and her heart beat at a normal rate. It must be because she knew she was right. In a steady voice, she continued. "This is a letter written by Emmet to me after he bought the River Queen. I'm going to read it." She smoothed out the folded pages and began, "'My Dear Rose...' I'll skip the personal part." She skimmed down to what was important and kept reading. "'You'll be interested to know I just bought a hotel called the River Queen. Although it needs work, I consider it a splendid piece of property, situated on a choice piece of land not far from the Sacramento River. It's all thanks to you, considering I used your twenty-five thousand from the sale of the Birchwood Inn to buy the River Queen. Without that, I could never have bought it.'" Rose lowered the paper and raised her eyes. "Well, Mr. Field? My money was used to buy the River Queen. Doesn't this prove it's mine?"

The solicitor allowed a long moment of silence to go by. "It appears that it does. Leave those documents with me. I'll run them by the judge, but if those are the facts, then yes, I can see why you'd have first claim on the property."

Rose got up and laid the envelope on the solicitor's desk. The hotel was hers! She looked to where her in-laws sat thunderstruck. She wasn't done yet. Seated again, she said, "I want to make it perfectly clear that all I want is the hotel. Whether or not I have a claim on the farm, it doesn't matter. I want the farm to go to my mother- and father-in-law. As for the money in Emmet's bank account, would it be possible that we could divide it equally?"

"I don't see why not." Mr. Field turned to Ben. "Would you agree to that, Mr. Peterson?"

Please say it's all right. Rose held her breath. She was doing her best to act sure of herself, but if she had to take much more of her in-law's hostility, she might break down and weep. Maybe she should give up. Be the docile daughter-in-law again. Maybe...

Ben glanced at Coralee, and when she nodded, he said, "This whole thing is a travesty. My daughter-in-law has lost her mind. However, because my wife and I have better things to do than fight her ridiculous claims, I shall agree to take the farm. She can have that den of iniquity and good riddance."

The solicitor solemnly inquired, "By 'den of iniquity' can I assume you mean the River Queen Hotel?"

Ben's lip curled in disgust. "It's a vile place of wickedness, Mr. Field. I cannot imagine how my daughter-in-law would want anything to do with it, but apparently that's her choice."

"Fine, then. The matter is settled." Archer Field made a show of gathering the papers on his desk and stacking them together. "As I understand it, you wish to divide the money in Emmet's account. This will take at least three days, possibly longer. When everything is ready to sign, I'll let you know."

She'd won! The River Queen was really hers. If she were alone, she'd have danced a little jig. Her in-laws got up to leave. Ben left without so much as a backward glance. Coralee turned to her and asked in a frosty voice, "Well, are you coming? We're going straight home."

Rose hesitated. She didn't want to be with them right now, not when they were showing such hostility. How could she make them see she was only standing up for herself?

Mason stepped forward. "Don't worry, Mrs. Peterson. I'll take her home. But first I'd like to give your daughter-in-law a tour of the town." His gaze shifted to Rose. "If you would like, of course."

With a hidden sigh of relief, Rose answered, "That would be lovely."

"Fine then." Mason offered her his arm. "You're about to see the sights of Sacramento. I might even give you a tour of my brewery."

* * * *

A tour of the town was just the distraction Rose needed. Ben and Coralee's hostility had lain like a heavy weight on her shoulders. Now, thanks to Mason, it had lifted, if only for a little while. Sitting by his side in his sporty phaeton, she couldn't help but notice how heads turned as they drove through the streets. Again, she heartily wished her new dresses and bonnets were ready, but they weren't, so no use fretting about it. At least Mason made her feel so comfortable she didn't feel awkward and dowdy sitting next to one of the town's prestigious civic leaders. The excursion was delightful. He'd shown her the beautiful wetlands where the American and Sacramento rivers came together. The tour of his brewery had been far more interesting than she'd expected. She learned how beer was made as he guided her through his three-story Talbot's Brewery. Several kinds were produced, including Talbot's Cream Ale which, according to Mason's proud description, had such a rich flavor, foaming appearance, and cooling qualities that it was the favorite of everyone, everywhere.

Toward the end, Mason took her to Walker's Emporium, a large store on Front Street that sold everything from farm equipment to furs, fans, lace, and all kinds of perfumery. Mason led her through the store to the perfume counter where he asked the female clerk if the store carried *Eau de Cologne Impériale*. Indeed it did, and soon an exquisitely cut glass bottle of perfume sat on the counter. Mason picked it up, removed the stopper, and offered it to Rose. "Take a sniff. It's from Pierre Guerlain, the favorite of Empress Eugenie, wife of Napoleon III."

Rose had never owned such expensive perfume, nor had anyone in her family. She'd never even smelled any. She held it to her nose and took a sniff. The delightful fragrance of rosemary, orange, and lemon verbena wafted past her nostrils. "It's very nice."

"Then it's yours."

She opened her mouth to say no, thank you, but before she could, he spoke again. "Yes, I know. The rule is a lady doesn't accept such a gift from a gentleman, but that's a Cairo, Illinois, rule. You're in the West now." He arched an eyebrow. "New state. New set of rules. I want you to have it, no obligation whatsoever."

How charming he was. How generous. He'd said no obligation. Looking into those honest blue eyes, how could she not believe him? Besides, after what he just said, she'd sound like a prig if she refused. "No obligation?"

"None whatsoever."

"Thank you, Mason. I shall treasure it."

After they left the store, the small package tucked safely in her reticule, he suggested they visit another store, but she declined. She'd been away from Lucy all day and really should get home. As they drove along Front Street in the center of town, they encountered a horse-drawn wagon piled high with big chunks of ice that was coming the other way. A man was driving, and it was…Deke! Her heart jumped when she saw him. Quickly she raised her hand and wiggled her fingers. She thought he nodded back but couldn't be sure.

* * * *

Deke turned his head to look after the phaeton that had just passed him by. He'd only caught a glimpse, but that definitely was Rose. But what was she doing with that low-down snake, Mason Talbot? Had she forgotten he was the man who'd shot her husband? And that wasn't the half of it. She ought to be set straight, but far be it for him to interfere. All his life, he'd kept to his own business, and he'd keep doing just that.

He flicked the reins. Better move along, or the ice would all melt and he wouldn't make a penny.

* * * *

In near darkness, Mason reined the horses to a stop in front of the farmhouse and sprang with alacrity from the carriage. He circled around and held out his arms. She would just as soon help herself down, but she clasped his hands and let him swing her to the ground. He didn't let go her hands, and when he started to draw her toward him, she knew he was going to kiss her. She could easily give in, but not having the least desire to find herself in the arms of Mason Talbot, she drew back. He immediately let her go. "You must forgive me. It's just that I am so damnably attracted to you that I…" He took a deep, shaky breath. "Am I forgiven?"

She had no wish to hurt his feelings. "I'm a widow in mourning. I hope you understand."

"Of course." Smooth as ever, he continued, "By society's rules, it's too soon, but may I take you to dinner sometime?"

She smiled up at him. "I suppose it's too soon according to Cairo, Illinois, rules, but as you've pointed out, this is the West, so yes, I would love to."

"When?"

"As soon as I'm the legal owner of the River Queen. I hope you understand."

"I understand perfectly. You have too much on your mind right now. We'll wait until you get the deed. Then we'll have something to celebrate."

As Mason drove away, Rose stood on the porch and looked after him. What a nice man, and how very considerate. She knew he wanted her, just from the way he'd tried to kiss her. He'd talked about waiting a decent interval, and that probably meant only one thing. Clearly things moved fast in the Old West. He was courting her, wanted to marry her, and she ought to be thrilled. Mason Talbot was a fantastic catch, the kind of man every woman dreamed of. What more could she ask for? If she wanted, she could give up all thought of running a hotel and live in luxury the rest of her life. The trouble was, she didn't want to give up the River Queen and wasn't in the least elated that a rich, handsome, charming man had wanted to kiss her. What was wrong with her? She ought to feel grateful, considering she hadn't been kissed since Emmet went away. And even then, Emmet and his quick little pecks was about as exciting as feeding the hogs. Come to think of it, only once in her life had she got the kind of kisses that made her toes curl, and that was when Anthony Parks lured her to his room and drove her wild. Even now, she felt a jolt inside remembering that night. One night out of a lifetime. She pressed her hand over the locket that lay hidden beneath the bodice of her dress. Not likely it would ever happen again.

One thing she realized: what she told Mason was a lie, partly anyway. True, she was a widow, but that didn't automatically mean she was in mourning. The truth was, although she was saddened by Emmet's death, she was far from being heartbroken and devastated. How could she be for a man she hadn't seen in two years and hadn't loved in the first place?

And that was an unfortunate fact she would keep to herself.

She found everyone in the parlor when she went inside. Not wanting to talk, she tiptoed by and headed straight to her room. She lit a candle and found Lucy in bed, wide awake, flinging her arms out to greet her. "Mommy, I missed you!"

"I missed you, sweetheart."

"Did you give Grandpa the farm?"

"Yes, I did, but I kept the hotel."

"Is he mad?"

"Maybe a little bit, but he'll get over it." Rose held her daughter tight. She hoped she was doing the right thing. Above all else, Lucy must be safe and happy. Perhaps the best thing to do would be give up this crazy idea of running a hotel and get married again. She'd have security. Lucy would have a father. But Mason Talbot? Well, perhaps...

Drifting off to sleep, her last thoughts were of Deke Fleming. What on earth was he doing with a wagon full of ice? She hoped they'd meet again soon so he could tell her what he was up to. And also... She wasn't sure why, but she enjoyed talking to him. Not that he flattered her liked Mason did. There was just something about Deke that made her want to see him again.

* * * *

In the morning, Rose found her sister-in-law in the kitchen. Ordinarily, at this early hour Drucilla didn't say much but today she was all bouncy, her usual taciturn expression replaced by a smile. "What are you so happy about?" Rose asked.

Drucilla's eyes lit. "You'd never guess. I was visiting Dulcee yesterday and discovered she loves to read, just like I do. She has got a whole shelf full of books. Nathaniel Hawthorne, William Thackeray, the Bronte sisters, and lots more. She loaned me *Jane Eyre*, and when I'm done with that, she'll let me have *Vanity Fair*. Think of it. Rose! I've got something to read again."

Rose remembered the day they left Illinois. There'd been no room in the wagons for her sister-in-law's huge collection of books. She'd come close to weeping when she learned she'd have to leave them all behind. "That's wonderful, Drucilla. I haven't seen you this happy since we left Illinois."

"Ma doesn't think it's so wonderful. She's still after me, thinks reading is a waste of time. What I should be doing is looking for a husband."

How many times had Rose heard this? "You're thirty years old. You should do what you want to do, not what anyone else wants."

"Around here, finding a husband wouldn't be hard. When I go into town, there's men everywhere, swarming the streets. They stare at me like I'm a great beauty, which is ridiculous. Even so, if I so much as crooked my little finger, they'd come running, I could get married tomorrow if I wanted to."

"But you don't, and that's that. You should read your books and stop worrying."

"You always manage to cheer me up, Rose. I just wish..." Drucilla heaved a sigh. "This thing with the hotel. Are you certain? Mother and Father are so upset. I hate it that you're hardly speaking to one another. It's like a funeral around here."

"You think I don't miss the chats and the laughter? I hate it too. I'd give anything if things were back to normal." Rose paused to think. "Well, almost anything. The River Queen is rightly mine, and I'm not backing down. Ben and Coralee haven't been very kind to me, but that doesn't matter. I couldn't ask for better grandparents for Lucy, and you know I still love them, no matter what. I promise you, when everything's settled, I'll do everything I can to make us a happy family again."

"But when will everything be settled?"

"I'm not going near the River Queen until the deed is mine. Mr. Field said it would take at least three days."

* * * *

Three very long, uncomfortable days. On the first day, Dulcee stopped by for a visit. She nodded with approval when Rose told her the news. "Good for you, missy. Didn't I tell you to have faith in yourself? Looks like you did and got what you wanted."

"But at what price? Ben and Coralee are hardly speaking to me."

"They'll come 'round. Just give it some time, and don't forget you're stronger than you think."

Was she? Dulcee's encouragement helped, but Ben and Coralee's disapproval weighed heavily upon her. The time passed slowly. Rose avoided her in-laws as much as she could, spending much of her time outdoors. There was plenty to do. Ben hadn't yet found a replacement for Deke, so a reluctant Raymond had been recruited to feed the horses and oxen, milk the cow, slop the pigs, and whatever else needed doing. Rose volunteered to take care of the chickens and kept herself busy scattering their feed, collecting eggs, and cleaning the coop. Every time she went into the tank house, she ran her hands through the chicken feed. The delightful feeling always made her think of Deke. How was he doing? Where was he hauling a wagon full of ice, and why? She hoped she'd see him next time she went to town.

* * * *

All his life, Deke Fleming had managed to take everything in his stride, prepared to cope with whatever problem came along. Now, sitting on the examining table in the office of Dr. Horace Andrews, he wasn't so sure. Saw in hand, the doctor was about to cut the cast off. When he took a look at the leg, what would he say?

Sorry, son, it didn't heal quite right and you'll have a permanent limp.

Or even worse: *What a shame. Well, it was a bad break and you shouldn't have expected it to heal properly. You'd better get accustomed to those crutches. You'll be using them the rest of your life.*

Oh, God.

Dr. Andrews started sawing. The two sides of the cast fell apart. He bent over the leg for a closer look. Carefully he felt along the shin bone, then looked up and smiled. "Excellent! It's healed perfectly. Considering the severity of the break, you're a lucky man, Deke."

"I won't have a limp?"

"Doesn't look that way. You'll have to try it out, but it looks like you'll walk as normally as ever."

Deke wasn't much of a praying man. He left all that religious business to his devout friend, Mitch. Even so, outside the doctor's office, he raised his eyes to the sky. He was a whole man again. Not a cripple. *Thank you, God.*

He headed back to the ice house, a bit shaky at first but soon was walking with long, sure strides. *Take a look at me now, Mrs. Rose Peterson.*

Chapter 8

As predicted, in exactly three days, Archer Field sent word the deed had been transferred to Rose's name. She was to stop by his office to pick it up, plus receive further information and instructions. Her mother used to say, "There's many a slip twixt the cup and the lip," so she tried to remain calm, yet her mind raced with all that she had to do. Today, in honor of the occasion, she'd take the buggy. In the stable, Raymond helped her hitch it up. "So you're going to get the deed today?" he asked.

"Yes, I am."

"Ma and Pa won't like it."

She laughed. "Not one little bit, Raymond, but don't you worry. Everything will be all right."

Would it? Driving into town, she contemplated the rift in the family she'd caused and again asked herself if she was doing the right thing. Stop! Right or wrong, she'd made her decision and there was no turning back. When she got to town, she first stopped at the dressmaker's. Yes, at last her dresses were ready. She'd ordered three: a full-skirted, blue silk taffeta trimmed with matching velvet ribbon; a deep ruby gown of patterned cotton with double-puffed sleeves and a full, three-flounce skirt that made her waist look incredibly small; a sensible, high-necked, brown wool bombazine for when she wanted to look serious.

She couldn't get out of the faded blue gingham fast enough. Trying each gown on in a full-length mirror, she tossed modesty to the winds, turning this way and that, unable to get enough of herself. What a difference! Funny what a new gown and bonnet did for her wounded spirits. She decided to wear the blue silk taffeta, with the matching silk bonnet, telling the dressmaker to please remove the faded gingham from her sight, and may she never see it again. Brimming with confidence, knowing she looked her very best, she proceeded to Mr. Field's office. He greeted her cordially, and in his stuffy way remarked, "You look absolutely splendid today, Mrs. Peterson." He gave her the deed and advised her to go immediately to Wells Fargo where he'd set up her account.

At the bank, she signed the required papers, discovering her account held nearly twenty thousand dollars, half the money that Emmet left and far more than she expected. Ben and Coralee would receive the same amount, and with the farm thrown in, how could they complain? For the first time in her life, she ordered checks of her own. A warm glow flowed through her as she left Wells Fargo. So far, the day had gone wonderfully well, a sure sign her luck would continue. Next stop, her very own hotel. Today was the day she was going to take over.

Rose swept through the lobby entrance of the River Queen with her head held high. Howie Sanders, the desk clerk whom she remembered as being a bit obsequious, was the first to spot her. Hand outstretched, he came around the counter to greet her. "Mrs. Peterson, good to see you. Is there something I can help you with?"

She shook his hand. "There certainly is, Howie. I've come to take over the running of my hotel, and you can be a big help."

"Take over?"

"That's right." With a purposeful lift of her chin, Rose continued, "Since I now own the hotel, I intend to personally be in charge. First off, I'd like to see my husband's office. I intend to move in there myself."

The little man's lips parted in surprise "Uh, well, now… I don't know as how… It, uh, might already be occupied, seeing as how Mr. Peterson is dead and all."

She'd prepared herself for minor problems such as this. "Let's not worry about it. Just show me Emmet's office."

"Yes, ma'am." Leading the way, the desk clerk guided her through the gambling hall. In the early afternoon, the huge room wasn't as crowded as the other night. Even so, gamblers crowded around every table and filled almost every stool at the bar. Not a woman in sight. Probably those painted ladies slept very late. Heads turned as she passed by, but she ignored all the stares and kept going.

"Watch your skirt," Howie warned.

Indeed she would. The tobacco-stained floor and discolored spittoons were utterly disgusting. She would soon be making many changes, and that included a quick removal of the spittoons and also those nude, disgraceful pictures hanging behind the bar.

At the back, they passed through an archway and down a short hallway to a closed door at the end. Howie knocked, opened the door, and poked his head in. "Mr. Grunion? Someone to see you." He turned to Rose. "I'd best get back. Go right in."

Entering the office, she found Jake Grunion sitting behind a large desk. Raising his eyes, he saw who it was and frowned. He caught himself immediately and leisurely arose to greet her with a smile that held no warmth. "Well, if it isn't Mrs. Peterson." He waved at a chair on the other side of the desk. "Have a seat. What a pleasure you've come to visit us again."

Ignoring the obvious insincerity in his voice, she sat and looked him in the eye. "It's more than a visit. This was my husband's office?"

He nodded warily.

Obviously Jake had moved in. She would be as tactful as possible. "I'm sorry, Mr. Grunion, but I shall want it back. As of today, the River Queen is officially mine, so I'll be in charge from now on." Seeing his slight flinch of surprise, she quickly added, "Oh, there's no hurry. And of course you're still the manager. If Emmet trusted you and thought you were doing a good job, then I do, too. First off, I'd like to examine the books. Are they handy?"

She'd expected he wouldn't be overjoyed at her announcement but wasn't prepared for the way his jaw dropped open in surprise. "You?" He was blinking his eyes as if he couldn't believe what he'd just heard.

"Yes, me, Mr. Grunion. I don't know if my husband ever mentioned it, but back in Cairo, Illinois, I helped run my family's hotel, so I'm quite experienced in such endeavors."

He returned a nasty laugh. "You might think you're experienced, but running a hotel in Illinois is a far cry from running a hotel in a Gold Rush town like Sacramento."

His remark caused her heart to sink, but he mustn't know. "Regardless of all that, I am here to run the hotel and I wish to see the books."

A look of contempt filled his eyes. "The books are not handy, Mrs. Peterson. Maybe you mean well, but I've gotta tell you, running a hotel like this is no job for a woman."

She remembered what Deke had told her. "Fanny Wentworth owns the Silver Star, does she not?"

"Fanny Wentworth is a whore who made good. She packs a revolver, a bowie knife, and gets drunk every night. Is that what you're planning?"

"Of course not. I…" Jake's response had so startled her, she couldn't think what to say.

"Good Lord." Jake rolled his eyes, as if he could hardly believe what he was hearing. "Look, Mrs. Peterson, a nice lady like you is way out of her element here. Those men you see in the gambling hall don't give a damn about good manners. They come here to gamble, drink whiskey, and pay for the services of a woman, which the River Queen gladly provides. They get a little whiskey in 'em, the least thing sets 'em off and we've got a fight on our hands, at least one or two every night, sometimes more. With luck, they use their fists. Otherwise, they pull out their pistols and bullets fly. The week doesn't go by we don't carry some poor sod feet-first out the door, shot dead by some idiot who thinks he was insulted or got cheated. Do you think you can handle that? You, with your good manners and your fancy bonnet?" His lip curled in a sneer. "I don't think so. My best advice to you is go home and make yourself a cup of tea. Do your embroidery. You don't belong here."

Jake didn't wait for her answer. Instead, he got up and walked out of the office, leaving her so dumbfounded she had to breathe deep and sit quietly until her heart slowed down. She should have known better. Obviously, Jake had been running the place since Emmet died and had planned to continue. How foolish to assume a crude man like that would give up his position without so much as a murmur. And what about the books? He'd downright flinched when she asked to see them. Something funny going on there.

She would not give up. She'd deal with Jake later, although what exactly she'd do, she had no idea. But for now, she would check out that awful excuse for a restaurant. Surely she'd have better luck there.

The restaurant was worse than she remembered. No tablecloths, just long tables and benches of rough wood. Walking in, she caught sight of a bearded old miner spitting a wad of tobacco directly onto the sawdust-covered floor. Such repulsive behavior would soon stop, she'd see to that. When she asked to see the head chef, a hefty, balding man came out of the kitchen wiping his hands on the stained white apron that covered his huge belly. He said his name was Gus Hurdlicka, and yes, he ran the restaurant. When she introduced herself and asked to see the kitchen, he squinted and asked, "Why?"

She further explained her reason for being there. "And I'll be looking to make some improvements in your restaurant, Mr. Hurdlicka."

The chef's face turned red. A vein twitched in his fat jaw. "What changes are you talking about, lady?"

"Well, I…" She certainly hadn't meant to make him angry and must be more tactful. "For one thing, I'd like to see your menu with the thought that I might expand it and—"

"We don't have a menu. For breakfast I give 'em scrambled eggs, beans, and biscuits. For lunch I put out cold cuts and let 'em serve themselves. For dinner I make beef stew. Along with sourdough bread, that's enough." He crossed his arms and glared at her. "The customers aren't complaining, so what more do you want?"

"I…uh…" This was not turning out as she had thought. Best to change the subject. "May I see the kitchen?"

Gus replied with a grunt and led her to the back of the restaurant and into the kitchen where two young men who appeared to be Chinese stood at a long table chopping vegetables. An awful smell slammed her nostrils, a combination of rancid fat, spoiled meat, and rotting vegetables. She couldn't help wrinkling her nose. "That's a rather bad smell."

He shrugged. "I'm used to it, and those chinks don't care. If they complained, they'd be out on their butts and no back pay."

She ignored his rude language and walked around the kitchen. Horrible! Dirty counters, dirty floor. Grease and grime everywhere. The stoves looked as if they hadn't been cleaned in years, if ever. She ran a finger over one of the stovetops, held it up, and regarded her greasy black fingertip. *Ugh.* Silently, she arched an eyebrow in disapproval. When she finished her tour of the kitchen, she chose her words carefully. "Well, Mr. Hurdlicka, I see room for improvement here. If I may point out—"

"Get out of my kitchen!" Gus Hurdlicka's eyes bulged. By now, his face was so red he appeared to be on the verge of apoplexy.

"Sorry, I didn't mean to—"

"Out!" He pointed a shaking finger toward the door.

There was nothing to do but go, and quickly. "Good day, Mr. Hurdlicka. We'll talk later." It was all she could do to maintain her dignity, walk slowly, head high as she made her way from the restaurant. Back in the gambling hall, she was heading for the entrance when she felt a tap on her shoulder. She instantly knew who it was from the overpowering reek of perfume. Turning, she found the painted woman she'd met the other night.

"Remember me?" the woman said. "Tillie LaTour?"

After the debacle of a meeting with the cook, Rose could hardly think straight. She desperately wanted to get out of there, but good manners required she nod pleasantly. "Of course, I remember you."

Tillie cocked her head and regarded her boldly. "I hear you're gonna make some changes."

Apparently that little weasel of a desk clerk had wasted no time spreading the word. "Why yes, as the new owner, I intend to change quite a few things around here." That had been her plan, anyway. Now she wasn't so sure.

"What about the girls on the third floor? You know, the hostesses."

Please, no more conflicts. After what she'd been through, she wasn't sure she could stand much more. All she wanted was to get out the door and breathe some fresh air. This woman deserved an answer, though, and she'd have to be honest. "Miss LaTour, you know and I know those girls are more than hostesses. I'll be honest. I own this hotel now, and I won't put up with what I consider sinful activities. Therefore, I'm afraid you and your, uh, ladies will have to go." She hoped the poor woman wouldn't be too upset but had felt compelled to give a truthful answer.

Tillie threw back her head and burst into laughter. "Are you joking?"

"Certainly not."

"Honey, you've got a lot to learn. Pigs will fly before the River Queen gets rid of its harlots."

They were standing next to a faro table surrounded by gamblers. A quick glance informed her they'd stopped the game and were listening to every word of their conversation. One of the gamblers spoke up. "Hey, lady, you can't get rid of the whores. The River Queen would shut down if you did. What d'ya say, boys?"

Rose inwardly cringed as everyone at the table laughed and hooted. Her cheeks burned. Never had she been so intensely humiliated. She murmured a quick "I must go," turned, and fled as fast as she could go without actually running, out the door of the River Queen and into the bustling street outside. When she reached her horse and buggy, she grabbed Star's halter, buried her head in Star's silky mane and whispered, "You wouldn't believe how I've made a complete fool of myself." How could she possibly have thought she could run a hotel that catered to just about every sin she'd ever heard of?

"Rose?"

It was Mason Talbot's voice. She breathed deep and turned to face him. He was dressed elegantly as always, sporting a top hat and cane. She put what she hoped was a smile on her face. "Hello, Mason."

He frowned with concern. "Is anything wrong? You look distressed."

"It's nothing." The words no sooner left her mouth than she changed her mind. Who better to talk to than this man who always seemed so wise, so considerate and understanding? "Oh, Mason, I never felt so humiliated, so..." Fighting back tears, she clamped her lips shut and looked toward the sky. She was absolutely not going to cry in front of him. "I did not have a very good day."

He took her elbow. "Come with me. We'll go for a little ride."

She didn't protest and soon sat beside Mason in his carriage. He flicked the reins and drove to a deserted spot overlooking the river. Facing him on the high seat, she told him about Jake Grunion and his hostility; about Gus Hurdlicka, the chef who, thanks to her, almost got apoplexy; about Tillie, the woman of ill repute, who'd laughed in her face; and how, in the end, she'd fled out the door, wanting nothing more than to escape what had been the most mortifying experience of her life. "I thought it would be so easy. Maybe a bit different from running the Birchwood Inn but nothing I couldn't handle. How wrong could I be?" She bit her lip. "What a disaster. I don't know what to do."

"Yes, you do." Mason drew both her hands into his. "My dear Rose, a beautiful woman like you is meant for better things than running a sordid, downright sinful hotel like the River Queen. I admire you immensely for trying, but at least you've found early on it's too much for you."

"I suppose you're right."

"I know I'm right. Here's what we'll do. As you know, I had offered to buy the River Queen. My offer still stands, and at the same price."

"That's...that's most kind of you." How generous he was, and how wonderful that he had offered a way out of her predicament. She opened her mouth to accept, but before she could, a sense of loss overcame her. Until this moment, she hadn't realized how much she'd been looking forward to making the River Queen a first class hotel. It had given her a whole new purpose in life, but what a foolish dream. She must be practical. As Mason had wisely pointed out, *It's too much for you.*

He must have noticed her slight hesitation. "You don't have to decide right now. Think about it. We'll have dinner tomorrow night, and you can tell me then."

"All right, but after what happened today, you know what my answer will be." She would look at the bright side. If she sold the hotel, she'd have more time with Lucy. Ben and Coralee would be relieved and happy. Best of all, she'd never have to set foot in the River Queen again. All to the good, of course, but even so, why did she feel so defeated, as if a heavy weight was pressing on her shoulders?

Mason drove her back to her carriage and said goodbye, remarking how much he looked forward to dinner tomorrow night. He would take her to Le Chantecler at his Egyptian Hotel, considered by many to be the best French restaurant in town. She started for home but had not driven far along Front Street when she noticed a large, square structure under construction on the right side of the street. In front, two men had nearly finished painting a sign that read Fleming & Carter's Ice House. She had nearly passed by when she realized...*Fleming?* That was Deke's last name. She pulled to the side and looked closer. "Deke?"

He dropped his paint brush and looked around. "'Pon my word, it's Rose."

He started toward her, walking straight and tall. No crutches. "Deke, your cast is gone!"

He reached the carriage and gazed up at her, a big smile lighting his face. "Too right. Got it off yesterday."

Somehow he'd changed, and it wasn't just the crutches. The strained frown that had etched his forehead had disappeared, replaced by a look of confidence that hadn't been there before. She nodded toward the unfinished building. "Is this what you meant by ice?"

"That's right." He nodded toward his companion. "That's my friend, Mitch. We're building an ice house."

"But why?"

Her question made him laugh. "Because a cold beer's a hundred times better than a warm beer. We've gone into the ice business. The saloons can't get enough of it. Already we've hauled a load down from the mountains and sold every last chunk of it for ten cents a pound."

"That's nice, Deke. I'm happy to see you've got a little money coming in."

Deke's friend Mitch joined them. A plain man with sandy hair, about the same age as Deke, he stuck out his hand in a friendly fashion and introduced himself. His accent was like Deke's. "Back home, we were neighbors. Now I've got to be nice to him because he saved my life."

She started to ask how, but before she could, Deke broke in. "Mitch just came from the diggings. He'd had enough."

"Really?" Surprised, she asked Mitch, "Don't you want to get rich?"

Deke's friend chuckled. "It's a crook deal now. The easy gold's disappearing. We may not make a fortune selling ice, but we're better off than those poor sods freezing their arses up at the diggings. Excuse the language. Deke tells me you now own the River Queen."

She nodded. No sense informing him she was about to sell.

"Then tell that bartender to get rid of that rotgut whiskey." Mitch clutched his throat and made a gagging sound. "I had a slug the other night and like to died."

"I shall indeed inform him, Mr. Carter." And she would have, if she wasn't going to sell.

"Pleased to meet you, Mrs. Peterson." Mitch tipped his hat and went back to his painting.

Deke took a long moment to look her up and down. "You look good. I see you got yourself a new dress and bonnet. So how's it going over at the River Queen? Last time we talked, you were about to take over."

"Not so well." Saying the words, she almost choked up.

"Oh, say now..." With a lithesome spring, he was beside her in the carriage. "Tell me what's wrong."

Just as she had with Mason, she related to Deke the terrible day she'd had. "So that's the end of it. Now I know I was in over my head. Mr. Talbot told me his offer's still good, so I'm going to sell."

"Blimey."

"It's for the best."

"For who? Mason Talbot?"

"For me, of course. He's a kind man, and he's doing me a favor."

He laid his hand on her cheek and turned her head directly toward him. "Look me in the eye. Do you really want to sell?"

"After today, I mostly do."

"What do you mean by 'mostly'?"

She thought carefully before she answered. "What I mean is, when I learned the hotel was mine, I got this joyful feeling. At last, here was something I could do besides help Coralee in the kitchen. I never even thought twice. I'd done a good job at the Birchwood Inn, so of course I thought I could handle the River Queen. And then today happened and I'm so completely mortified that I..." She heaved a defeated sigh. "What was I thinking? I'm lucky Mason will buy the hotel and get me out of this...'disaster' best describes it."

Deke cocked his head and gave her a long, puzzled stare. "I don't get it."

"Get what?"

"Why you're quitting after one day."

"Because they didn't respect me. Nobody took me seriously."

"Will you tell me about it? When you first saw Jake Grunion, what did you say?"

"I told him I now owned the hotel. Then, as tactfully as I could, I informed him I'd be in charge from now on. I said I was sorry but wanted him to move out of Emmet's old office because I wanted to move in. I was nice as I could be and let him know there wasn't any hurry. Then I asked politely if I could see the books and couldn't imagine why he got so angry. Also, I assured him he'd still be manager because if Emmet trusted him then I would, too." She flung out her hands. "Is there anything wrong with that?"

"Oh, my word." He seemed to be struggling, as if he could hardly keep from saying something he knew he shouldn't say. "And I suppose you were 'nice as you could be' to Gus, that worthless cook?"

"Of course, Deke. I know my manners."

"Oh, my word." For a moment he looked skyward, as if some kind of divine intervention was necessary after what he'd just heard. He let some time go by, as if he had to calm himself before he spoke. "Manners are important to women, bless their hearts. They don't want to hurt anyone's feelings, so they go out of their way to be nice. Men are different, especially when it comes to business. What you didn't realize is, whoever runs the River Queen lives in a cutthroat world where no one gives a damn about manners and hurt feelings. That's the way it is, so if you think you're not tough enough to handle it, then you made a good decision when you said you'd sell."

"You're absolutely right, and that's why I'm selling." *But wait.* She didn't want Deke Fleming to think she wasn't tough enough, that she was a cowardly quitter. "I don't understand. What should I have said?"

"To be honest, I wouldn't know where to begin."

"Out with it. Don't spare my feelings."

"Here's where you went wrong. The River Queen Hotel is not the Birchwood Inn."

"I know that."

"No, you don't. What worked in Illinois isn't going to work here. This is the Gold Rush. Up at the diggings, men die every day and nobody gives a hoot. All they care about is finding gold to make themselves rich. Here in town, the saloons are out to get every last nugget, every last speck of gold dust from the poor suckers who've worked like dogs at the diggings for whatever they've got. Greed drives them all. Nobody gives a damn how nice and considerate you are, and that includes that lowlife crook, Jake Grunion. You think he's going to let you see the books? From what I hear he's been skimming for years, and who knows what else he's been up to? What I mean is, you handled him all wrong. You and your good manners don't mean a thing in Sacramento."

What a surprise. Since she'd known Deke, he'd always seemed so easygoing. Now he spoke with an intensity she'd never heard before. "Then, if you don't mind my asking, what does work?"

"You've got to think like a man."

"Well, I'm not a man, I'm a woman."

A corner of his lip lifted in the slightest of smiles. "You think I'm not aware of that, Mrs. Peterson? What I mean is, you don't have to be a man, you have to think like one."

"How do you mean?"

"I'll show you." He sprang from the carriage and helped her down. "You've got to use your imagination." He swept an arm over the rubble-covered ground. "This is Emmet's office. I'm Jake Grunion. I've taken over the office and I'm sitting behind his desk over there." He nodded toward a short stack of lumber lying nearby. "You've just knocked on the door." Deke went to the lumber pile and sat on top. "Come in, Mrs. Peterson. I'm busy. What do you want?"

She wasn't sure what he was up to, but she'd play along. She pretended to open a door, stepped inside his imaginary office and up to his "desk." "Good afternoon, Mr. Grunion. I'm sorry to bother you—"

"No! You're not sorry you bothered me. This is your office and you want it right now. Try again."

"Very well." She retreated, then went through the pretend door again. "Good afternoon, Mr. Grunion. I want my office back, and if it isn't too much trouble, I'd like to take a look at the books."

"No! Men don't ask if it's too much trouble. They don't say they're sorry, and they don't apologize. Try again."

She went through the routine again, and again was informed she hadn't got it right. She tried for the fourth time. "Good afternoon, Mr. Grunion. I want my office back, and I mean right now. The River Queen is mine. If you have any doubts, you can check with Mr. Archer Field, my solicitor. If you're still not convinced, I shall call the sheriff, show him my deed to the property, and then let him decide. I shall also call the sheriff if those books aren't on my desk by five o'clock this afternoon."

Deke clapped his hands. "That's it. You've got the hang of it."

At last. She delighted in his praise. "Now I see what I should have said. Too bad it's too late."

"Is it? Let's do Gus."

She agreed and listened to Deke's advice on how to deal with Gus Hurdlicka. "You handle him same as Jake. The man's all bluster and no backbone. Don't ask for the menu. Demand to see the menu. You make it clear who's boss and he'll crumble."

She practiced only once this time, and Deke said she got it right.

Tillie LaTour was another matter. Deke cocked an eyebrow in surprise when Rose described how she'd told Tillie the third-floor ladies had to go.

"'Pon my word, are you sure? The River Queen will lose a lot of business if you chase the fancy ladies away."

A small shadow of doubt crossed her mind, but she quickly dismissed it. "I've gone along with this, but does it matter? I haven't said I wanted to try again. The trouble is, I'm bold and brave when I'm talking to someone friendly like you, but Jake Grunion? If I were to go back, and I'm not saying I would, when he looks at me with those mean little eyes and gets that nasty expression on his face, will I turn and run? I'm not sure."

"You don't know until you try."

Could she do it? Had she acted in haste? Maybe she had. The more she thought about it… Yes! Deke had made her see she'd given up far too soon. And Mason hadn't helped with his offer of an easy way out. "All right, I'll try again. I don't suppose you could…?"

"Could what?"

"Nothing." She was about to ask if he'd come with her when she went back to the River Queen. How comforting it would be to have a man by her side when she faced Jake Grunion. Not a good idea, though. She had to be strong, and that meant she would rely on no one but herself. "I forgot about Mason. I pretty much told him I'd sell. He's not going to like that I've changed my mind."

"To hell with him. This is your decision, not his."

"He's invited me to dinner tomorrow night. I'll tell him then." The weight pressing on her shoulders had disappeared. It was almost as if she could stand straighter, hold her head higher. She could do it! With what she knew now, she wouldn't make the same mistakes again.

* * * *

After Rose left, Deke stood looking after her as she drove down Front Street. Mitch joined him and gazed after her, too. "Do you like her?" he asked.

"She's a bonza girl, all right, but she wouldn't be interested. She just lost her husband."

"That so? Can't say she looks much like a grieving widow."

"She hadn't seen him for two years." Deke nodded toward the ice house. "She said she was glad I'd have a little money coming in."

Mitch chuckled. "You didn't tell her we're about to make a fortune?"

"And sound like I'm bragging? Didn't think it was necessary." Deke had been tempted, though. The Fleming & Carter Ice House was nearly finished. With its double-thick, charcoal-lined walls it could store up to a thousand tons of ice. Orders were pouring in. Everybody wanted cold beer now. That meant every saloon in town would gladly buy all the ice they could lay their hands on. At ten cents a pound, how could they lose? Unless something went wrong, and he couldn't think what, they were bound to end up rich. Thank God, the crutches were gone. At least he hadn't seen any pity in her eyes today, not like before, but so what? She was having dinner with Mason Talbot tomorrow night. He clenched his jaw at the thought of how she might get hurt at the hands of that evil man.

Chapter 9

The closer Rose got to the farm, the lower her spirits sank. She was about to spend another cold, awkward evening with her in-laws. But maybe...? Deke had opened her eyes to a new way of handling things. She should speak up, be firm but honest, like she planned to do tomorrow at the River Queen.

It was worth a try. Anything was worth a try if she could avoid another miserable night of being shunned at the dinner table.

When she arrived, she stepped into the entryway, removed her bonnet, and smoothed her dress. She squared her shoulders and stepped into the parlor where Ben was reading his Bible and Coralee was knitting. "Good evening. We need to talk."

Ben looked up and frowned. "What about?"

She sat on the sofa, taking extra time to smooth her skirt while putting her thoughts together. Total honesty was best. Now was the time to pour her heart out, which wouldn't be easy considering they both sat stiffly, eyes filled with dislike. She opened her mouth to speak, then had to clear her throat and try again. "I want you to know I love the both of you and wouldn't hurt you for the world."

"Ha!" Coralee gave a scornful sniff.

"I don't blame you, Coralee. You must think I've been horribly selfish, and perhaps I have been. It's hard to explain, but when I learned the River Queen could be mine, I saw it as a challenge, a chance to do something special in my life. I know it sounds vain, but I could see my name on the door—Rose Peterson, Owner and Manager."

"You weren't content being a wife and mother?" Ben's voice was heavy with sarcasm.

"I mostly was, except I've always yearned for a home of my own. But besides all that, I've felt something was missing from my life. The River Queen is the answer. I'm eager for the challenge. I want it to be a first class hotel, and why shouldn't it be? Thanks to Emmet's bank account, I've got the money. I plan a new restaurant, nicer hotel rooms, a better—"

"What good will that do?" Ben gave her a hostile glare. "First class or not, Emmet's hotel will still be a den of iniquity."

"Not so much. It's true they serve spirits, but, to be honest, Ben, don't you take a drink now and then yourself? As for the gambling, from all I've heard, the Gold Rush will soon be over. That means we won't have thousands of miners pouring into town on a Saturday night, bent on throwing their money away on the gaming tables. Looking ahead, I see a time when I could get rid of the gambling and simply run a first class hotel."

Coralee slammed her knitting into her lap. "What about those women of ill repute? You think everyone will admire you for owning a hotel, but the way I see it, you'll be running a common whorehouse, and you know what that makes you."

"I'm getting rid of them immediately. I've already made it clear they've got to go." Surely that last would please them both. Rose sat back and waited.

Both appeared to be caught off guard. Ben said nothing. "Truly?" asked Coralee.

"They'll be gone first thing."

Ben still looked skeptical. "You know how much we love our granddaughter. For all we know, you plan to move to the River Queen and take her with you."

"Never! Lucy's home is here with you, and so is mine. That is, if you want me. The only reason I'd leave would be because you continue not speaking to me. I can't tell you how hurtful it is when you…" Rose's voice almost broke. She gulped and continued, "You don't have to approve of everything I do. Just try to understand I'd never do anything to hurt you or Lucy."

Ben looked at his wife. "Should we believe her?"

"I think she means it."

Rose could easily have leaped from her chair and done a joyful little dance, but her straight-laced in-laws wouldn't appreciate such recklessness. "Of course I mean it." She watched as Ben and Coralee exchanged a long, meaningful look. Finally Ben gave a slight nod.

Coralee stood and gave her a smile. "Time to start dinner. Come along. You can peel the potatoes."

* * * *

Late that night, Rose had just crawled into bed next to Lucy when Drucilla came in, perched on the bed, and began to chat. "I see Ma and Pa are talking to you again."

"They are, thank goodness. I paid a price, though. It wasn't easy standing up to them like I did."

"I admire you for it. I wish I could."

"You?" Rose couldn't keep the surprise from her voice. "You're the most strong-minded woman I know. Look at how you've managed to stay single all these years, despite all that pressure from your mother."

"But what have I got to show for it?" Drucilla's faint smile held a touch of sadness.

"I'm surprised. I thought you were perfectly happy."

"I've been thinking a lot about it lately. I've let my parents rule my life. I ask myself, what am I living for? Helping around the house and going to church on Sunday? I have my horse and my books, of course, but when I look at you and see all the exciting things you're doing, I have the most dismal feeling that life's passing me by. What's worse, I don't know what to do about it. All I know is I need to get away—do something different."

"There's no reason why you couldn't do the same as I've done. You're a grown woman. You don't have to do what your parents say."

"That's what I'm thinking. The problem is, what can I do? I refuse to marry, as you know, but when the time comes, do you suppose I could work in your hotel? There must be something I could do—make beds, maybe, or sweep the floors? I just need to be more like you and have the courage to break away."

Rose hid her surprise. Her sarcastic sister-in-law had always seemed so satisfied with her life, but apparently not. "I'm not that brave. With a little help, I realized I had to stand up for myself. If I didn't, I'd live to regret it, so I took the chance and it worked—at least so far, it has." Considering the bad day she'd had, she wasn't being entirely truthful, but now was the time to sound positive. "Of course you can work in the hotel. Only…"

"Only what?"

"You're the smartest woman I know. I'd hate to see you scrubbing floors when you know so much about so many subjects. You speak French, for heaven's sake! How many women can say that?"

Drucilla frowned in concentration. "I'd love to do something with my French. I do speak it well, as you know, and though I've never been to France, I've studied that country so much I could have been born and raised there."

"Then why don't you teach it?"

"That's a good idea, but where? Sacramento's such a primitive town I doubt it has any schools."

"I'll find out." Rose had no idea whom she could ask, but she'd do her best. How wonderful that for the first time ever, Drucilla was showing signs of wanting to break away from her domineering parents. She'd do everything she could to help.

The next morning, Rose dressed with care. She didn't need Deke to tell her not to wear the frilly blue silk taffeta gown and fancy bonnet. She'd wear the practical brown wool bombazine and no hat at all. Standing before the mirror, she liked what she saw. The modest cut of the high-necked bombazine couldn't hide her trim waist and full bosom. She hated to wear her hair pulled into such a severe bun, but she looked more serious-minded that way, not like some giddy female without a brain in her head. She would make sure she had plenty of time to come home and change before Mason picked her up for dinner. When the time came, she'd look her absolute best in the deep ruby gown with the double-puffed sleeves. Maybe put some flowers in her hair.

With Raymond's help, she hitched up the buggy and started for the River Queen. Strangely, she felt no butterflies in her stomach. Maybe that was because Deke's advice had made her realize exactly what she'd done wrong. That wasn't going to happen again. Even the thought of facing Jake Grunion didn't faze her. She'd imposed an iron will on herself. This time no apologies. No saying she was sorry.

When she reached the hotel, she went straight to the reception desk. Howie raised his eyebrows in surprise when he saw her. "Uh, Mrs. Peterson? I didn't think you'd be back so soon, I...uh, I mean after yesterday."

She smiled serenely at his confusion. "I shall be in my husband's old office."

"But didn't Jake tell you—?"

"The office is mine now." She glanced at the wall clock. "It's eight thirty. This next half hour I shall be having a talk with Mr. Grunion. Will you inform Mr. Hurdlicka I wish to see him in my office at nine o'clock?"

"Uh...yes, ma'am, of course."

She left with the desk clerk gawking at her and continued through the gambling hall, more sure of herself than ever. When she reached Emmet's office, she entered without knocking. Sitting at the desk, Jake looked up in surprise. "Well, well, if it isn't Mrs. Peterson. Why are you here? I thought I told you yesterday—"

"I'll make this brief, Mr. Grunion." She swept in and seated herself across from him. "I'm the new owner of the River Queen, and that makes me the boss. If you have any doubt about that, I suggest you visit my solicitor, Mr. Archer Field, who will gladly show you the newly transferred deed. If you have further doubts, and wish to dispute me, I shall call the sheriff, an action which I wish to avoid, of course, but will if I have to." She cocked her head. "Any questions?"

A corner of Jake's mouth lifted in a sneer. "Since when can a wife own her own property?"

"Since the new California Constitution said so. Now, here's want I want you to do..."

She continued on. Jake sat speechless as she discussed how they must aim for improvements. Some would take time, but items such as the disgusting spittoons would be removed immediately. Not only that, any guest caught spitting on the floor would be banned from the premises. Also to be removed: those degrading pictures of women that hung behind the bar, to be replaced by portraits in a more tasteful mode. Regarding the bar, she hadn't tasted the whiskey herself but had heard it was of low quality rotgut and must be replaced with liquor of a higher quality. "We aim to be a first class hotel, Mr. Grunion." And speaking of the bar, it would remain for men only, but she had in mind a separate "women's ordinary" to accommodate ladies who might enjoy an occasional refreshment. They could use a private entrance alone or with an escort.

And another thing: the ladies on the third floor would be asked to leave immediately.

"What!" Jake slammed his palm on the desk. "You can't do that."

Up to now, she'd ignored his slowly reddening face and deepening scowl. "Calm yourself. I can, and I will. Prostitution is a dirty business, and I won't have it in my hotel."

Jake leaped from his chair. "Are you out of your mind? A good part of our profit comes from the whores."

"You heard me."

"So what do you care if we serve rotgut? Anything better, you'd be wasting your money. Those miners will drink anything that comes from a bottle."

"You heard me."

"Then I quit."

Oh, no. She didn't want him to quit. Despite his faults, she needed him, but she'd have to take a chance and call his bluff. "Fine with me if you quit. I'll expect you to leave immediately."

Jake got a startled look on his face. Obviously he'd expected her to argue. "You can't fire me. You're crazy if you think you can manage this hotel by yourself."

"Perhaps, but I'm going to try."

"See here…" He struggled for words but soon gave up. With a curse, he stamped out of the office and slammed the door behind him.

She'd done it! Rose sank back in her chair and breathed a huge sigh of relief. Amazing, how she'd managed to stay calm on the outside while her insides trembled. But no matter. She'd got rid of Jake. Maybe that was a mistake, but she'd worry about that later.

There was another knock on the door. When she called, "Come in," Mason Talbot entered the office. "Mason! I'm surprised to see you at this early hour. Do sit down."

"Good morning, Rose." A strange look she couldn't quite read covered his face. He remained standing. "News travels fast in this town. I just heard you're not selling the River Queen. Is that true?"

"Yes, it is." Was that a flash of anger in his eyes? Surely not. She must have been mistaken because now he was smiling.

"Well, I am surprised, Rose. What changed your mind?"

"I talked to a friend." He didn't need to know who.

"You plan to manage it yourself?"

"I just fired Jake Grunion." Again, she could have sworn anger flashed in his eyes, this time accompanied by the slight twitch of a muscle in his jaw. "I do apologize, Mason. I told you I'd sell. Now I've gone back on my word, and for that I'm truly sorry. I planned to tell you when we went to dinner tonight, and try to make amends. I hope you'll forgive me."

Mason broke into his usual friendly smile. Smooth as ever, he declared, "Of course I forgive you. Shall I come here to pick you up for dinner?"

She glanced down at the plain brown bombazine. "I'll be at the farm. I want to change into something fancier than this. Can you pick me up there?"

"I'd be delighted." Mason gave her such a warm smile she decided she must have been mistaken about that flash of anger. He liked her. Of course, he'd forgiven her.

Directly after he left, Gus Hurdlicka arrived. Without bothering with a greeting, he asked what she wanted. Ignoring his obvious displeasure, she asked him to be seated and proceeded to inform him what in essence she'd told Jake—the hotel was hers and if he didn't like it, he could leave.

"So what did Jake do?" he asked.

"Jake is no longer with us."

Gus sat silent so she continued on, pleasant but firm. "We'll go about it gradually. Wouldn't you find it a lot easier to work in a nice, clean kitchen? That's where we'll start. Good heavens, there must be a ton of grease on those stoves. Then we'll tackle the dining area, a thorough cleaning, and then I think some red-and-white checkered tablecloths would look nice on those awful bare tables." She smiled sweetly. "Don't you agree, Mr. Hurdlicka?"

Gus replied with a boorish grunt, which she ignored.

"And then we shall work on revising the menu..." As she talked, Gus seemed to relax a bit, apparently realizing she was indeed in charge. He even began nodding his head as she went through her list of new items for the menu. By the time she finished, he appeared to be satisfied his position was secure, at least Rose hoped he was. She hadn't mentioned any plans for the grandiose restaurant she'd envisioned, and that was because she wasn't sure about it herself.

After Gus left, she sat back in her chair, content. Jake gone. Gus at least agreeable. Everything had gone well. All her fears were for nothing. Next, she would deal with the ladies on the third floor. She would give them a week, and then out they'd go. Judging from Sacramento's large number of hotels and saloons, they could easily find employment elsewhere.

The door burst open. A small woman in her fifties, maybe sixties, stood in the doorway. Dressed in a long-sleeved black gown adorned by a lace collar and cuffs, she would have looked like somebody's grandmother except for the pistol in a holster resting on her hip. "Are you Rose Peterson?"

"Yes, I am, and who might you be?"

The woman entered and stood peering down at Rose from across the desk. "I'm Fanny Wentworth. I own the Silver Star down the street."

"I've heard of you." Rose gestured politely. "Won't you sit down?"

"I don't have time to sit." Fanny got an icy look in her eye. "So you're the woman who married Emmet Peterson."

"You're correct. I'm Emmet's widow. We were married for several years before...well, I'm sure you know what happened."

"What happened was, that fool husband of yours got himself killed in a duel, and it was all his own fault. How stupid was that?"

"Well, I—"

"You're not to blame, although for the life of me, I don't know why you married Emmet in the first place. Dull as a post."

Rose half rose from her chair. "Now see here! You can't—"

Fanny raised a palm. "Sorry. He was good man, dull or not. But I didn't come here to talk about your late husband."

Rose settled back in her chair. "Then why did you come?" Again she gestured. "Won't you please sit down?"

With a grunt of acquiescence, Fanny seated herself, carefully clasping the holster as she settled into her chair. Seeing Rose's wary eyes upon it, she casually remarked, "Wouldn't want it to go off accidentally."

"I should hope not."

"I don't like carrying a gun, but when you work in a saloon, it comes in handy. You should get one."

Rose couldn't imagine walking around with a gun strapped to her hip. "Is there something I can help you with?"

"It's the other way around." A half smile crossed Fanny Wentworth's face. "Honey, I'm here to give you a piece of advice."

"Fine. I can use all the advice I can get."

"You're making a big mistake."

"In what way?"

"Word travels fast in this town, so I heard right away you intend to run the River Queen yourself. I've no objection to that. God knows, Jake Grunion is crooked as they come, and I hope you get rid of him."

"I just did."

"Good for you. You're off to a good start, but one thing you're doing wrong. I hear you want to get rid of—how shall I say it to a lady like you?—River Queen's ladies of the night? Soiled doves? Girls on the third floor?"

"Please continue. I know what you mean."

"You can't get rid of them."

"Why not? It's my hotel now. I can do as I please, and what pleases me is to get rid of what has got to be the most sordid, sinful occupation in the world."

Her visitor didn't look the least perturbed. "Have you been to the third floor?"

"Certainly not."

"I didn't think so." Fanny rose from her chair and beckoned with a finger. "Come along."

"Where to?"

"Where else? The third floor. It's time you saw it."

"Enter a brothel? Are you out of your mind?"

Fanny sighed patiently. "Tillie LaTour's an old friend of mine, and so are most of the girls. Believe me, you won't find any customers up there at ten o'clock in the morning."

"You're sure?" Up to now Rose hadn't given a thought to actually viewing River Queen's brothel even if it was her own hotel.

"There won't be a man in sight, I guarantee."

"All right, then." She didn't know what she was letting herself in for, but after all, the River Queen was hers now, and common sense told her she should be familiar with every inch of it, third floor included.

Following Fanny, Rose climbed three flights of stairs to where the third-floor landing expanded into a large, open sitting room furnished with plush, red velvet-upholstered couches and chairs, a piano, and a long mahogany bar. A woman in a flowered silk wrapper lounged on one of the sofas. At first, Rose didn't recognize her, but closer up she saw it was Tillie, the brazen woman she'd already met in the saloon. But she didn't look so brazen now. The vivacious, painted lady from last night hardly resembled this pale, tired-looking woman who wore no rouge and whose red hair now hung limp and straggly around her shoulders. When she saw Rose, she gave a languid wave. "Ah, there's Mrs. Peterson." Her voice held a bitter edge. "Are you still planning to shut us down?"

Fanny quickly spoke up. "Not so fast, Tillie." She cast a meaningful glance at Rose. "Nothing is settled yet."

"Well, I hope not. This is our home. We got no place to go."

Fanny took Rose's arm. "Come on, I'll show you the rooms. Each girl has her own." She led Rose down a hallway lined with a long row of doors. A wooden sign with a girl's name painted on it hung on every door. Joy, Evette, Ruby, and so on. Each sign was different, some plain, some colorfully painted. Fanny stopped in front of a sign that read "Cherry" and was decorated with pastel-colored flowers and butterflies. She knocked, and a pretty young woman with big brown eyes and long, honey-colored hair answered. She was heavy with child.

"Can we come in, Cherry? This is the River Queen's new owner, Mrs. Peterson. She wanted to meet you."

Cherry broke into a smile and swung the door wide. "If I'd known you was coming, I'd have tidied the place up a bit." Her voice had an immature sound to it. She couldn't have been more than eighteen.

They stepped inside a tiny room furnished with a bed, small chest, and one chair. Drapes of purple velvet hung over the one window and part of the walls. A heavy perfume filled the air. Fanny asked, "How are you feeling, Cherry? You're looking good."

"As well as could be expected, I guess." Cherry placed both hands on her protruding belly. "I had to stop work, though. They said the last month would be the hardest, and it surely is. Even those randy miners don't want a woman who looks like this." She frowned and glanced around her tiny room. "I wish I could offer you something, but—"

"Please don't bother." Fanny raised her hand. "We won't stay. I just wanted Mrs. Peterson to meet some of the girls who work on the third floor."

Rose wasn't sure what to say to a prostitute, but a normal greeting seemed appropriate. "I'm pleased to meet you, Cherry. Are you excited about the new baby?" The second the words left her mouth, she knew she'd said the wrong thing.

The young woman's face clouded. She looked close to tears. "I hear you're going to throw all of us out, Mrs. Peterson. Is that so?"

Rose was so taken aback she couldn't think what to say.

"That's a good question." Fanny's eyes widened innocently as she looked at Rose. "Considering Cherry has no place to go, you wouldn't do a thing like that, would you? I can see what a kind heart you have. Surely you wouldn't want her to end up out in the cold, giving birth in some gutter."

Rose recognized the trap Fanny Wentworth had so very cleverly set for her. Now what should she do? If she threw Cherry out, she'd look like some kind of heartless monster. If she allowed Cherry to stay, she'd be breaking her promise to Ben and Coralee. Both Fanny and Cherry were looking at her expectantly. She let out a frustrated sigh and gave the only charitable answer she could give. "Don't worry, Cherry, I'm not going to throw you out. You can stay, at least until after your baby is born."

Cherry burst into tears of gratitude. "Thank you, Mrs. Peterson. I'm ever so grateful. You won't be sorry, I promise."

"What about the rest of the girls?" Fanny asked.

"You realize this will cause me no end of trouble."

At least Fanny had the decency to shrug apologetically. "I'm sorry for that, but I'm doing what I had to do."

At this point, she could give only one answer. "They can all stay until after Cherry's baby is born. After that, they'll have to go, although there might be a few jobs available here in the hotel. Maids, for instance." Rose didn't regret her decision. In her heart, she knew she'd done the right thing. As for Ben and Coralee, she didn't even want to think how angry they'd be, especially Ben, who wanted them gone right now. She would deal with all that later, though. She'd done what she had to do.

As the day went by, Rose's confidence grew. She'd made her wishes known concerning the quality of the whiskey and other alcoholic beverages. Only quality products would be served. The head bartender, an amiable Englishman named Cecil, readily agreed. He'd been forced to follow Jake Grunion's instructions and hadn't been happy about cutting good whiskey with turpentine, ammonia, or sometimes even gunpowder.

At her request, Howie gave her a tour of the second floor, where she discovered the deplorable condition of the guest rooms. All had dirty floors, unmade beds, towels and linens that looked none too clean. The bathroom at the end of the hall was a disgrace. Where was the housekeeper?

"We don't have a housekeeper," Howie replied with a shrug. "Emmet hired a woman to come in and clean every now and then, but she drinks, so you can't count on her."

"So you rent out the rooms even if they're dirty?"

"If they've come from the diggings, what do they care? They're just happy to sleep in a real bed."

To her ever-lengthening list of things to be done, Rose added: Find housekeeper.

* * * *

At the end of the day, she was just getting started, but it was time to quit. She must get home and change in time for her dinner with Mason. And also, she wanted to stop at the ice house and see if Deke was around. She'd been dying to tell him—brag, she supposed—about how she'd gotten rid of Jake; how she'd brought Gus, the surly cook, into line; how the words "I'm sorry" hadn't crossed her lips, nor had she never once said, "I apologize."

Just before she was going to leave, after a quick knock, Deke stuck his head in the door. "I say, are you busy?"

"Deke! So good to see you. Do come in." After he entered and sank comfortably in a chair, spreading his long legs before him, she proceeded to tell him all about how her day had gone. "Thanks to your advice. I'm now convinced I can run this hotel. I feel wonderful."

His mouth twitched with humor. "Almost as wonderful as when you ran your hands through a barrel of chicken feed?"

She burst into laughter. "Well, almost."

"I knew you could do it."

She could tell he was pleased. "And what about you? Are you and your friend selling a lot of ice?"

"Enough."

What did that mean? Obviously Deke and Mitch were just getting by. How could they make any money selling chunks of ice? "Perhaps I'll buy some for the hotel."

"You can't."

"And why is that?"

Shirley Kennedy

"Because you need a cellar to store the ice, and the River Queen doesn't have one."

"Do the other saloons?"

"You're about the only one that doesn't."

Rose sighed. Had Emmet done anything right? "There's another thing to add to my list of things to do."

"I wouldn't worry about it," Deke said comfortably. "Shall we celebrate your successful day? Mitch and I are going over to the Alhambra for fish and chips. Want to come?"

"Oh, I..." She hated to ruin the moment but had no choice. "Thank you, but I have other plans." That didn't sound right, a line she would use as an excuse to get out of doing something she didn't want to do. "I'd really love to go, but don't you remember? Tonight I'm having dinner with Mason Talbot at the Egyptian."

"Of course. I forgot." Only a slight squint of his eyes revealed his annoyance. "You should order the oysters. I hear you can have them any way you like." He stood. "Time to get along."

She watched him leave. *Damn.* A moment ago there'd been a warm and special closeness between them. Deke's expression hadn't changed, but somehow she knew she'd disappointed him, and that special moment was gone.

Chapter 10

Beneath sparkling crystal chandeliers, sitting at a linen-covered table set with delicate china and the finest of silverware, Rose couldn't stop marveling at the magnificence of Le Chantecler. On a stage at one end, backed by a full band, a famous group of Tyrolean singers entertained the diners throughout dinner. Pierre, the French chef, "imported direct from Paris," served up such culinary delights that at the end of the meal Rose sat back and exclaimed, "That was the best meal I ever had." It was true. Turtle soup, lobster salad, oysters from Oregon, a quail pâté cooked in Malaga wine—she'd never had such a fabulous meal in all her life.

Mason proudly proclaimed, "You have your choice of every variety of fish, flesh, and fowl which the country affords." This was food she couldn't even have imagined those months on the wagon train, all of it served with faultless precision by waiters in formal evening wear. She couldn't help but compare this elegant restaurant to the sad debacle at the River Queen.

She took the last bite of her French pastry with the incredibly light meringue. "Do you suppose it's possible I could find a French chef for the River Queen? Not now, of course, but after I get it cleaned up and remodeled."

"Very possible. Pierre has a friend, another French chef who's just left France. He'll be arriving soon and will be looking for employment."

"Is he from Paris?"

"Lived there all his life."

"Perfect." She wanted to clap her hands but refrained. "Please do get in touch with him. A French restaurant would be my dream." She thought of Gus with his dirty apron and surly face. What would she do with him? Another problem she must put aside till later.

"Glad you enjoyed the dinner." In his perfectly cut dinner jacket and white bow tie, Mason looked as if he belonged here. After lighting an after-dinner cigar, he waxed eloquent about the delights of Sacramento's leading hotel. "When you stroll down the street, you see block after block of hotels and gambling houses, all of an inferior nature until you reach the Egyptian. It's superior in every way."

After they left the restaurant, he gave her a tour of the three-storied building. With its imposing façade and a terrace that overlooked the river, the Egyptian appeared to contain practically every luxury a hotel could have. That included a billiards room and reading room which, according to Mason, "Provides an admirable retreat for a gentleman who might wish to retire and peruse his newspaper or try his hand at dominoes or checkers." Rose wondered what the ladies were supposed to do but politely didn't ask.

They moved on to what was obviously Mason's pride and joy: an art gallery that housed his special collection of Renaissance art. "I don't let everyone in here," he said as he unlocked the door to a small room on the first floor. "This town is full of rubes who wouldn't know how to spell 'Renaissance,' let alone appreciate the art form." The room was unfurnished except for an upholstered bench situated in the middle. Paintings of various sizes hung on the surrounding walls. Mason motioned proudly at the largest picture in the room, a gilt-framed portrait of a young boy dressed in medieval clothing. "It's a Raphael, titled 'Portrait of a Young Boy.' It's priceless, actually." His chest puffed with pride. "This is only the beginning. I aim to have the most prestigious art collection in Sacramento. Are you interested in art, my dear?"

He sounded a bit condescending, no doubt assuming she knew nothing. Thanks to Drucilla, her art-loving sister-in-law, she did. "I've seen copies of Raphael's paintings. His 'Portrait of a Young Man' is quite remarkable." She flashed him a look of genuine delight. "How exciting to see an original painting by one of the great artists of the world."

Mason couldn't quite cover his surprise and looked properly impressed. Suddenly he frowned. "I love my art collection, but it's a big responsibility. Less than two years ago, the Egyptian and every other hotel in this area burned to the ground."

"And they rebuilt so quickly? That's hard to believe."

"Not when money is involved. What with thousands of miners waiting to be relieved of the gold in their pockets, new gambling saloons sprang up practically overnight."

"Then I must be extra careful, and thank you for the warning." An unsettling thought struck her. "What caused the fire?"

"No one knows for sure. An overturned lamp, perhaps. The whole row of hotels went up in a gigantic blaze in no time. No wonder, considering they were constructed mostly of canvas and flimsy wood."

"What about the River Queen?"

"It, too, was made of wood, so it went up with the rest. Your husband bought it right after it had been rebuilt, this time more sensibly of brick."

"Then I have nothing to worry about?"

"Hopefully not, but you never know. The threat of another fire always exists. And then there's… That's enough. I don't wish to alarm you."

"You have already," she said with a laugh. "And then there's what? Now you've got to tell me. You can't keep me in suspense."

Mason frowned thoughtfully. "In case you hadn't noticed, my hotel sits next to a rather large river."

"You mean…?"

"I mean the Sacramento River has been known on occasion to overflow its banks."

"I hadn't thought, but surely… It doesn't go far over its banks, does it? Are we safe on J Street? The Egyptian is on the river, but the River Queen is at least two blocks away."

Mason reached across the table and took her hand. "I apologize for even bringing the subject up. I assure you, we're perfectly safe here. Let's enjoy the evening and forget such unpleasantness as fires and floods."

"If you say so." She made a note to herself to learn more. After only a day, she was beginning to feel a special affection for the River Queen. It might be in a muddle of disorder, but now it was *her* muddle of disorder, and if it was in danger, she needed to know.

Later, when Mason brought her home, he swung her down from the carriage as he'd done before. Again, he held her hands tight and wouldn't let go. "Ah, Rose, I'm having a difficult time remembering you're still in mourning."

Now was the time to remind him she most certainly was in mourning and politely back off, but he'd been so generous—showed her such a lovely evening—that the least she could do to repay him was to let him go ahead and kiss her. Perhaps this time she'd feel something, maybe even enjoy it. His arms encircled her and pulled her close. She relaxed and sank into his embrace. His lips captured hers and pressed eagerly. She waited for the thrill, but it didn't happen. All she wanted to do was break away. When he finally lifted his lips, he was breathing hard and trembling. "You're a beautiful woman, my dear. Is that my perfume you're wearing?"

"Yes, it is, Mason. The *Eau de Cologne Impériale*. It's very nice." She very much wanted to go inside and wished he would let her go, but next she knew, he was wanting to kiss her again. She placed a firm palm on his chest. "Not tonight."

He backed away. "Is it too soon?"

"Yes, too soon, I'm afraid." She'd included a note of sadness in her voice, as if the mere reminder of Emmet deepened her great sorrow. "Good night, Mason, and thank you for a lovely evening." Before he could answer, she spun on her heel and hastened into the house, trying to keep from running. What was wrong with her? Why was she pretending a grief she didn't feel? Why did she continue to reject Mason Talbot? He was a great catch by any woman's standard, but for some unfathomable reason, she wasn't interested.

Finding Ben and Coralee still up and sitting in the parlor, Rose poked her head in. "Hello, I'm home." She decided to be honest. "I'm late because I had dinner with Mason Talbot." If they objected, they'd surely speak up.

"That's nice," Coralee said, hardly raising her head from her knitting.

Ben spoke up. "Did you get rid of them?"

"You mean...?"

"I mean the whores."

Rose got a tight feeling in her chest. "Uh...no, not yet. Of course, they're going to go, but it will take a little time. I mean, I can't just throw them out on the street."

Ben studied her a moment, his eyes sharp and inquiring. "I don't see why not."

"Don't worry, they're going soon. I'm tired, so good night." Rose hastily left the parlor and headed for the kitchen. What had gotten into her? She'd let Mason kiss her when she really didn't want him to. Just now, she'd practically lied to Ben. What had happened to her resolve to be brave and strong? Tonight she'd been weak and indecisive with both Mason and Ben. Of course, she hadn't told Ben an out-and-out lie because she really did plan to "get rid of the whores," as he so crudely put it. What she'd failed to explain was she now realized those so-called whores were human beings, too. She wasn't going to treat them like so much trash no matter what he said.

Deke would not have been proud of her tonight. Why she should care what some down-and-out Australian would think of her, she didn't know, but for some reason, she did.

Drucilla was in the kitchen. "How did your day go?" she asked. "Will you go back tomorrow?"

How nice to have a friendly family member to talk to. Rose described her second day at the River Queen, including a description of the deplorable state of the hotel rooms and how she must quickly find a dependable housekeeper. As she talked, Drucilla's face slowly lit. When she finished, her sister-in-law clapped her hands and gleefully declared, "That's it! Forget about the school. I'm your new housekeeper."

"You?" Rose asked in a skeptical voice. "First off, I doubt Ben and Coralee would approve."

"I don't care if they approve or not. Don't you see? It's the perfect job for me. You know how neat I am. You know I believe in a place for everything and everything in its place. What better qualifications for a housekeeper? That job is just what I was hoping for but didn't know quite what it was."

Rose wasn't so sure. "But I thought you wanted to teach French. That would make much more sense than you working at the River Queen. I don't think you'd like it."

"And why not?"

"Because..." Rose hated to be so honest, but she must speak the truth. "You're accustomed to gentlemen with good manners, but men are different at the River Queen. You have no idea how rough and disorderly some of them are. They spit on the floor. They get drunk and get into fist fights and brawls. Sometimes some drunken fool will pull a gun and shoot someone. They make lewd and vulgar remarks to the women who work there, who themselves, by the way, aren't all that genteel."

"What you're trying to say is they're prostitutes. I know that. I don't care about that." Drucilla set her jaw in a stubborn line. "I want that job, Rose. Nobody could do it better than I could. What do you say?"

"Well..." Rose had her reservations, but never before had she seen her unadventurous sister-in-law with such an eager gleam in her eye. Why not at least let her give it try? "Even though your ma and pa won't like it?"

"You let me worry about that."

"All right then, you're hired." Although reluctant, Rose was struck by a positive thought. "Here's something to think about. You'll be working with men, *surrounded* by men, all kinds of them, so who knows? You might meet your knight in shining armor."

"Thank you, thank you!" With uncharacteristic abandon, Drucilla got up and literally danced around the table to give Rose a hug. "You won't be sorry. No knight in shining armor, though. That's never going to happen."

* * * *

To Rose's surprise, her in-laws didn't put up much of a fuss when Drucilla announced she was going to be the new housekeeper at the River Queen. "Probably thanks to you, Rose," Drucilla told her privately. "They're still so shocked over what you did, I could announce I was going to be a hootchy-kootchy dancer in the circus, and they wouldn't be surprised."

Next morning, Rose drove the horse and buggy to the River Queen, a talkative passenger by her side. Drucilla kept asking questions. Which project would Rose tackle first? If she was going to remodel the restaurant, how would she go about it when she knew nothing about construction, let alone architecture? The same with the lobby she planned to remodel and the women's ordinary. Where would she put it? And what about the ice cellar? Would she just dig a hole in the ground, or was there more to it than that? What about the nude pictures behind the bar? Would she replace them with pictures more tasteful? If so, where would she find them? On and on she went until by the time Rose reached the stable behind the hotel, and turned the buggy over to the stableboy, all those questions struck home. She'd been so proud of herself, in such a state of delight that she'd successfully acquired the hotel that she hadn't looked beyond that. Now the reality was sinking in. She couldn't possibly do it all by herself.

Once inside, Drucilla, self-sufficient as always, announced she didn't need Rose to show her around. She'd inspect the rooms herself and go from there. Rose went to her office and sat at her desk for a while, doing nothing but gazing into space, contemplating the daunting task ahead. How could she make her hotel one of the best, if not the best hotel and saloon in all of Sacramento? Where could she find enough help?

After a brief knock, the door partly opened and Jake Grunion stuck his head in. "Are you busy, Mrs. Peterson?"

"Uh, no, Mr. Grunion. Please do come in."

He entered, hat in hand, and stood at the desk in front of her. "I've come to ask for my job back."

"Really?" She didn't try to conceal her surprise. "Seems the last time we talked, you could hardly wait to get out of here."

Jake nervously licked his lips. "I got to thinking. I like it here at the River Queen. If you give me my job back, I'll see to it you get the books whenever you want to see them. There won't be nothing wrong with them, either."

"No more skimming?"

He had the decency to hang his head. "No more, I promise." He looked her in the eye. "And besides that, you need me. You can't run this place by yourself, Mrs. Peterson. Nobody knows what this hotel needs more than I do."

"Why do you want to come back? Can't you get a job at another hotel?"

"Sure I can, but there's no hotel like the River Queen." Jake's mouth curved into an unconscious smile. "She's something special."

"I'll think about it, Jake. Come back tomorrow, and I'll let you know.

After he left, she sat wondering if she'd done the right thing. Maybe she hadn't been tough enough, should have told him straight out he could never come back. Meantime, she'd better get practical. First off, it was time to visit the bank.

At Wells Fargo she picked up the checks she'd ordered, with her very own name on them. It was a new experience. "I shall be making some rather extensive renovations," she told the clerk. "Is there a limit?"

"You can write as many checks as you please, as long as you have money in your account."

Twenty thousand dollars! And all she had to do was fill out a little piece of paper to get her hands on it. Her mind swirled with the possibilities. With that kind of money, the River Queen would look as good as the Egyptian, maybe better. But how would she go about it? And what about Jake? Her mind was foundering. Maybe if she talked to Deke, he would at least help her think straight.

On her way back to the hotel, she stopped off at the ice house where she found Deke standing in a wagon full of ice, holding a pair of tongs. As she watched, he hooked a large block of ice and effortlessly tossed it onto the dock below. For a moment, she couldn't take her eyes off his well-muscled frame as he moved gracefully, making what must be a heavy burden look like he was lifting cobwebs. Hard to believe this was the same man who'd looked so weak and pathetic when he was on crutches. She called up to him, "Where did you get all that ice?"

He stopped when he saw her and broke into a pleased smile. "Rose? Nice to see you. The ice comes from high in the mountains. Mitch and I chopped out the first couple of loads ourselves. Now we've hired a few down-and-out miners to do it for us."

"So you must be doing well."

"We're getting by." Deke threw down the tongs and waved toward the front steps of the ice house. "Come sit down. What's with the River Queen?"

She settled herself on the steps. "Jake wants to come back. He says I can trust him now. Says he's learned his lesson."

Deke let out a low whistle. "That puts me in mind of a roustabout I once hired for Amalie Station. I soon found out he was stealing me blind, making off with my newborn lambs."

"What's a roustabout?"

"He does lots of things, like cleaning up the shearing sheds."

She'd never really asked what he did in Australia. "You owned some sheep?"

"Sixty thousand, give or take."

"Really! That's a lot of sheep."

He shrugged as if it were nothing. "There are lots of stations bigger than Amalie."

So Deke was a land owner? How wrong she'd been. One of her mother's favorite sayings was, "Don't judge a book by its cover," yet that's what she'd done with Deke when she saw him as a down-and-out loser because of his crutches and the way he looked. And he, unpretentious man that he was, had never told her otherwise. She had lots to think about, and she'd deal with it later. "So of course you got rid of him."

"Hell no. If I'd let him go, he'd have been free to steal even more lambs, so I kept him on. He never stole from me again, I saw to that. There's a saying, 'It's better to deal with the devil you know than the devil you don't know.' Do you get my meaning?"

"That settles it. I'll rehire him." Rose sighed. "Jake can handle all the ordinary, everyday things, but that doesn't solve all my problems. I'm not sure how to start. There's so much to do, and I must confess, I'm not sure how to go about it. There's the cellar that needs to be dug. The dining room and that awful-looking lobby must be completely designed and remodeled. Then there's the women's ordinary I want to build, and then—"

"Stop." Deke held up his hand. "You can't do all of that by yourself and neither can Jake."

"You're so right. I'm beginning to realize that. Running a hotel is one thing, but renovating and remodeling? That's another matter entirely and I'm not sure—"

"You need help and I've got just the man for you. Name's Tim Delahunty. He's an Irishman from New York. Worked as an architect and built buildings. Right now, he's chopping ice for me, one of those down-and-out miners I was telling you about. He worked the diggings for a while, but never found so much as an ounce of gold. Then caught pneumonia and nearly died. Now all he wants is to make enough money to get home to his family. I'm not sure he'd say yes, but I could ask."

"Would you?" Relieved, she continued, "You're a good friend, Deke. It seems you always come through for me."

A wry smile played at the corners of his mouth. "At your service, Mrs. Peterson. Always glad to help a grieving widow."

Was her less-than-deep grief for her husband that obvious? She stifled an impulse to giggle. "You know me too well."

His smile disappeared. "Well enough. So tell me, how was your dinner last night with the great Mason Talbot?"

She ignored his sarcasm. "It went beautifully, thank you. The food was wonderful. I was so impressed I plan to open a French restaurant at the River Queen. Mason knows of a French chef who's absolutely fabulous." She could stop right there, but couldn't resist a playful urge to annoy him. "Mason was the perfect host, so thoughtful and generous. He's a wonderful person, and I really can't understand why you don't like him."

For once, Deke lost the amiable expression she was accustomed to. For a long moment he sat silent. "He killed your husband, Rose."

She could have sworn he'd uttered those last words through clenched teeth. "I know all that. I don't want to sound disloyal to Emmet, but you know the circumstances even better than I. My husband brought it all on himself, and that's the truth of it. Mason isn't to blame, and I wish you could see that."

For the longest time, Deke simply stared at her until his continued scrutiny caused her to ask, "Aren't you going to say something?"

Finally he spoke. "I don't want to hear another word about Mason Talbot, not now, not ever."

She had planned a further argument, but the gritty firmness in Deke's voice stopped her cold. For the first time, she saw a side to her friend from Australia she'd never seen before. He wasn't all light-hearted and friendly as she'd thought. He had a deeper side, too, but right now she couldn't figure it out.

He was wrong about Mason, though. She would continue to see him, despite Deke's low opinion of the man.

That afternoon, upon Deke's recommendation, Rose summoned Tim Delahunty to her office. A tall man with a full head of curly dark hair, he possessed a jovial laugh and friendly, outgoing nature. Only his pallid face and thin appearance disclosed how he'd toiled at the diggings and barely survived. "I should never have left New York," he told Rose. "Left my wife and three kids so I could rush to the gold fields and get rich. What a fool. Now all I want is to make enough money to get back to New York."

Rose liked the man but had a concern. "If I hire you to oversee the renovation of the River Queen, would you run out on me the minute you had enough money and head for home?"

"Absolutely not. I'd stay till the job was done. I'm a man of my word, Mrs. Peterson. What have I left but my honor?"

She believed him and hired him on the spot.

After Tim left Rose's office, such an overwhelming sense of apprehension suddenly ran through her that a knot formed in her stomach, and she had to breathe deep and sit back in her chair. Dear Lord, what had she done? Not long ago, she was Mrs. Emmet Peterson, wife, mother, and that was all. Now she was Rose Peterson, owner of a notorious, run-down hotel and saloon that she, with little experience, without the least idea of what she was doing, planned to turn into a luxury hotel better than the Egyptian. She wasn't at all sure she could do it, but she'd burned her bridges behind her, and by God, she'd give it a try.

Chapter 11

The first thing Rose did the next morning was to take Deke's advice and hire Jake back. She still had her doubts, but she'd keep a close eye on him.

In the days that followed, she threw herself into the daunting task of improving and expanding the River Queen. She took care of the easy things first, like removing the obscene pictures behind the bar. They needed to be replaced, and when Mason offered to loan her a few "more tasteful" portraits from the Egyptian, she gladly accepted. "Until I can get to San Francisco to buy my own."

She worked hard at the hotel all day, but Lucy came first in her life, so when night came, she went home and let Jake run the place. So far, he seemed to be doing a good job. Even so, she remained vigilant so he wouldn't rob her blind.

Other than their daily buggy ride from home and back, she didn't see much of Drucilla, who had thrown herself into her housekeeping responsibilities with joyful zeal. Since women were scarce in Sacramento, Rose had warned her she'd have trouble finding maids, but Drucilla easily found the answer. She visited the third floor and hired two of the younger girls, both of them happy to leave the oldest profession.

After checking the hotel's inventory, Drucilla found the entire supply of linens and towels in such deplorable condition she ordered everything new from San Francisco. The bathrooms at each end of the hall which had been, as she put it, "too disgusting to discuss," now sparkled with cleanliness. To Rose's relief, nothing upset Drucilla, not even the drunken, disorderly behavior she daily witnessed among the River Queen's regular clientele. She did her job, did not complain, and kept her opinions to herself. Only once, after seeing a particularly disheveled and rowdy customer tossed out on the street, did she cast a skeptical glance at Rose and remark, "What a shame. There goes my knight in shining armor. Do you suppose he'll sober up by morning so we can tie the knot?"

Rose had little time to devote to her sister-in-law's skeptical attitude toward romance. Her biggest concern was what to do about the wretched condition of the River Queen's one and only restaurant until one day Mason stopped by with exciting news. "I've found that French chef you wanted, the one who's a friend of Pierre. He has just arrived from San Francisco."

Ever since she'd eaten that fabulous meal at Le Chantecler, she'd dreamed of a similar restaurant for the River Queen. "That's wonderful, Mason. Who is he, and when can I see him?"

Next morning, Monsieur Gaston Bernier presented himself in Rose's office. Of medium height and slim, thirty-five or so, he fulfilled her image of a gallant Frenchman when he bowed and with a flourish kissed her hand. "Madame Peterson, I presume?"

Oh, my. His dark, snappy eyes and flirtatious smile made her heart flutter, but only for a moment. She must get serious. "You're the chef who worked with Pierre? And you're from Paris? Please do sit down."

She had prepared a list of questions but had hardly started to ask them when Monsieur Bernier made it clear who would be in charge of the interview, and it wasn't her. He told her of his greatest successes: his steak au poivre, his blanquette de veau. At the end, with an arrogant lift of his chin, he declared in his charming French accent, "In Paris, I worked only in the finest of restaurants. Some of my dishes are famous. My coquilles St-Jacques?"—he kissed his fingers and tossed his hand in the air—"Superb! In the spirit of adventure, I 'ave come to America to, shall we say, seek new worlds to conquer. You need to know I will not lower my standards. I must inspect your kitchen and the entire restaurant at length before making a commitment."

Despite his arrogance, she immediately knew she must have him. But oh, dear God! What would he say when he laid eyes on River Queen's restaurant as it was now with its greasy stoves, rough plank tables, and worst of all, fat Gus in his sweaty headband and dirty apron. Well, she'd do the best she could. She stood and put on a confident smile. "I want you to see our restaurant but hope you'll keep in mind it's about to be renovated and currently doesn't look…uh…quite what I know you would like."

He stood and bowed. "Lead the way, madame."

When they arrived at the restaurant, her worries were confirmed. Monsieur Bernier took one look through the door, flinched, and wrinkled his nose. "This is the best you 'ave?"

Before she could answer, Tim Delahunty walked up. In the few days he'd been at the River Queen, he'd pitched into his job with endless energy and enthusiasm. Already he'd begun to draw plans for remodeling the restaurant. Rose introduced him. "Monsieur Bernier, this is my man in charge of the remodeling."

Tim must have noted the sour look on the French chef's face. After a quick glance at Rose, he declared in his booming voice, "Wait till you see the plans!" He slung a friendly arm around Bernier's shoulders. "Come with me, my friend. We'll take in the kitchen first. We're just getting started. Want any changes? We'll be glad to oblige."

If the chef was offended by Tim's over friendly behavior, he showed no signs of it. Rose trailed silently behind as the two toured the entire restaurant with Tim urging Monsieur Bernier to ignore the shoddy present and look at the glowing future when the River Queen Restaurant would be transformed into "The best damn restaurant in town, and that includes Le Chantecler at the Egyptian."

By now, the Frenchman's sour expression had disappeared. He beamed with interest. "But that name! It won't do. Mon Dieu! You cannot call a first class French restaurant by a name as common as 'The River Queen Restaurant.'"

Rose thought fast and took advantage of the opportunity. "But that will be up to you, monsieur. If you stay, *you* will be the one to pick a new name. I give you my word, whatever you choose, we shall honor it."

Gaston Bernier's eyes lit. Although he said nothing more, Rose could see she'd found just the right thing to say.

When they finished the tour and had walked through the saloon, they encountered Drucilla headed down the staircase, hair flying in all directions, a harried expression on her face. "Some of our guests are like pigs!" she exclaimed.

She was about to move on when Rose stopped her at the bottom of the stairs. "Drucilla, I would like you to meet Gaston Bernier, who might be our first French chef." She turned to Bernier. "Monsieur, may I introduce Miss Drucilla Peterson, my sister-in-law and the hotel's housekeeper?"

Drucilla stuck out her arm and blurted a hasty, "*Bonjour, monsieur! Ravi de faire votre connaissance.*"

Obviously she'd planned on a fast handshake and get-away, but before she could move on, the Frenchman uttered, "*Enchanté,*" and with a gracious bow, kissed the back of Drucilla's hand. Rising up, he inquired, "*Vous parlez francais, mademoiselle?*"

"*Un peu.*"

"Vous avez de beaux yeux."

"Mes yeux sont ordinaires, et n'ont rien de special."

"Ah non! Vous etes une femme magnifique!"

Drucilla rolled her eyes, uttered a quick, "I must go," and hurried away. Bernier looked after her. "Charming!"

"Yes, isn't she?" *Really?* Rose couldn't believe anyone could find her blunt sister-in-law charming, but then, he was looking at her through a man's eyes, seeing something that had somehow escaped her attention.

Before the chef departed, she made herself clear with her final words. "The job is yours if you want it, Monsieur Bernier. What do you think? Would you like to work here?"

He frowned, as if in deep thought. "Perhaps... Yes, I will indeed consider it. You will 'ave my answer tomorrow."

"Thank you, monsieur. I shall be anxiously waiting to hear from you." *Not true.* She wasn't anxious at all. Thanks to buoyant Tim Delahunty and his infectious optimism, she had no doubt that Gaston Bernier was going to be the new French chef at the River Queen. And maybe a bit of thanks to Drucilla? Whatever she'd said in French must have impressed him.

Later, Rose caught up with her sister-in-law in the hallway. "What was all that French about?"

Drucilla gave an impatient shrug. "It was nothing. The man's a flirt. He told me I had beautiful eyes."

"And what did you say?"

"I informed him I had ordinary eyes and there was nothing special about them."

"And then what did he say?"

"He said I was a beautiful woman. *Me.* Can you believe that? I let him know he was being ridiculous."

"Perhaps he meant it."

Drucilla burst out laughing. "Of course, he didn't mean it, but what if he did? I'm not the least bit interested in finding a man, as you very well know. And besides, he's shorter than I am."

"Only an inch or so."

"Ha! Be it an inch or a foot, I will never have a man I can't look up to."

She stalked off with her nose in the air, leaving Rose shaking her head. What a shame. Why did Drucilla have to be so bull-headed? But still...

Despite all the nonsense, she'd sensed a spark between her obstinate sister-in-law and the arrogant French chef.

* * * *

Rose's biggest problem hung over her like a dark cloud. Over a week had gone by since she'd told Ben she would end prostitution at the River Queen. Ben remained adamant that the River Queen's ladies of the night must go. Every day when she got home, he asked in his caustic voice, "Are they gone yet?" So far, she'd held him off by explaining she'd been so busy she hadn't had time to deal with the situation. Up to now, Ben replied with a grunt and said nothing more. That wouldn't last, though. "He's running out of patience," she told Dulcee one evening when she'd gone to visit. "You know how he is. He won't bend."

"Ben's right for all the wrong reasons," came Dulcee's surprising reply. "He says prostitution is a sin. I say the fate of those poor girls is where the sin lies. They might look like they're having a fine time, but they live a life of degradation, and don't tell me otherwise. They never last long. If they don't die from some disease, they soon lose their looks and end up on the streets, hungry and destitute."

Dulcee's wise words strengthened Rose's resolve. If she wanted to do the right thing, as well as keep the peace with her in-laws, she'd have to take action, and soon.

But how? More than once, Tillie dropped by Rose's office. Hand on hip, in her usual cheeky manner, she'd inquire, "Made up your mind yet? What will you do after Cherry's baby is born?"

All Rose could do was reply, "I'm not sure yet." What a dilemma. She was getting pressured by both sides and kept putting off her final decision. Occasionally, early in the day when no men were around, she visited the third floor to see how Cherry was doing. Oddly enough, she didn't feel in the least uncomfortable, mainly because in the cold morning light, the third floor dwellers of the River Queen didn't look so much like tarts, harlots, and whores as much as they looked like ordinary women, relaxing in their wrappers, sipping their coffee, engaging in gossip and friendly conversation. They were all concerned about Cherry. "She cries a lot," Tillie said. "Stays in her room all the time. She needs you to cheer her up, Mrs. Peterson."

On Rose's latest visit to Cherry's tiny room, she'd found the girl lying on the bed, her eyes red from crying. "But why the tears, Cherry? You know you can stay. I promised I wouldn't throw you out, and I assure you I won't."

Cherry turned her face to the wall. "It's not that, Mrs. Peterson. You've been very kind. It's just…"

"Just what? You know you can tell me anything."

Cherry turned toward her, her face a mask of despair. "I didn't want to do this in the first place…"

She went on to describe how, as a child, her father had beaten and abused her. "He did things to me a father ought not to do." Finally she ran away. Then, even worse, she, a naïve girl of fourteen, with no place to go and starving, fell into the hands of a depraved individual who forced her into this life of sin. A tear rolled down her cheek. "I don't want to give my baby up. Tillie and the other girls say I have to if I want to keep working, but I love it already, be it a he or a she, and I don't know how I can do it. Sometimes I think I'll kill myself so I can get out of this misery."

Rose hated to be honest but had no choice. "I must confess I haven't given a thought to the fate of your baby. I will think about it, though. I promise. And maybe…well, maybe I can come up with something."

"Oh, would you? I would be much obliged if you could."

"I shall do my very best."

On her way down the staircase, Rose met Drucilla on the second floor landing. "What's the matter?" her sister-in-law inquired. "You look troubled."

"I am troubled." Rose described how the thought of Cherry's plight hung heavy on her mind. She put herself in Cherry's place. What would she have done under the same circumstances? Could she have given up her own child at birth? No! How horrible if she'd lost her precious Lucy. The trouble was, she still had no idea what to do, and it wasn't just Cherry, it was all the third-floor girls. "Why can't I make up my mind, Drucilla?"

"Well, you certainly ought to. If you're waiting for a sign from God, that's not likely to happen."

"I suppose not." Shaking her head, Rose continued down the staircase. What was she waiting for? Why couldn't she make up her mind? How nice it would be if somehow she did get a sign from God.

Hardly the day went by that she didn't see Mason. He never declared he was courting her but always seemed to be around, bringing small gifts, offering invitations to dinner. One day he took her for a drive and showed her the nearly completed house he was building. Situated on a rise overlooking the river, it resembled an English mansion, at least three stories high, with quaint turrets and massive chimneys.

"Pretty fancy," she declared. "You'll be lord of the manor in a place like this."

He got a teasing smile on his face. "Then I shall need a lady of the manor, won't I?"

So of course he was courting her and was only holding back because of her status as a new and supposedly grieving widow. Occasionally, she was struck by the irony of it all. Mason Talbot had made her a widow.

Now he wanted to marry her himself? How very strange, but she had no time to sort it all out, and besides, why should she? The day might come when she would indeed seriously consider becoming Mrs. Mason Talbot. Meantime, each of her days was so busy she had no time to think about what might or might not happen in the future. Mostly she turned down Mason's invitations because she needed time with her daughter. Every morning when she left the farm, she got a pang of guilt, but it never lasted. Coralee might have her faults, but she remained the loving, caring grandmother Lucy adored. She couldn't have been in better hands.

Rose had been so busy she'd hardly seen Deke, and she missed him. The day workmen finished the new ice cellar, she hastened to invite him to come take a look. Built directly back of the hotel, the cellar had a large trap door for lowering blocks of ice, a wooden staircase, and plenty of space for the storage of beer. "What do you think?" she asked Deke after they'd descended the staircase and stood in the good-sized cellar.

He looked around and nodded with approval. "Plenty of room. You did a good job."

"Tim Delahunty did it all. Designed it and hired the workmen to do the digging. He's truly a godsend."

Deke's gaze swept her critically. "How are you doing? I've hardly seen you."

"I'm doing fine."

"No, I don't mean that." In the dim light of the cellar, he studied her with eyes both sharp and shrewd. "You've made some big changes in your life. Are you happy? Has it been worthwhile?"

How perceptive of him. Certainly no one else had asked how she truly felt about the momentous decision she'd made. Actually, she'd been so busy she hadn't taken a moment to question herself, but now that she thought about it? Despite all the difficulties, a mounting wave of satisfaction flowed through her. "I'm glad you asked. I'm doing what I want to do, and I love it. There's problems…one after another, it seems, but at the end of the day when I go home all tired, I get this…this…"

"Feeling of a job well done?"

"Yes! That's it. I've accomplished something. Because of me, the River Queen is a better hotel than it was the day before." She touched his arm. "It's all thanks to you."

"And how is that?"

"Remember what you said about courage? You got me to see what I really wanted in this world. That's why I got brave and stood up for myself."

"Ah, Rose." He stepped closer. His hands gripped her shoulders. "You're quite the girl."

In the dimness of the cellar, she felt, more than saw, the warmth and tenderness of his gaze. "Deke, I..."

He pulled her close and bent to kiss her. Her heart jolted, and she leaned toward him, eager for his kiss. When his lips pressed against hers, then gently covered her mouth, she wanted more, but after one long, passionate moment, he broke off and thrust her away. "Don't worry, that was a friendship kiss."

"I know. Of course it was." But it wasn't. She hadn't missed the tremor in his voice or the searing, devouring way his mouth had moved over hers. *Friendship kiss, my foot.* But the moment was past. Best to let it go. She stepped away and gestured toward the empty depths of her ice cellar. "Will you sell me some ice?"

He laughed, and she heard the relief in his voice. "If you like, a whole cellar full."

"Fine, then. I shall aim to have the coldest beer in town."

Her knees felt a little wobbly as they climbed back up the stairs. What had happened? How could it be that a casual kiss from the man she'd always felt sorry for had sent tiny shivers down her spine? Ridiculous. He was just plain Deke, good friend and nothing more. Besides, she already had a suitor. Mason Talbot—rich, handsome, successful. Every woman's dream. She knew he loved her. If she gave him a sign, he'd propose in a second. What a fool she'd be if she threw him away.

* * * *

It was late. Deke sat on the steps of the ice house long after he should have been in bed. Soon Mitch joined him, asking, "Why are you up so late?"

"Can't sleep."

"Neither can I." Mitch sank down beside him. "We're a long way from home, aren't we?" He looked upward, taking in the millions of stars in the sky. "Did you ever think those are the same stars that shine over Amalie Station?"

"Don't get all sentimental on me, Mitch."

"I think about it a lot. Here we are, thousands of miles from home, and I ask myself, was it worth it?"

Deke laughed with irony. "You tell me. You never found a speck of gold. You're living over a stable in back of an ice house. You spend your days delivering ice."

"But making a fortune doing it. We're getting rich, Deke. Did you stop to think about that? We began this business at the right time, and we're just getting started." Mitch paused for a wistful sigh. "I like it here. The river, the mountains; it's beautiful country. I'd like to stay, only… Too bad there aren't any women around." He tipped his head toward the saloons down the street. "Well, except *those* women."

"That'll change, Mitch. Already this Gold Rush has begun to run its course. Give Sacramento another ten years—no, five years—and it'll be a city of solid citizens where you can go to church and find all the virtuous women you want."

"Easy for you to say. You've got Rose Peterson." Mitch looked over at his friend. "Right?"

"Sure, right." Hearing her name gave Deke a stab in his heart. One little slip was all, so why was he torturing himself? But damn, why had he kissed her? All right, he knew the reason. No woman he'd ever met could hold a candle to Mrs. Rose Peterson. And when she'd stood there in the ice cellar, holding her chin high, telling him in her soft voice how proud she was of herself, and how he'd helped her, he'd had to touch her, kiss her. It wouldn't happen again. She didn't love him. Considered him a helpful friend. *Down-and-out Deke, the crippled farmhand.* He would never beg, never plead. The last thing he wanted was for her to discover how he truly felt about her.

Ever since he'd kissed her, he'd played the scene over and over in his head. The intimate feel of her breasts when she'd pressed against him, the softness of her mouth, the sweet smell of her. Was it perfume Mason gave her? *Damn.* She made him feel things he'd never felt for another woman. Call it love, he supposed. All he knew was, he wanted her so bad he could hardly act like a normal man around her. He'd do it, though. Do it if it killed him. Despite the eager way she kissed him today, he'd seen her around town, riding with that lowlife, Mason Talbot, in his fancy phaeton. Incredible as it seemed, she had feelings for that cold-blooded murderer, and as long as she did, he would not interfere.

Deke stood and stretched. "Let's turn in. Big day tomorrow."

Mitch stood too. "We're going to get richer, and that's what counts, right?" He clapped Deke on the shoulder. "Don't get yourself in a twist over the widow. There's no finer man in the world than you, Deke. If she can't see that, the hell with her."

Chapter 12

Thanks to the efforts of Monsieur Gaston Bernier, the French restaurant was not only taking shape, it was going to be far finer than Rose had even imagined. When she told him "Spend what you need," he took her at her word. Soon every steamboat arriving from San Francisco contained items meant for the River Queen's fancy new restaurant. Gaston had shut the old restaurant down. Whenever Rose peeked inside, she was met with a disarray of unpacked boxes, rolls of carpeting, and stacks of what looked to be new tables, but she wasn't sure. "Do not worry," Gaston would reply when she asked. "It will all come together in due time."

Meantime, a lunch counter had been hastily erected next to the bar in the saloon. Run by Gus, dirty apron and all, it provided a simple fare of soup, hard boiled eggs, and sandwiches. To Rose's surprise, Gaston hadn't yet fired the surly cook. "So what will you do about Gus when the new restaurant opens?" she asked him one day. "Will he still be running the lunch counter?"

The Frenchman flashed his little enigmatic smile, the one she'd become quite familiar with. "Maybe yes, maybe no. Do not worry, madame."

That wasn't all. In a moment of rashness, she'd left the choosing of the restaurant's new name entirely up to Gaston. Now she wished she hadn't. She was dying to know what he planned to call it, but he remained cagey. "Perhaps I'll name it after one of Paris's oldest restaurants. La Petite Chaise. It's been there since 1680. Louis XIV ate there. Their onion soup, their steak tartare! *Mon Dieu!*" He blew a kiss in the air.

"La Petite Chaise has a nice ring to it, Gaston. I'd be happy with—"

"But on the other hand, La Tour d'Argent has been open since 1582. It was there that King Henri III used a fork for the first time."

"Fine. La Tour d'Argent, then."

"I will let you know in good time, madame." Gaston gave her his eyebrows-lifted "end of conversation" look with which she never argued. Funny, for all his outrageous arrogance, she liked him and trusted him completely. Judging from what she'd seen so far, he was doing an excellent job. The new restaurant was taking shape nicely and she couldn't be more pleased. Not only that, from what she'd seen of his cooking, she was sure she'd found an outstanding French chef who would soon dazzle Sacramento with his culinary skills.

Too bad Drucilla didn't feel the same. Strange though it seemed, the Frenchman obviously found her attractive, although how that was possible, Rose didn't know. All the same, his eyes lit whenever he saw her no-nonsense sister-in-law. No matter how busy he was, he would stop and engage her in a conversation all in French. In return, she would remain impatiently polite and always hurry off at the first opportunity.

More than once, Rose tried to convince her sister-in-law that a miracle had occurred and she'd attracted an admirer. "The man really likes you."

The slight curl of Drucilla's lip revealed her disdain. "He just wants to practice his French so he won't get rusty."

"Not so! I can tell he likes you, just from the way he looks at you with that little gleam in his eye. He's a fine man, a successful man, and not bad looking, besides. You could do far worse—"

"He's an inch shorter than I am."

More than once, Rose threw up her hands. Why must her sister-in-law be so hardheaded? Gaston and Drucilla would make the ideal couple, perfectly suited to one another, but oh, well. She'd learned a long time ago that people didn't always do what she wanted them to do. That was surely the case with stubborn Drucilla.

Early one afternoon, when renovations were nearly complete and the restaurant due to open in a week, Gaston came to her office and announced, "I 'ave decided on a name."

She refrained from remarking it was about time. "What did you decide on?" She expected he'd chosen either La Petite Chaise or La Tour d'Argent.

"It will be called Gaston's."

For a moment the name didn't sink in. "You mean you're naming it after yourself?"

"But of course. It all comes together." As if envisioning a sign high above, Monsieur Bernier raised his arm and gazed upward. "Gaston's! Famed for his *coquilles a la Normandie*, his *soupe à l'oignon*."

"That sounds like onion soup, but what is *coquilles a la Normandie*?"

The French chef beamed. "It's the dish I'm best known for. Scallops poached in white wine, placed atop a puree of mushrooms in a scallop shell, covered with a sauce so delicious you will call it the best meal you ever ate."

She thought a moment and had to smile. "I guess I can't argue with that. Gaston's it is then. The perfect name, and your dish with the scallops sounds absolutely wonderful."

"It will be." Gaston frowned. "My poaching pans haven't arrived. I ordered them over a month ago."

"They're coming by ship?"

"On the steamship *Mary Jane*. She's overdue."

"Let's hope she arrives today."

* * * *

In the late afternoon, Rose was in her office when from a distance she heard the tooting of a ship's whistle. She hurried to the restaurant and found Gaston. "Did you hear that? I'd wager it's the *Mary Jane* arriving."

More tooting followed. Gaston tipped his head. "Sounds like more than one ship."

"Maybe they're racing." Rose had heard about the dubious sport of steamboat racing on the Sacramento River. Arrogant captains weren't past taking dangerous chances in order to prove their ship was the fastest and therefore the best.

"At last, my poaching pans." Gaston made a fast exit. Curious, Rose followed close behind.

The landing dock lay only a short distance from the River Queen. Rose and Gaston weren't the only ones hurrying in that direction. Drawn by the sound of the ships' dueling whistles, a steady stream of curiosity seekers was gathering on the dock and along the riverbank. Drucilla joined Rose as she and Gaston found places on the dock. Deke and Mitch had already arrived and were peering downstream. "They're coming fast," Mitch remarked.

Rose looked downstream. Two steamboats, their paddlewheels rotating at a furious speed, were heading for the dock practically side by side. Were they racing? The churning white wake behind each ship and the constant tooting of their whistles told her they were, especially when people standing on the decks of both ships appeared to be shouting and waving, no doubt urging their ship on.

"Damn fools!" cried someone in the crowd.

"They'd better watch out," said a grizzled old miner. "Them boilers blow all the time."

Rose couldn't take her eyes off the ships. As she watched, one pulled ahead of the other. "Look," she said to Gaston, "one's ahead. I wonder if it's the *Mary Jane*."

She never heard his answer. As she watched, a sheet of flame shot upward from the bridge of the ship that had gone ahead, closely followed by an explosion so strong the force of it drove her backward along with everyone else on the dock. As she staggered to keep her balance, Deke's strong arms caught her and brought her straight again. Gaston caught Drucilla. In horrified silence, the onlookers watched as flames billowed in all directions from the doomed ship. It was literally coming apart, masses of burning timber flying in all directions. In the gathering darkness, Rose could barely make out men, women, and children either jumping or being hurled into the river.

And then, as if things couldn't possibly get any worse, flames shot up from the other steamboat, apparently caused by the burning debris blown off the first ship.

Many of the witnesses on the dock and along the waterfront remained stunned by the shock of the explosion. They gazed in horror, unable to move. Others fled the dock screaming. A few kept their heads and leaped into action.

"We'll need boats," Deke called. Rose watched as Deke, Mitch, and Gaston raced from the dock to an area along the waterfront where small boats were drawn ashore. Without hesitation, they jumped into a rowboat, shoved off, and started rowing toward the flaming remains of the stricken ship. Other men followed, Tim and Gus among them, until soon, in the gathering darkness, an armada of small boats headed toward the wreckage.

Rose couldn't hear well. Her ears were ringing and numb from the explosion. Otherwise, she hadn't been hurt and neither had Drucilla. Rose grabbed her arm. "There's going to be survivors and they're going to need help."

Chaos reigned on the dock. Many women were screaming and weeping, but not Drucilla. She nodded in agreement. "Let's get to the River Queen. We're going to need blankets, lots of them, and whatever else we can think of."

Hems held high, Rose and Drucilla raced the short distance to the hotel. They hurried through the saloon. How strange it looked, almost empty, the patrons having deserted their games and whiskey to rush to the waterfront. From the linen closet on the second floor, they grabbed as many blankets as they could carry and started back. Rose could hardly see her way over the top of the pile she was carrying, but when they reached the river, she was glad she'd made the effort.

Steered by Deke and Mitch, a boatload of survivors had pulled ashore. Spying Rose, Deke called, "Good, we'll need all the blankets we can get."

Some of the survivors climbed from the boat on their own, all of them soaking wet and shivering. Rose and others helped them ashore and gave each a blanket. They were the lucky ones. Others had been badly injured, some with broken bones, some with burns. With infinite care, Deke, Mitch, and others lifted and carried them ashore. Just when Rose thought the boat was empty, she saw two unmoving bodies lying on the bottom. "They...they're dead?"

Deke nodded grimly. "We pulled them out of the water, but it was too late. Worse thing is, we'll be going back because there's more, lots more."

A black-robed priest had arrived. Standing on the shore, he made the sign of the cross and implored, "Dear God, please help us on this terrible night."

Rose sent up her own silent prayer. Many were badly burned. Many were dead. As the night wore on, Rose learned the ship that exploded and sunk was indeed the *Mary Jane*. Flames still blazed on the other ship, the *Excalibur*. It remained afloat but had to be abandoned. She lost track of time as she gave what help she could to victims rescued from the water and brought ashore. Worst of all was the sickening, near-unbelievable sight of the growing row of blanket-covered bodies lined up along the shore, and that included men, women, and children, too. Until now, she'd never seen a dead body before except for funerals and once on the wagon train when a careless young man had accidentally shot himself. She would never forget that ever-lengthening row of the dead, but right now must force herself not to dwell upon it. If she did, she'd fall apart, and that couldn't happen. She must concentrate on helping the survivors. Only later, and in retrospect, would she ponder upon this heart-rending tragedy and how this night was unlike anything she'd ever lived through before, and, if God had mercy, never would again.

At least one good thing emerged from the catastrophe. At one point in that long, horrible night, the thought crossed her mind that for once, there were no distinctions of class, gender, race, or anything else. Only one thing mattered: helping the poor souls who came from the stricken ship. Everyone worked together. The Chinese kitchen workers labored alongside hotel owners, miners, and ordinary citizens. Every doctor in town had rushed to the scene to aid the badly burned, the cut and bruised, those with broken limbs. A desperate call went out for morphine, as well as linseed oil and lime-water, termed carron oil, to treat burns. A steady stream of wagons and carriages hauled the most badly injured to Sacramento's one small hospital, located near Sutter's Fort. A tent was hastily erected for the rest. Every hotel along the waterfront opened its doors for survivors who had no place to go. During the course of the night, Rose noticed Joy, Evette, Ruby—all the third floor girls—had come to the river. Still in their gaudy dresses, their cheeks rouged, they'd pitched in to help like everyone else. Once, when Rose was lifting a little girl from one of the rescue boats, Cherry, now heavy and awkward, stood beside her, lifting another child. "You shouldn't be doing that," Rose said.

"Oh, yes, I should." Cherry had tears in her eyes. "These poor people! Seems like this is the least I can do."

During the night, Rose threw a blanket over the shoulders of a white-haired, older crewman, one of the relatively uninjured survivors who had stepped ashore from one of the rowboats. "Thank you, ma'am," he remarked through chattering teeth.

She asked, "Were you aboard the *Mary Jane*?"

"I was the engineer."

"Were you really racing?"

The engineer responded with a bitter laugh. "I told the captain how dangerous it was, but did he listen? He points at the boiler and shouts, 'Shove it up!' Wants top speed. Wants to get there first and to hell with all the lives on board. Then the fool tells me to lash an oar to the safety valve so it won't close."

"That doesn't sound smart."

"It sure as hell wasn't. T'wasn't long before the whole damn boiler blew and landed us all in the river."

Rescuers made trip after trip by boat to the disaster scene. At first, their goal was to find passengers and crewmen who were either treading water or clinging to wreckage and pull them to safety before they drowned. Later on, all those still alive had been rescued, and rescuers were pulling only dead bodies from the river. By then, Rose and Drucilla had moved from the beach to the tent set up for the victims where doctors worked at a frantic pace to aid the injured. Rose did what she could, applying carron oil to burns, fetching water, helping find a lost child. Far into the night—Rose lost all track of time— she was placing a bandage on a little girl's cut face when Ben appeared, frowning with concern.

"Ah, Rose, there you are. I've been searching all over. Are you and Drucilla all right? We heard the explosion. Coralee was worried and sent me to fetch you home."

Rose stood straight and wearily pushed back a wayward strand of hair. "Drucilla's fine. She's around somewhere. I can't go yet. Look around at these poor people. Some are badly hurt. Many are dead. It's all just so horrible, but I want to stay as long as they need me. Tell Coralee I'll come home when I can."

"Terrible tragedy," Ben muttered as he looked around the tent. Rose didn't miss his slight recoil when he caught sight of Tillie, face rouged, fancy coiffeur in ruins, still dressed in her red plumed finery. At the moment, she was comforting a crying child who sat on her lap while a doctor applied a bandage.

Ben's lips pressed into a thin, disapproving line. "Is that one of your bawdy girls?"

Anger swelled within her. At a time like this, how dare he criticize? In fact, why should he criticize at all? She could easily say Tillie wasn't from the River Queen, but she didn't feel like lying. Through gritted teeth, she replied, "Yes, that's one of my bawdy girls. Everyone has pitched in to help, and that includes *all* the employees of the River Queen."

Ben's cold, hard gaze bored into her. "You gave your word you were going to get rid of them."

That's enough. If ever there was a sign from God, this was it. Something snapped, and the words she'd suppressed up to this moment, came pouring out. "I said I would, but guess what? I've changed my mind. I am *not* getting rid of them, is that clear?" She braced herself for his tirade. Whatever he said would do no good. After the selfless manner in which the ladies from the third floor had conducted themselves tonight, she would not throw them out, no matter how much Ben Peterson disapproved.

She waited for his rant but it never came. Ben continued with his granite glare until he said in an icy cold voice, "You will live to regret this," and walked away.

Drucilla had overheard. "I'm afraid you're in for it now. Pa's really mad."

"I'll worry about it later." Not easy. She'd finally made a stand. There would be consequences, but for the moment, she put all thoughts of Ben out of her head. These poor people needed her help, and her own problems would have to wait.

Minutes later, Cherry, who'd been working beside her, clutched her stomach and doubled over. "My stars! I think my time has come."

No, not now. This couldn't be happening, but one look at Cherry's pain-twisted face told Rose that it was. At all costs, she must keep her composure. She worked at keeping her voice calm. "Then you must lie down." But where? A few cots had been brought to the tent, but they were all taken. Like most of the victims, Cherry would have to lie on the ground with nothing but a blanket to protect her. "At least the doctors are here, so you've got plenty of help."

Cherry clenched her jaw. "No! I won't be having this child in front of everybody. I want my own room and my own bed. Oh, what's that?" A horrified look crossed her face. "I think my water just broke."

From her limited experience, Rose was aware that when the mother's water breaks, the baby could be coming fast. Cherry would be better off staying here, but if she wanted to go home, then by God, home she would go. Looking for help, Rose gazed around the tent. Drucilla, the third-floor girls—everyone was working at a frantic pace, trying to ease the suffering of the poor victims. She would not disturb them, could do this herself. Nothing to it. All she had to do was somehow get Cherry back to her room and then... She wasn't sure what, but she'd deal with that later. She wrapped an arm around Cherry's waist. "Come on, I'll help you home."

Cherry was able to walk from the tent on her own, but as they started up the street to the hotel, she called, "Wait!" bent over, and groaned. "There's another pain. I dunno if I can make it, but I've got to."

"We'll stop a minute and rest and then keep on." Rose kept her voice calm, but panic was building inside her. Cherry was too far gone. She'd never get back on her own. Over the top of Cherry's head, she peered into the darkness. *Somebody—anybody—please, I need help.*

A figure emerged. "Rose, is that you?"

A miracle! It was Deke.

"Yes, it's me."

Mitch appeared alongside Deke. They hurried to where Rose was standing over Cherry who had just sunk to the ground. By a sliver of moonlight, Rose looked into their tired, strained faces. They'd been working nonstop and it showed. She stretched out her hand. "Can you help? She has to get home." Cherry groaned, this time louder. "I mean, right now, this instant! She's... she's..."

"About to have a baby." Deke took a close look. "Looks like there's no time to waste. We'll get her back to the tent and—"

"No!" Cherry cried. "I don't care if I have this baby all alone. I want my own room and my own bed. Please, please, get me home."

Mitch stepped forward. After a close look at Cherry, he turned to Deke. "Take the boat by yourself. If the little lady wants to go home, I'll take her."

Deke didn't hesitate. "Rose, Mitch will help. I've got to get back. We're still looking for bodies, and I—"

"I understand. You need to go." As Deke disappeared into the darkness, Rose gazed at Mitch with pleading eyes. "Please, if you could just get her to her room?"

"Don't worry." Mitch bent and scooped Cherry into his arms and started up the road. Since he wasn't a big man, his strength surprised her. He'd picked Cherry up like a feather and was now taking such long, fast strides, Rose could hardly keep up.

"I'm so grateful," she remarked as she trotted alongside. "Don't know what I would have done."

"Glad to help," Mitch replied, not slowing down.

"We won't be able to find a doctor. They're all down here or at the hospital."

"No, we won't."

"Maybe I can find a midwife."

Cherry moaned aloud. Mitch increased his pace. "By the looks of things, there's no time to look for a midwife."

Rose had to work hard to keep up with him. "But what shall we do?"

Mitch didn't answer. They got to the hotel and through the entrance. Rose pointed toward the stairs. "Third floor."

As Mitch carried Cherry up the stairs, he spoke again. "Don't worry, I'll handle it."

Breathless, she struggled to keep up. "*You*?"

They got to the third-floor landing before he spoke again, this time to Cherry. "What's your last name?"

"I'm Cherry Foley," she gasped.

"Back in Australia, I've delivered maybe a million lambs, some not so easy, so I know how it's done." He looked down the hallway. "Is this where you live, Mrs. Foley? Which is your room?"

"I'll show you." Rose led the way to Cherry's room and swung the door open. Mitch came through and gently laid his burden on the bed as Rose, drawing a breath of determination, closed the door behind him.

Chapter 13

James Alan Foley's arrival into the world was met with a complication. "It's a breech birth," Mitch said after his first look. "His little bum is coming out first."

Rose sat at the head of Cherry's bed, holding her hand, lending encouragement. "That's nothing serious, is it?"

"Not to worry. Ewes give breech births all the time."

Once, when she was between pains, Cherry called, "What are you doing down there?"

"Just turning the baby, Mrs. Foley. Don't you worry. Nothing to it. Lots of lambs come into the world this way."

Whatever Mitch did worked fine. The baby literally slipped into the world soon after. He had lots of dark hair and all his fingers and toes. The moment he arrived, he let out a lusty cry and kept on crying. Even though Rose had never assisted in a birth before, she knew enough to clean the baby, wrapped him in a soft blue blanket, and placed him in his mother's arms.

Cherry's first glimpse of her newborn was a joy to see. "My son," she murmured. With the tenderest of touches, she ran her finger over his forehead, down his nose to his tiny chin. Eyes shining with love, she announced, "He's perfect."

Soon Baby James stopped crying and fell asleep. Exhausted but happy, Cherry gazed up at Mitch, a world of gratitude in her eyes. "You brought my baby into the world, and I'll always be grateful."

"Nothing to it."

Rose spoke up. "That's not so, Mitch. What would we have done without you?"

"You'd have managed."

Cherry soon fell asleep. Mitch sat back and took his first opportunity to look around the tiny room. Since he'd had no time to examine his surroundings, Rose guessed he had no idea where he was. When she opened the door to get some fresh air, his gaze fell upon the fancy sign with the flowers that hung on the door. He looked at Rose. "Why is her name on the door?"

Rose remained silent. She couldn't think what to say.

Mitch took another look at the sign. "Blimey. Is this place what I think it is?"

Rose remembered Deke telling her about how religious Mitch was. Lived by God's word. Read his Bible every night. Now that he'd realized what kind of place this was, no doubt he couldn't get out of here fast enough. She looked into his kind grey eyes. "I'm afraid it's what you think it is."

Mitch looked toward the sleeping new mother. "And she...?"

"She is."

"I see." Slowly Mitch got to his feet. "I'll be leaving now. Mrs. Foley will be fine, and the baby, too."

She could tell nothing from his blank expression. Well-mannered man that he was, he must be hiding his disgust. "Thanks so much, Mitch."

He gave her a quick "You're welcome" and left. What a shame. She thought back to when Cherry had reached the worst of her labor. Stoic up to then, she'd cried out in pain. Mitch had patted her hand and reassured her. "There, there, little mother, be brave. It's almost over." He'd been so kind, so compassionate, that Rose, in what she now saw as a moment of madness, had considered the possibility that here was the perfect solution for Cherry. Mitch would fall in love with her, and she with him. She would keep her baby. They would marry and have a wonderful life.

Ah, well. Only a fairy tale.

Tillie poked her head in. She and the other girls had done all they could do for the victims and had finally returned. When Tillie saw Cherry and her newborn, she uttered one of her choice expletives and called, "Girls, come see! She's popped the baby."

Soon the third-floor girls were crowding around Cherry's bed, waking her up, oohing and ahhing over her newborn. Cherry would be fine and it was time for Rose to leave. She looked through the window and saw dawn was about to break. She'd been up all night, so engrossed in helping the victims, and then Cherry, she'd never given a thought to herself. A tide of weariness engulfed her whole body. As she hurried down the stairs and out to the stable, she shivered with chill and fatigue. Her legs ached. Her eyes felt heavy from lack of sleep. So much had happened this night. To her dying day, she'd remember all of it, from the horror of the accident to the joy of helping a new baby into this world. She'd think of all that tomorrow, though. All she wanted now was to get home, crawl into bed, and hug her daughter before she fell into a long, deep, merciful sleep.

To the sound of roosters crowing, Rose drove the buggy down the long driveway that led to the farmhouse. Tired though she was, she would drive around to the back like she always did, unhitch Star, feed and water her, and then—what a joyous thought!—get to bed. But something in front of the house caught her eye.

What on earth?

She reined in the horse and stepped to the ground. Some kind of objects were heaped in a pile directly in front of the porch steps. She drew closer. Her dresses! Her shoes, bonnets, pearl reticule—everything she owned lay in a heap before her. What were all her possessions doing out here on the ground? Who would do such a thing? Her stomach clenched tight as she rushed up the front steps. She grasped the doorknob and turned it. The door didn't open. But it was never locked, and it always opened. She pushed hard. Nothing. The door was barred on the inside. With both fists, she started pounding, she didn't know how long. She waited. Nothing happened, and she pounded again. At last she heard a noise. Someone was sliding the bar on the inside back. *Thank God.* Someone had made a mistake. Soon it would be all straightened out and she could get to bed.

The door opened a crack. Raymond peeked out. "I can't let you in."

She gasped. "What do you mean you can't let me in?"

"I just can't is all."

"Raymond, you open the door this minute and talk to me."

Her brother-in-law slowly swung open the door. Sleepy eyed, he scratched his head, looking acutely uncomfortable. "Pa's mad at you. He says to tell you that you don't live here anymore."

This couldn't be happening. A flood of desperation swept through her, but she would try to stay calm. "What did he say exactly?"

"Well..." Raymond's eyebrows drew together in an agonized expression. "He says you're a sinner because you're running a den of in...in..."

"Iniquity?"

"That's it, iniquity. And he says you're not a fit mother, and he's going to take Lucy away from you."

Her blood pounded. She felt her face get hot from a combination of rage and humiliation. "Call him down here. I want to talk to him."

Raymond shook his head. "He won't come, Rose. You know how he gets sometimes."

"Then call Coralee."

"Even if she wanted to, Pa wouldn't let her."

"Does she want to?"

"I don't think so. She sides with Pa."

"Drucilla?"

"She was up all night. I hate to wake her up."

She needed to get away, go someplace where she could think. "Is Lucy all right?"

"Oh, she's fine." Raymond frowned in sympathy. "I'm sorry, Rose. It was Pa who did this, not me."

Poor Raymond looked miserable. He wasn't accustomed to any kind of a crisis in his life. No use standing here. Nothing to do but leave. "None of this is your fault, Raymond, so don't you worry."

"Where will you go?"

"I have lots of places to go." She had no idea. She turned and headed down the porch steps, calling over her shoulder, "Get back to bed. I'll be fine."

She passed the pitiful pile of her belongings without touching anything. To do so would have been utterly humiliating. Without a backward glance, she climbed in the buggy and headed back to town. Where could she stay? She must think straight, but the raw, naked hurt of being thrown out of her home was so overwhelming she could hardly manage a rational thought and kept having to swallow the sobs that rose in her throat. How could Ben and Coralee do such a thing? How could they keep her from seeing her child? But she mustn't dwell on that now. She absolutely must keep her wits about her, get back to town and go...where?

If not for the accident, she could have gotten a room at her own hotel, but at the moment, the River Queen was full to overflowing with shipwreck survivors. So was every hotel in town, and she knew for a fact there was not a room to be had. Perhaps Mason could help her, but come to think about it, where was he and where had he been? Oddly enough, she hadn't seen him last night during all the excitement. How very strange that every man she knew, every woman too, had rushed to the river to help. *Except Mason Talbot.* No doubt he had an explanation, but it did seem strange.

Deke. At the thought of him, a spark of hope rose from the depths of her despair. Deke with his kind, warm eyes, his laid-back humor, his wise advice. Deke with his practical, no-nonsense view of life.

Of course, that's where she'd go.

* * * *

In the early morning sunshine, Deke was bending over the water pump when Rose guided her buggy past the ice house and stopped in front of the stable. Bare to the waist, wiping his face with a towel, he rose to see who it was. "Rose?"

"Yes, it's me." She'd never seen him half-dressed before. Despite her distress, she couldn't help but notice how flat his stomach was, and how the lean, hard muscles rippled in his chest. "Did you get any sleep?"

"Not much. Maybe an hour." He pulled on his shirt and started buttoning. "This is a surprise."

She laid down the reins and stepped from the buggy. Until this moment, she hadn't realized how happy she was to see him. What a relief it would be to talk to him and confide the awful thing that had happened. The telling of it would be painful, but she would *not* cry. Above all else, she would maintain her dignity and control.

She walked toward him. "I thought I'd stop by because..." The sob lurking in her throat—the very one she'd so far managed to suppress—came surging up. No way could she stop it. "Oh, Deke, I..." Her voice choked. Tears so blinded her eyes she staggered and would have fallen if two strong arms hadn't encircled her and pulled her close.

He didn't ask what happened or why she was crying. "Whatever it is, we'll fix it," he said in a perfectly reasonable voice, as if sobbing women fell into his arms all the time. "Come on, we're going upstairs."

A bed, bureau, chair, and washstand made up the Spartan furnishings of Deke's room over the stable. A few pegs on the wall held his clothes. The room wasn't much, but for Rose it provided a welcome shelter from the turmoil her life was in. One arm circling her shoulder, uttering soft words of comfort, Deke sat with her on the bed and waited patiently until she finished her bout of crying. When at last the tears stopped and she dried her eyes, he got off the bed, pulled up a chair, and faced her. "Are you upset because of the accident? You've seen too many things you should never have seen. You're not the only one. I hope to never have a night like that again."

"Last night was a nightmare. If I live to be a hundred, I'll never forget what those poor people went through." She tried to keep her voice from shaking. "But it's more than that."

"There's more? Tell me what happened."

With a final gulp and dab at her eyes—he'd loaned her a handkerchief—she told him how she'd returned to the farm and found her belongings piled in a heap out front. She recounted her devastating conversation with Raymond. "So there you have it. My father-in-law has thrown me out and threatened to take my child away from me. Coralee agrees, so where does that leave me? I'm desperate, Deke. I don't care about the farm. They can have it. All I care about is Lucy and howI can get her back."

Deke rubbed his chin. Concerned and attentive, he'd carefully listened to every word she said. "First off, Ben should have talked to you himself, not left the dirty work to poor Raymond."

"I'm not so sure. Maybe I should have pushed past Raymond, or gone around back and broken a window. Then gone upstairs and talked to Ben."

"I can't see you doing that. You were right to leave. Most important, don't act in haste. There's a solution, but we've got to work on it."

"*We*? You mean you'll help me?"

"You're a good mother, and Ben is being an arse. Of course, I'll help you."

Up to now, she'd felt so alone, so utterly without support. She pressed a palm to her heart. "I'm very glad and so utterly grateful, so—"

"Stop right there. Have you had any sleep?"

"None."

"Hungry?"

"I couldn't eat a bite."

"Here's what we'll do. First off, I'm going to bring you some water so you can wash up. And then"—he arose and pulled a long, red plaid shirt from one of the pegs—"you'll get out of those clothes, into this shirt, and go to bed. Don't worry, I'll be elsewhere."

She started to protest that she wasn't really tired, that the ugly scene at the farm had so upset her she'd entirely forgotten how exhausted she was. Now her aching body reminded her how much she needed some rest. She took the shirt Deke offered. "Maybe I will sleep for a while, that is, if I'm not putting you out."

The warmth of Deke's smile echoed in his voice. "No, you're not putting me out, Mrs. Peterson. Sleep as long as you want. When you wake up, we'll decide what to do."

* * * *

The sinking sun cast long shadows through the pine trees that lined the river when Rose awoke and looked out the window. She hadn't meant to sleep so long. Surely they must need her at the hotel and were wondering what had become of her. She would dress and hurry there now. But first… She looked around. So this was where Deke lived. Curious, she slipped from the bed. In the plaid shirt that was way too big, she wandered around his room. Everything clean and neat. At his bureau, a near-irresistible urge struck her to peek in the drawers. She would do no such thing, of course. She was above all that. Mother had taught her that snooping through somebody's things was not only bad-mannered, it showed a distinct lack of character.

Only...

She couldn't resist, opened the top drawer halfway and peeked inside. Nothing special, just a pair of long johns neatly folded, matching socks tied together, handkerchiefs stacked in a tidy pile. Everything perfect, as she might have suspected of a man like Deke Fleming. If he had any character flaws, she had yet to spot them. Such a nice man...but "nice" didn't quite cover the way she was beginning to feel about him. He wasn't even here, yet she felt comfortable and protected in his room.

One drawer was enough before shame stopped her from opening the rest. She hoped no one would see her, but before she dressed, she needed to wash at the pump and use the privy. She needn't have worried. After sneaking cautiously down the steps, she discovered no one was around, and the stables couldn't be seen from the street. She had just gone upstairs again when she heard a knock on the door followed by, "It's me."

Sitting on the bed, still wearing his red plaid shirt, she called, "Come in, Deke."

He entered and asked, "Did you get some rest?"

She smiled up at him. He looked the same as ever, dressed in dark pants and a blue cotton shirt. Remembering this morning when she'd seen him without it, she got a tingling in the pit of her stomach. But that was silly. After all, this was only Deke. "I slept all day."

"Feel better?"

"Yes." To her surprise, she meant what she said. Earlier, she'd been in a state of dark despair and could see no way out. But things didn't look quite so bleak now. Perhaps it wasn't the end of the world after all. With Deke standing by to help her, she'd regained at least some of her confidence. Gazing down, she realized the plaid shirt wasn't nearly long enough, and her legs were exposed. "Oh, dear." She reached for a blanket to cover herself.

The gesture seemed to amuse him. "Don't bother. I've seen more than a few female limbs in my time and managed to control myself."

She dropped the blanket. Such false modesty was ridiculous, and besides, she'd always been proud of her shapely legs and didn't mind in the least if he saw them. Not like her at all, but then, this wasn't an ordinary day, and this strange attraction she was feeling for Deke right now wasn't part of her ordinary feelings. "Come sit down and talk to me, Deke. I've got to get to the hotel, but I wanted to tell you how much I appreciate your letting me sleep here."

He sat beside her on the bed. "It's always my pleasure to help you. You know that, don't you?"

The look in his eyes—so deeply caring, so…was that desire she was seeing? Unexpected words popped into her head. If this were an ordinary day and she was thinking rationally, she wouldn't dream of saying them, but in the current mood she was in, she deemed them ultimately suitable. "Do you remember that day you kissed me in the ice cellar?"

"Of course I do."

She took the plunge, knowing full well what would happen. "I haven't forgotten either. It was very nice, Deke. I liked your kissing me."

His reaction was what she expected, and wanted. With a shuddering breath, he wrapped his arms around her and brushed his lips against hers. "Happy to oblige. I liked it, too."

As she wrapped her arms around his neck, he pressed his lips to hers, caressing her mouth more than kissing it. At the same time, he lowered her to the bed, swinging her legs up so that they were lying flat, he half on top of her. His hand skidded down her side as he kissed her devouringly. When finally he lifted his lips, she murmured, "No, come back," and drew his face to hers in a renewed embrace. Why was she doing this? She hadn't planned anything beyond a quick kiss, but now she wanted more, and it was all her own doing. The trouble was, this was a Deke she didn't know, not the poor cripple she felt sorry for but a strong, virile man in every sense of the word, a man whose hands at the moment were slowly, tantalizingly unbuttoning the red plaid shirt.

An explosion of pleasure and need went off inside her. "Don't stop," she said.

* * * *

When it was over, she lay in Deke's arms, head resting on his chest, feeling more warm and content than she could ever remember. She never knew passion could feel like this, certainly not whatever that was with Emmet. A sliver of guilt struck her. Her poor dead husband hadn't been gone six months, and here she was, making love with another man. How downright wicked. Also how shameless and immoral. She smiled and snuggled closer, cherishing the steady beat of Deke's heart against her ear.

He laughed from his exhaustion. "That was a bit of all right," he said.

"Just all right?" She gave him a gentle nudge. "You Australians and your understatements."

He tangled his fingers in her hair. "I can't get enough of you."

She was turning to press a kiss against the pulse in his neck when her practical side intruded and the outside world closed in. *The shipwreck. Ben. Lucy. The River Queen.* What was she doing? How could she actually be enjoying herself after the horror of the ship explosion, let alone her shock at finding she'd been locked out of her home? "I must go, Deke. I shouldn't be here. I—"

"Yes, you should go. I understand." Deke raised on one elbow and gazed down at her, a mixture of desire and understanding in his eyes. "Go do what you have to do. Don't worry about Lucy, and for God's sake, don't do anything rash. Bide your time. Sooner or later you'll know what to do. Much as you'll miss Lucy, from what I've seen of Coralee, she's in good hands."

He'd given her good advice, much as she hated to admit it. "Thanks, I suppose you're right."

Aside from her anguish over Lucy, a jumble of other anxieties assailed her as she slid from Deke's bed. Had they missed her at the River Queen? What about Mason? He'd practically asked her to marry him, and, face it, she'd led him to believe she might say yes. What if he'd somehow found out she'd spent the night with Deke? What if everyone knew? Oh, dear God, what a mess.

Deke watched in silence as she washed and dressed at a frantic pace. Only then did she remember the gold locket that hung around her neck, the one she thought so precious because it contained a lock of Anthony's hair. What a naïve little fool she'd been. Why hadn't she seen how he'd used her? When Deke wasn't looking, she yanked the locket from her neck. Not only would she never wear it again, it was destined for the trash.

When she was ready to leave, she stood with her hand on the doorknob, her mind fumbling for the right thing to say. Not easy when her life was in such a turmoil.

Deke blew her a kiss. "Don't forget what I said, Rose. Don't do anything rash. Now go. They need you."

"Goodbye." She opened the door, then looked back and gave him a playful grin. "In case you hadn't noticed, I had a lovely time."

Chapter 14

When Rose reached the hotel, to her surprise she found a near state of normalcy. Many of the survivors had already left. In the saloon, the usual throng of miners crowded around the tables and stood three-deep at the bar. Last night's angels of mercy, the third-floor girls, were back to mingling with the customers, coarse and flirtatious as always in their gaudy finery. Rose found Tillie and drew her aside. Her words came easily, perhaps because she'd made up her mind and knew exactly what she was going to say. "When I saw what you and your girls did last night, I knew I could never throw you out. You can stay as long as you need to. Of course, you know how I feel about prostitution. I won't have it at the River Queen. I'd like to end it right now, but I'll give you one more month before I shut it down."

Tillie stared at her in surprise. "You really mean it, don't you?"

"I give you my word I mean it, so if you stay, you must agree to look for another line of work. Meanwhile, I'll make sure there are other jobs available. If you prefer to remain in your profession, all I ask is that you don't delay looking elsewhere."

"That's fair. We'll start looking." Tillie actually smiled. "You didn't do too bad yourself last night, Mrs. Peterson. Goes to show you're not all bad."

Pleased at her conversation with Tillie, Rose headed for the restaurant, where she found Gaston unpacking dishes in the newly refurbished kitchen. When he saw her, a look of relief crossed his face. "Ah, there you are, madame. We were beginning to worry about you."

"I was up all night but finally got some sleep." She remembered his part in the harrowing hours after the *Mary Jane* exploded. "I so admire what you did last night. Every time I looked, you were either pulling people from the river or carrying the injured to the tent. If not for you and a few others, many more would have drowned."

He ducked his head modestly, a rare occurrence for the arrogant Monsieur Bernier. "Like everyone else, I did what I could. Tell me..." He seemed at an unusual loss of words. "Is Mademoiselle Drucilla all right? She was up all night helping in the tent, and I haven't seen her today."

"She's fine. I haven't seen her either, but I know she went home to get some sleep."

Gaston bit his lip, seeming to struggle for words. "Perhaps...you could do me this favor."

"Of course, anything." She could already guess what he was going to say.

"This may come as a surprise to you, but I have grown fond of your sister-in-law."

"Really? I had no idea." Whenever he saw Drucilla, he resembled a lovesick puppy, but she wouldn't tell him that.

"But I don't know how she feels about me. Would it be possible...? I don't suppose you could—?"

"Find out how she feels?"

"Yes, that's it." He smiled with relief. "Up to now, she has ignored me, but last night at the river, when I was carrying a child to safety, I thought I saw a look of admiration in her eye. I'm not sure, though. So if you could do it without...without—"

"Letting her know? Of course, I'd be happy to." She touched his arm and bent close. "This is between you and me."

He gave her a heartfelt thank you. Quickly reverting to his usual superior self, he launched into a discussion of what was still needed for the nearly finished restaurant. Before she left, she asked about the date for the opening. Because of the accident, would he delay it?

He tilted his head back and looked down his nose. "Certainly not. I may have lost my poaching pans, but I assure you, madame, Gaston's will open on time."

Rose found her sister-in-law on the second floor, checking the near-empty linen closet. "Well, there you are," said Drucilla. "I was beginning to worry. Raymond told me you came to the farm last night, and of course—"

"I discovered Ben threw all my things out." Rose didn't quite succeed in keeping the bitterness from her voice. "Sorry. You're not to blame. I worry about Lucy. I never dreamed they'd keep me from my daughter."

A pained expression crossed Drucilla's face. "I know. It's terrible what Pa did. I tried to talk him out of it, but you know how he is when he gets stubborn. The trouble is, he doesn't understand. Frankly, neither did I, before

I started working here. I would have agreed with him about getting rid of the third-floor girls, but now that I've met them and heard their stories, I can see how cruel you would be to throw them out."

Grateful for her sister-in-law's support, Rose repeated the conversation she'd had with Tillie. "So prostitution ends at the River Queen in a month, but the girls can stay if they want to."

"Good for you. That's the perfect solution." Drucilla heaved a sigh. "Although I suspect Pa will still be mad. He's too rigid in his thinking ever to understand a compromise."

"Don't worry about it," Rose replied. "You've done your best to help me, and it's not your fault. Are my clothes still lying on the ground?"

"Not anymore. Raymond and I packed up all your belongings. I brought them to the River Queen and had them placed in an empty room. So you've got your clothes and you'll have a place to stay tonight, as long as you want." Drucilla cocked her head. "Where did you go after you left the farm? I knew the hotel was full, and I was worried."

Rose felt her face turning red. "I found a place."

Drucilla, who was certainly nobody's fool, raised an eyebrow. "You either went to Mason Talbot or to a certain good-looking Australian. I'd wager it was the Australian, but I'll say no more."

"That would be wise."

Rose remembered Gaston's request. Now she had the perfect opening. "Speaking of good-looking men, did you happen to notice our new French chef during the rescue last night? Who would have thought he would be that brave, the way he worked alongside Deke and Mitch the whole night long. So admirable, I thought, the way he put own life in danger to pull those poor drowning people from the river."

"We saw lots of brave deeds last night." Drucilla paused to reflect. "Although I will admit I noticed how Gaston worked nonstop. Frankly, I was surprised. I would have thought he'd consider himself too important to lend a hand, but from what I saw, he conducted himself splendidly."

Rose phrased her next sentence carefully. "He's quite fit, I noticed. Not an ounce of extra fat on him, despite those fancy meals he prepares."

"And strong," Drucilla added with enthusiasm. "Did you see how he lifted a grown man out of the boat and carried him to the tent by himself?"

So Drucilla had been watching him, a good sign she was interested. "I certainly did notice how strong he is, and intelligent, too. He's quite well read, you know, and has a variety of interests beyond the culinary. In fact"—she may as well go all out—"in my humble opinion, you two are eminently suited to one another. You both speak French and I don't know how many other languages. You both have varied interests and love to read. You both—"

"It's hopeless. I must admit, I find him admirable in many respects, but there's one thing wrong with him that he can't change."

"He's too short?"

"Only by an inch, but that's too much."

Rose hid her disappointment. If she could wave a magic wand and add a couple of inches to Gaston's splendidly masculine frame, she would do so, but the best she could tell him was she'd tried and sadly failed. Perhaps somehow, some way, he might find something that would change Drucilla's opinion, but she couldn't imagine what.

As soon as she could, Rose made her way to the third floor to visit Cherry and the baby. The new mother was sitting on the side of the bed, the newly arrived James Alan Foley wrapped snug in a blanket in her arms.

"Mrs. Peterson, I'm glad you came. Ain't he precious?" Her voice filled with pride. "Ain't he the most beautiful baby you ever seen?"

"He certainly is." Rose smiled. "Except for my own, of course. I have a little girl."

"You do? How old is she?"

"She's five." At the thought of Lucy, a flash of desolation ripped through her, but now was not the time to be thinking of herself. "I see you're out of bed already."

"And doing fine, only..." Cherry's mouth trembled. "Tillie says he can't stay here. I've got to give him up, and it's going to be harder than I ever imagined. I told myself I wouldn't care, but now that I've seen him, I love him so much I don't know what I'll do without him, and what will he do without me?"

"I'm surprised. Didn't Tillie tell you I'm closing the third floor in just a month?"

Cherry nodded sadly. "She said it didn't make any difference. Whether I go or stay, I'm not capable enough to care for my own child, and it's best he goes. She won't tell me where. I'm better off not knowing, she says. She won't give me the names of the people who'll take him, and neither will Jake."

How cruel. Rose searched for words, but nothing she could say would ease Cherry's pain at losing her child. She could speak with Tillie and Jake. After all, she owned the place, and if she told them not to take Cherry's child away, they'd have to do what she said. But then what? No getting around it, the third floor was the absolute worst place in the world for a baby. Of course, it would soon be closing, but this was a problem that needed solving now. Perhaps Cherry could find another kind of work. "Have you ever considered doing something else other than this?"

"Like what?"

Rose tried to recall all she knew about available jobs for unskilled females in the town of Sacramento. There wasn't much, except… "All the hotels need maids, including the River Queen. I could ask Drucilla."

Cherry sadly shook her head. "Do you know how much those maid jobs pay? I wouldn't mind the work, but I could hardly earn enough to support myself, let alone a child."

Unfortunately, Cherry was right. Rose had no other ideas. "I'll speak to Tillie and make sure you have more time. So don't worry, they won't be coming up here tomorrow to take James away." She heaved a sigh. "I'm so sorry, Cherry. I'm hoping there's a solution, but I've yet to find it."

Cherry put on a brave face. "There ain't no solution for me. I'm only a whore, and you shouldn't go to all that trouble to help me. I know better than anyone my baby can't stay here long."

Rose left Cherry's room with a heavy heart. At the moment, she could think of no happy ending for Cherry's heartbreaking dilemma and wasn't at all sure she'd find one. She found Tillie in her room and got down to business immediately. "I'd like to talk to you about Cherry."

Tillie's granite-eyed expression told her she had no time for sympathy. "She can't keep it."

"Are you sure?"

Tillie smirked. "What do you suppose our customers are looking for when they get to the third floor? Do you think they want to hear a baby bawling?"

"I suppose not."

"Look, you're the boss, but listen to what I'm telling you. I don't like to be tough, but a baby doesn't belong in a brothel. And what's she going to do after it shuts down? She's got no other way to support herself. I've got a farm family that'll take the kid in. It wouldn't be the first one. The farmer works 'em hard, but at least they get three meals a day and a roof over their heads."

Hopeless. Why had she even tried? "Could you wait a few more days? I promised Cherry you would."

"A few more days won't matter, one way or another."

The words stuck in her throat, and she had to force them out. "Thank you, Tillie. That's most considerate."

Rose got to her office and had hardly settled at her desk when Mason knocked and came in. Looking dapper as always, he dropped into the chair across, remarking, "Did you get some rest after last night?"

"Not much." Curiosity got the better of her. "I didn't see you at the river last night." She refrained from adding, *not like nearly every able-bodied man in this town.*

If her question annoyed him, he didn't let on. "Quite a night, wasn't it? I was at the Egyptian. Spent the night finding shelter for those poor souls from the ship."

Was he telling the truth or did he consider himself too important to join the others and help? She suspected he did, but she might as well drop the subject. He'd never admit it.

He examined her closely. "You look tired."

"That's because I've had a few problems." She hadn't planned on telling him, but he did seem concerned, and besides, with his knowledge and the connections he had in this town, he might have some good advice. She told him all of it: how she'd gone home dead tired and exhausted, only to find Ben had kicked her out. Of course, she made no mention of how she'd gone to Deke. Fortunately he didn't ask.

Mason listened to her story, eyes full of concern. When she finished, he asked, "So what will you do?"

"I don't know. I've hardly had time to think."

"Do you need a place to stay? You're always welcome at the Egyptian."

"Thank you, but Drucilla saved me a room here in the hotel. I want to go home, though." He'd been so warm and friendly, she didn't hold back. "They can't keep me away from my daughter. There's got to be law against such a thing. Should I see Mr. Field? If you think he might help, please tell me."

"I don't see it would do much good. My best advice is simply be patient and wait. Sooner or later these little family tiffs will settle themselves. If there's anything I can do to help, you can count on me."

She didn't appreciate his calling her dilemma a "little family tiff," but still, his soothing words made her feel better. "Thank you for that. You know I value your advice."

After they chatted for a while, Mason rose to leave. Up to that moment, he'd been warm and friendly, but now his face settled into a stony expression of warning. "You want my advice? You're making a mistake."

Taken aback, she asked, "In what way?"

"Ben's right. You're a genteel woman, and you're out of your depth. It takes a man to run a hotel like the River Queen with its prostitution and gambling. Frankly, as a friend who's concerned only for your best interests, the best advice I can give you is to sell the hotel and devote yourself to raising your child."

Her mouth dropped open. She couldn't find words.

He hadn't finished. "You're a beautiful woman, meant for better things than dealing with a bunch of lowlifes." His expression softened. "Think over what I said, and meantime, will you have dinner with me tomorrow night? If you like, I'll take you to Le Chantecler again."

"I…I'll let you know."

After Mason left, she sat stunned at her desk for she didn't know how long. Was he right? Everyone admired and respected Mason Talbot, highly successful businessman, all-around pillar of strength and respectability in the community. He was right, at least in one respect. She was, after all, only a woman and knew full well that not only Mason but most everyone would agree she was out her depth. Certainly Ben would. Only a deep belief in herself had kept her going, but now…?

Only twenty-four hours ago, her life was going well and she was bursting with confidence. No longer. She buried her head in her hands. She'd lost her daughter, lost her home, and a man she greatly respected had just informed her she wasn't fit to run her own hotel. She thought of Deke. At least he believed in her, but was that enough?

Chapter 15

The next morning, despite Mason's opinion that it wouldn't do any good, Rose hastened to the office of Archer Field, solicitor. He sat at his desk, his bushy white eyebrows slanted in a frown. Sitting across, she told him what had happened. "So can you help? There must be a law that says Ben hasn't the right to keep me from my daughter."

After a long moment of pondering, the solicitor sighed and shook his head. "Bear in mind, California is a new state with new laws and more being written every day. Certain areas aren't completely covered yet, and I'm afraid your specific problem is among them. So to be honest, in answer to your question, I'm not sure. Frankly, I don't see how a mother can be kept from her child, although under the circumstances, we might have a problem."

"What circumstances?"

"Well, now..." Mr. Field paused to gather his thoughts. "There are some who consider every saloon in this town an abomination. You've got your Women's Christian Temperance Union, your Sons of Temperance, and more of that type of organization popping up every day. In their view, those who own a saloon, or even work in one, are to be condemned."

"I see." Rose's spirits dropped to a new low. "But you'll try?"

"Of course. Meantime—"

"Don't do anything rash?"

He gave her a fatherly smile. "Exactly, Mrs. Peterson. From what I understand, your daughter is being well cared for. Have patience. Meanwhile, I'll see what I can do."

Walking back to the hotel from the solicitor's office, she spotted Mitch driving a wagon loaded with ice. A big sign on the side read, Fleming &

Carter's Ice House. She gave him a friendly wave, and he pulled over. "Rose! Just the person I wanted to see."

How fortunate, considering Mitch was just the person she wanted to see. She hadn't forgotten his compassion and caring when he delivered Cherry's baby. Somehow she'd sensed a special feeling forming between the two, only to be destroyed when he found out what Cherry did for a living. What a shame. If she could do something to revive it, she would. In fact, she'd already planned what she was going to say. She walked over to the wagon. "How's the ice business, Mitch?"

"Booming," he replied with a pleased smile. "We're selling ice to every saloon in town and then some."

"You wanted to see me?"

He didn't hesitate. "I've been thinking about Cherry. Is she doing all right?"

"Yes and no. She's recovering nicely from the birth, but of course..." She heaved a sigh. "So sad."

Mitch frowned with concern. "How do you mean?"

"As I'm sure you know, she can't keep her baby in a place like that. They'll soon be taking him away, and she's devastated."

"That's terrible." Mitch frowned in thought. "Isn't there something...? I mean, a baby should be with its mother."

"It's the price she has to pay for being"—Rose cast her gaze down discreetly—"in the profession she's in."

"She hasn't gone back to work yet, has she?"

"Not yet, but what choice does she have? I'll be closing the third floor soon, but she can always go elsewhere." Rose took advantage of the perfect opening. "It's so unfair. The poor girl didn't choose to do what she's doing..."

She went on to repeat the story Cherry had told her on one of her visits. The father who beat her. The depraved individual who forced her into... "I can't say the words, Mitch. Suffice to say, I hold her blameless. Even if she weren't, there's such a thing as forgiveness. Do you know your Bible?" She already knew he did.

Mitch nodded solemnly. "Read it every night."

She remembered a Bible verse from Sunday school. "'The Lord is gracious and righteous; our God is full of compassion.'"

Mitch nodded solemnly. "Psalm 116:5."

"You ought to at least go see her."

He pondered a moment. "I'd like to, but knowing what I know now, I want nothing to do with the occupants of the third floor."

"Really? I'm surprised. You risked your life to rescue those poor people from the water, but now you're afraid of a few ladies of the night? They're harmless, I assure you."

He took her remark good humoredly and nodded to himself, as if he'd reach some sort of private decision. "Is there any place she can stay other than the third floor?"

"She could have a room on the second floor. Those are just plain hotel rooms."

"Then move her and the baby to the second floor. I'll pay for her room and the rest of her expenses."

"That's wonderful, Mitch, and so very generous."

"Just one more thing," he said with a thoughtful frown. "She mustn't know who's paying."

Rose nodded agreeably. "I shall refer to you simply as her benefactor, but are you sure? I think Cherry should know—"

"No! I'm a devout Christian. In my wildest dreams I never thought I'd have anything to do with a brothel. But Cherry is special. She…she…"

"Say no more, Mitch. You have my word Cherry will never know."

After they parted, Rose had to congratulate herself. She'd done it! Got Mitch to help, as she'd intended. The poor man needed to get his thoughts in order, though. He ought to decide what really mattered in his life. She hoped someday soon he would.

* * * *

During the next few days, Rose fought through spells of despair. She and Lucy had never been apart before, and she missed her terribly. Thankfully, the pending opening of Gaston's left little time to dwell on all the tumult in her life. A kind of controlled chaos reigned in the kitchen and dining room as her iron-willed French chef confronted a myriad of last minute crises. His poaching pans were missing. Two waiters he'd hired direct from Paris had yet to arrive. She pitched in to help, sometimes chafing under Gaston's despotic rule. She hardly ever questioned his judgment, though, having every faith he knew what he was doing.

One day, while she was working in her office, Drucilla opened the door and peeked in. "I have a surprise." She opened the door wide.

To Rose's joy, Lucy was standing there, holding her aunt's hand. At the sight of Rose, she cried, "Mommy," and rushed to throw her arms around her.

Rose held back tears as she knelt to embrace her daughter. No words were necessary. Finally, over the top of Lucy's head, she asked Drucilla, "How did you manage?"

"Ben was going to be gone for a while, so I took the chance. I've got to get her back soon, but I'll leave you two alone for a little while."

After Drucilla left, Lucy peered around the room with her usual curiosity. "Is this your office?"

"Yes, it is."

"Is this your hotel?"

"Yes, this is the River Queen. First it was Daddy's and now it's mine."

Lucy looked toward the desk. "Can I sit in your chair?"

"Indeed you can."

Lucy perched herself in the big mahogany chair and immediately discovered she could swivel back and forth. "This is fun. Do you tell everybody what to do?"

"I'm the boss, so I guess I do."

Lucy stopped swiveling and gazed at Rose with troubled eyes. "Grandpa doesn't like that you work here. He says you ought to be home, taking care of me."

Rose wasn't going to lie. No sense trying to convince Lucy everything was fine when it wasn't. She was a smart little girl who wouldn't believe her anyway. "Grownups have problems sometimes, and that's why I'm not living at home right now."

"Are you mad at Grandma and Grandpa?"

"No, I'm not. I love them both very much and want us to be together again. Meantime, you're to stay with your grandparents and be a good little girl."

"You promise you'll come home?"

"I promise." Her voice almost broke. "I love you more than anything else in this world, Lucy. Of course, I'm coming home."

Rose knew she'd given the right answer when she saw the relief in her little girl's eyes.

After Drucilla came back and took Lucy away, Rose sat for a time in dark, brooding silence. Only with the greatest effort did she pull herself together. She hated being so muddle-headed, so unsure of herself. She only knew she couldn't give up now, when she was beginning to see improvements in the hotel, and the opening of Gaston's was in just a week. She must stay strong. Mustn't let the world know how her heart ached for her daughter. Someday soon all would be well. She wouldn't let herself think otherwise.

She'd kept dodging Mason's invitation for dinner, claiming she had too much work to do. True, of course, but whenever she thought of his advice that she should sell the River Queen, an icy resentment rose within her, and she had no desire to see him. That might change, though. He'd been good to her in so many ways, she would certainly see him again—when she had the time.

As for Deke...

They'd both been so busy she'd hardly seen him since that day she spent in his room. She thought about him, though, and whenever she did, which was far more often than she liked, her mind spun in such a tangle of emotions that she quickly blocked him out each time. Not easy, considering the memory of his making love to her with his tough, sinewy body did strange things to her insides. Despite that, she couldn't possibly be in love with him. He wasn't on crutches anymore, so he wasn't the cripple she'd felt so sorry for. Even so, much as he'd changed, first impressions were hard to forget. Of course, she had to admit her heart did a little leap whenever she caught a glimpse of him. As soon as she had the time, if she ever did, she'd sort it all out, but not right now. She was far too busy.

* * * *

Deke Fleming considered himself a lucky fellow. Only weeks ago, he'd been a miserable cripple, left to fend for himself while his companions made their fortunes in the gold fields. Although he took no pleasure from reports of their various miseries and dismal failures, he couldn't help but be proud of his own success. Thanks to his and Mitch's hard work, profits from their ice business had spiraled to heights they hadn't dreamed of. "We're rich," Mitch declared. "All because the customers like their beer cold."

Only one area of his life caused Deke to lose sleep at night. *Rose.* Since that day she'd come to his room, he longed to see her again, but his ice business had kept him at least as busy as she with her hotel, and somehow the days had slipped by without their even talking. Since he'd never been the kind of man who sat on his arse and waited for something to happen, he took action. On the day before the grand opening of Gaston's, he went to the River Queen and stopped by the lunch counter. Next, he found Rose in her office, poring over some kind of list, no doubt having to do with tomorrow night's big event. She was wearing a blue dress he hadn't yet seen, which he liked very much. Her hair was nicely done up in a bun. Only little strands of it had escaped and framed her pretty face.

"We're going on a picnic," he said.

Startled, she looked up. "The restaurant's opening tomorrow. I couldn't possibly."

He nailed her with a firm and unrelenting gaze. "Yes, you could. You've got to eat sometime. It's time we talked."

After a long moment, she nodded, more to herself than him. "You're right. I could use a little time to myself, and besides, it's been a while, hasn't it?"

He took her to the banks of the American River, where tall oak trees shaded a grassy spot below. Facing her over a checkered tablecloth spread on the ground, Deke pulled all sorts of items from a basket, which Gus himself had prepared. "Beef sandwiches. Potato salad. Boiled eggs. Chocolate cake, which I hope didn't get squashed."

Gazing at the feast before her, Rose burst out laughing. "What a wonderful idea. I've been so busy I've forgotten how to enjoy myself."

"Why do you think we're here?"

While they ate, he saw to it they talked only of pleasantries, taking time to watch the river flowing by while a group of white herons waded along the shallow edges. Finishing her cake, she remarked, "It's beautiful here, and so peaceful. I should do this more often instead of letting my stomach get in knots over…so many things."

Only then did he ask, "Has Ben relented?"

"No, he has not." She told him about her visit to the solicitor, and how she was still waiting to hear. How she'd seen Lucy the one heart-wrenching time, and how she couldn't hold on much longer. As soon as Gaston's opened and the excitement died down, she'd take some kind of action, but as yet she didn't know what.

As always, Deke listened with full attention. There was one subject she hadn't mentioned, the most important of all, as far as he was concerned, and he needed to know. "I haven't seen you with Mason Talbot lately." He waited. She knew damn well what he meant.

"Well…" Looking down at her plate, she busily rearranged the remaining crumbs of her chocolate cake with her fork. "I haven't seen him for a while." As if she'd finally reached a decision, she looked up and gazed directly into his eyes. "It's not anything to do with us. Mason said something I didn't like, and I've been avoiding him."

"Do you think you'll see him again?"

Again she hesitated. He waited, his heart beating like a hammer in his chest. A large bird with a streaked belly landed on a branch nearby. He pointed. "Red-tailed hawk." Damned if he'd let her know how much her answer meant to him.

She finally spoke. "I've been trying to make myself like him. He's been kind to me, at least most of the time, and of course, even you can see he's a desirable man in so many ways. Only…" After a moment more of thought, she continued, "The farthest thing from my mind right now is finding a husband. Be that as it may, as far as Mason Talbot is concerned, I could never love him. In fact, I'm not even sure I like him."

He was hard put to quell the joyous shout that rose in his throat, but he stayed straight-faced and asked in a mildly interested voice, "You're sure about that?"

"I'm sure about that." A smile trembled on her lips. "You and I have lots to talk about. Are you busy tomorrow night? If you're not, you're invited to Gaston's for the grand opening. Drucilla and I are planning to be there, and I'd love to have you join us. Mitch, too, if you like."

Deke chuckled. "I'll ask, but I can tell you right now Mitch prefers to stay home and read his Bible."

"But you?"

"I'll be there."

She began to pick up the remains of the lunch. "We'd best get back. There's still lots to do before the grand opening."

He quickly arose and joined in the cleanup. *Tomorrow night. After dinner.* That's when he'd get her alone. He'd never been all that good at expressing himself, especially to a woman, but the time had come to tell her how he felt.

* * * *

Rose greeted the opening night of Gaston's with mixed feelings. On the bad side, she'd so focused all her energies on the restaurant, she'd put off any and all decisions concerning her in-laws until after the opening. But now the big night had arrived. Starting tomorrow, no more excuses. She must start making some decisions. On the good side, she could hardly contain her excitement that at last her hotel could boast a major attraction. The Egyptian had its Le Chantecler. The Woodcock Hotel had a dining saloon which was, according to the *Sacramento Union*, "in point of comfort and elegance, unsurpassed by anything of the kind that we have seen in the country." Sacramento boasted other fabulous restaurants besides, but Rose had every confidence that Gaston's at the River Queen, run by one of the great chefs of Paris, would soon become the most elegant French restaurant in town.

To her relief, in the last days before the opening, Gaston had calmed his jitters and now exuded such confidence that everyone, she included, had no doubt opening night would be a big success. She'd ordered a new gown for the occasion. Now, with only minutes left before she must go downstairs, she stood before the full-length mirror in her room, twisting this way and that for a good look at herself. She had to admit she didn't look half-bad in her new off-shouldered gown of cream satin and chiffon. Embroidered with gold coral beads and spangles, it was by far the most elegant she'd ever owned.

Drucilla knocked and entered. She cared nothing for fancy clothes, but when Rose had firmly informed her she couldn't possibly attend such an elegant event in anything she owned, she, too, ordered a new gown, a low-cut Nile-green chiffon velvet, trimmed in gold. She'd even done something with her hair, sweeping it up into curls atop her head, fastened with a jeweled comb. Stepping to the mirror, she took a close look at herself. "Well? Do I look all right?"

Rose refrained from declaring she'd never seen her look as good, a two-way compliment if ever there was one. She absolutely did, though. "You look gorgeous in that gown. It's your height that carries it off."

Drucilla responded with her usual scornful sniff, yet Rose knew she was pleased. Even though her sister-in-law had worked at the River Queen for only a few weeks, already she seemed to be standing taller, holding her chin higher. All due, Rose very much suspected, to Drucilla's finally escaping her mother's stifling criticism. Not that she realized it yet, but if she could see how beautifully regal she looked in that gown, she'd gain even more confidence in herself.

"Don't forget Deke is joining us," Rose said. "We're to meet him downstairs."

"What happened to Mason?"

She might have known Drucilla would ask. "I have no idea."

"At least Mason knows how to dress, but does Deke?" Drucilla frowned with concern. "I've never seen him in anything but work clothes. Does he even know what a frock coat looks like?"

Rose had wondered the same thing. When she invited Deke, she'd failed to mention the opening was a formal affair. Judging from what she'd seen of the clothes hanging from pegs in his room, he owned nothing that could pass for evening clothes. She'd taken care of it, though. "I spoke to Gaston. If Deke shows up in ordinary clothes, the maître d' is to let him in regardless."

"Is that wise?"

"Deke has been helpful to me in many ways, and I don't care if it's wise or not."

Rose's snappish answer had its effect. Drucilla shrugged and changed the subject. "By the way, rumors are flying about who Gaston hired for his maître d'hôtel. Nobody seems to know. Have you heard anything?"

"All I know is, all the waiters are French, but I have no idea who the maître d' might be, or the kitchen help or everyone else. Gaston was quite secretive about it. I suspect we're in for some surprises." She glanced at the clock. "It's time to go."

During the course of the day, Rose went up and down the stairs thinking nothing of it. So did Drucilla, but tonight the River Queen's main staircase served more like a theater stage. Dressed in their stylish new gowns, aware of the many eyes upon them, Rose and Drucilla slowed their pace as they paraded down, heads held high, gloved hands lightly touching the railing.

A man stood at the bottom of the staircase looking up at them. Halfway down, Rose realized who it was. Deke! And dressed to the nines in a black frock coat and trousers, starched, pleated high-collared white shirt, cravat and—incredible!—white gloves. *Oh my God, he looks amazing.* She'd never thought of him as handsome, but seeing him dressed the way he was, with those great wide shoulders and his tall, lean build, she was hard put to conceal her admiration. Arriving at the bottom of the stairs, she smiled and said, "Good evening," hoping she sounded casual, as if she saw him dressed this way all the time.

Deke gave a slight but gracious bow. His gaze swept over them. "Good evening, ladies. You both look beautiful."

"You don't look so bad yourself." Rose hid her amusement at her considerable understatement.

His mouth hinted at a smile. "Hard to believe, but we've been known to wear frock coats even in Australia."

Tilting her head, she declared, "Fancy that. Then let's go to dinner, shall we?"

They made their way through the saloon to where a crowd of patrons, all dressed in their best finery, had formed a line in front of the entrance to Gaston's. They joined the line. After a short wait, they reached the maître d's station inside the door.

What? Rose couldn't quite grasp who was standing there. "Gus, is that you?"

"It's me." A pleased expression crossed the face of Gus Hurdlicka. "Monsieur Bernier has been training me. He didn't want you to know. Said it would be a big surprise."

"I'm surprised all right." Flabbergasted would be more like it. Gaston had performed a miracle on the sly. Gone were the stained apron, the surly expression. Dressed in elegant evening attire, Gus resembled the ideal maître d', especially when his friendly smile disappeared, replaced by a disdainful lift of his chin.

"You will have a table by the orchestra," he loftily declared. He raised his arm and imperiously snapped his fingers. A waiter came running. "Table number ten, Julien."

"Thank you, Gus," Rose said.

He peered down his nose at her. "It's 'Guillaume' now, if you don't mind."

"Of course." Rose stifled her laughter, happy Gaston had chosen to keep Gus, despite all his faults. Judging from what she'd just seen, he'd do fine. As they followed the waiter to their table, she got her first good look at the magnificence Gaston had created. What a difference! Thick, red Axminster carpet covered what had once been a sawdust floor. Overhead, six chandeliers, bigger than Le Chantecler's, twinkled and sparkled from newly installed gas lighting. At one end of the room, partially hidden by potted palms, a four-piece orchestra played the classical music of Haydn and Mozart.

At the table, the waiter seated Drucilla, pulling her chair back with an extra flourish. Deke did the same for Rose, without the flourish but with the composure of someone who had dined in fancy restaurants all his life. "Well done," she whispered as she sat. "Do they have restaurants in Australia, too?"

The waiter brought the menus. Gaston had outdone himself. Starting with *canapes of caviar*, there were so many courses, Rose could hardly count them all. She marveled at the list of mouth-watering entrees: *Escargots à la Bourguignonne, Huitres Thermidor...*

From across the table came a gasp from Drucilla. She'd been holding the large menu with both hands. Now she slapped one hand to her mouth and stared wide-eyed at something she'd just read.

Rose and Deke exchanged questioning glances. Never had she seen her sister-in-law anything but cool and composed. "Drucilla, what is it?"

"Look, look!" Drucilla pointed at the menu. "It's under the entrees. Oh, I don't believe it." She slapped her hand over her mouth again.

Rose went back to her own menu and scanned the entrees. "Oh, I see it! '*Coquilles a la Drucilla.*' Oh, my goodness, Gaston has named a dish after you."

"I... I..." Drucilla choked up and couldn't go on. Her eyes got watery. Finally she managed, "Did you know about this?"

"Are you joking? Gaston kept almost everything a secret."

"I've never had anything named after me before."

"Who has?" said Deke.

With a twinkle in her eye, Rose declared, "*Coquilles* are scallops, aren't they? That's what I'll order. And why shouldn't you have a dish named after you? Gaston obviously thinks you're an exceptional woman, and I think so, too."

"Why, thank you," Drucilla softly replied, casting her gaze modestly downward. Amazing. For the first time, Rose's obstinate sister-in-law had accepted a compliment without some kind of sarcastic denial.

A jovial mood prevailed throughout the dinner. Whenever Rose looked around, she saw every table full and everyone enjoying themselves. At her own table, she couldn't remember when she'd laughed so much, what with Drucilla's dry humor and Deke's funny stories about herding sheep in Australia. And the food was marvelous. Without question, Gaston's was an overnight sensation and would take its place as the best French restaurant outside of San Francisco, if not in San Francisco, too.

Julien had just served dessert when a stir swept through the crowded restaurant. "It's him!" Rose heard someone say. "Gaston himself!" Looking toward the kitchen, she spotted her French chef threading his way through the tables. For the first time, he was wearing his full chef's regalia: white double-breasted jacket, hound's-tooth-patterned black and white pants, an amazingly high white chef's hat. "It's called a *toque blanche*," Gaston had told her. "The higher it is, the more important you are." That certainly fit, considering Gaston's lofty opinion of himself.

Ignoring proffered compliments along the way, Gaston headed straight to their table. When he arrived, Rose and Deke might just as well not have been there. The chef had eyes only for Drucilla. In turn, she wasn't acting her normal self at all but was gazing up at him as if she were spellbound.

Gaston regarded her with a piercing gaze. "So, Mademoiselle Drucilla, did you enjoy your dinner?"

Drucilla's cheeks colored a deep red. "I did indeed, monsieur."

"And what did you have?"

"The *Coquilles a la Drucilla*." A little smile crossed her face. "I've never had a dish named after me before."

"Perhaps it will be the first of many. We will talk later."

"Yes, I would like that."

Gaston finally turned his attention to Rose. "Well, what do you think?"

"About the restaurant? I think you've done a fantastic job. I couldn't be happier."

Gaston nodded with satisfaction, said a quick goodbye, and headed back to his kitchen. Rose turned to Drucilla. "Perhaps Gaston has a few tiny faults, but he's a brilliant man, so talented in so many ways."

Drucilla got a grin on her face. "I must say, I agree."

"Maybe an inch or two isn't so much after all."

"Perhaps. At least he looks taller with that hat on."

Would wonders never cease? Gaston was a genius for finding the one thing that would make an impression on her prickly sister-in-law. What a relief that Drucilla appeared to have come to her senses. As for her own self...

She had a lot to sort out. All through dinner, she'd looked at Deke through different eyes, as if a new awareness had awakened inside her. Maybe the crutches had blinded her to what an exceptional man he was in so many ways, but whatever the reason, up to now she'd failed to notice how witty he was, what a compassionate heart he had. And besides all that, she'd worried he wouldn't know how to handle himself in elegant surroundings, would act like some ill-mannered rube. Instead, his impeccable dress and manners were a match for the most refined gentleman in the place. Up to now, he'd been just a friend, even after those hours she'd spent in his room, but how did she feel now? Was she falling in love with him because he looked good in his evening clothes? She laughed to herself. She couldn't be that shallow. She needed to talk to him. Alone. What would he suggest after dinner? A buggy ride in the moonlight would be a good choice. After that, she would end up in his room over the stable. In his bed. In his arms. And when that happened, he would know, and she would know, too, that with all her heart, with every fiber of her being, she was falling in love with Deke Fleming.

At the end of dinner, the three were wending their way through the tables toward the exit when Rose spotted Mason Talbot dining with two men she recognized as among Sacramento's most prominent citizens. Oh no! The last person in the world she wanted to see. She turned her head away, hoping she could slip by without his noticing, but no such luck.

"Rose?"

No way out. She had to stop and talk to him. "Why, Mason, how nice to see you. What a pleasant surprise."

He stood, threw his napkin down, and strode around the table to greet her. Dressed impeccably as always, he was all congeniality as he reached to shake her hand. "May I offer my congratulations? My friends and I have been enjoying a most excellent dinner. Your new restaurant is an instant success." He peered over her shoulder to where Deke and Drucilla stood waiting. "Good evening, Miss Peterson, and this is...?"

Deke stepped forward. "We've met before." He did not extend his hand.

"Ah, yes." Mason lost his smile. "The Australian. I remember."

"How could you forget?"

"I hear you're peddling ice now."

Rose couldn't miss the nasty undertone in Mason's voice. She hastily broke in before Deke could answer. "We must move on. Lovely seeing you, Mason."

Once outside the restaurant, Drucilla made a quick escape, claiming she must get home. Rose turned to Deke. "What was that all about? You looked as if you'd like to punch him in the nose."

"Did I?" Deke shrugged his shoulders. "Let's not let the likes of Mason Talbot ruin our evening. Want to go for a buggy ride?"

Indeed she did. Any further discussion concerning Mason could wait. "That would be lovely. I must stop by my room first to freshen up."

He flashed a smile that grabbed at her heart. "I'll get my carriage and meet you in front."

Her spirits soared as she practically ran upstairs to her room on the second floor. She'd had high hopes for this evening. So far, it had gone even better than she'd expected, and it wasn't over yet. She made haste to freshen up, left her room, and started down the staircase. A man was waiting at the bottom, only this time it wasn't Deke. "Hello again, Mason." She tried to ignore the cold, hard stare he was giving her. "So you enjoyed the dinner?"

"We must talk."

He was angry. She could tell not only from the tight set of his jaw but from the fast, short breaths he was taking. She heartily wished she could put him off, but her good sense warned her she'd better not. "Shall we go to my office?"

"Fine."

Filled with anxiety, she led him toward the back of the hotel. Except for that one occasion when he'd told her she ought to sell the River Queen, Mason had always been so friendly and congenial. Obviously something she'd done had set him off, but she wasn't sure what it was. He followed her down the dimly lit hallway until they reached her office, now nearly pitch black inside. "Wait a second, Mason, while I light the lamp."

"Don't bother. Leave the door open. There's enough light from the hallway."

He gripped her arm and led her inside. She went willingly and didn't pull back, not sure he'd have let her get away. In front of the desk, he turned to face her. Even in the dim light from the hallway she could see enough of his expression to know how furious he was. She would try to keep her voice calm. "Why are you so angry?"

"Do you know who I am?" His voice held a strangled quality, as if he could hardly keep himself under control.

"Of course, I know who you are."

"Apparently you don't. What you don't understand is, I am not a man to be trifled with."

"I've never trifled with you in my life. What have I done?"

"What have you done? How can you ask after all the help I've given you? The time I've taken to advise you? All the gifts I've given you?"

"You know I'm grateful."

He burst into bitter laughter. "So grateful you chose to dine with someone else."

Ah, so that was it. He was jealous she'd invited Deke for dinner. What could she say? Mason had good reason to be jealous, and she wasn't going to lie. "I appreciate all you've done for me, but I'm not obligated to you in any way."

Cursing softly, he gripped her shoulders. "I've tried to be patient, but this is the thanks I get?"

Such venom in his voice! No sense reasoning with him, just get out of here. She tried to back away. With a snarl of anger, he pulled her close. "You need to be taught a lesson, my dear." His arms locked tight around her and pulled her toward him so roughly the breath went out of her. Before she could even begin to struggle, he bent her over his arm and kissed her, his lips crushing hers, not in a loving way but in a cruel, hard way that made her skin crawl. Locked tight in his arms, she couldn't begin to struggle. All she could do was gather her strength and try to get out of here the second he let her go. *If* he let her go. In a panic, she started to struggle.

"Blimey! What the hell?"

Mason let her go. She pushed away from him and looked toward the door. Even in the dim light, she could see it was Deke standing there. She searched for words, but before she could get them out, he spoke again.

"Sorry. Don't let me interrupt you."

The next second he was gone. She stared at the empty doorway. *Dear Lord, what have I done?* But she hadn't done anything. How would Deke know that, though? Judging from what he'd seen, he must be thinking the worst of her. She must find him, tell him he was wrong. She started toward the door, but Mason grabbed her arm. "I'm not through with you."

"Oh, yes you are." She gave him a swift kick in the shin. He grunted and dropped her arm. Fast as she could go, she ran from her office and along the dim corridor. When she reached the saloon, she slowed her pace and gazed with desperation around the crowded room. No Deke. He must have already gone outside. She lifted her skirt and hurried through the saloon, vaguely aware of the many curious eyes that were following her. No doubt she was making a spectacle of herself, but she didn't care. Let them laugh at the finely dressed lady who'd lost her decorum. All she cared about was finding Deke before he got away.

She pushed through the swinging doors. He'd parked his carriage directly in front. He had just climbed in and was picking up the reins. She ran to the carriage, grabbed hold of Sidney's harness, and looked up at him. "Don't go. Let me explain."

"What is there to explain? I have eyes, haven't I?"

The coldness in his voice stabbed at her heart. "I know what it looked like, but it wasn't what it seemed. Mason Talbot means nothing to me."

"It didn't look that way."

"But it wasn't my idea. Didn't you see he was forcing me? He—" What was she doing? The more she defended herself, the guiltier she sounded. "Please, Deke, we need to talk."

"Why? I have nothing say to you." He gazed down at her, a lethal calmness in his eyes. "He's the man who killed your husband. Had you forgotten?"

What was he getting at? "Of course I haven't forgotten, but Mason wasn't to blame. It was Emmet who insisted on the duel."

His mouth took on a cynical twist. So unlike him. "You're a fool, Rose Peterson. Go talk to Jake Grunion. He'll set you straight about your wonderful Mason Talbot. Let go of the harness."

She released the harness and stepped away. Flinging her hands out in simple despair, she watched as Deke drove away without another word, never once glancing back.

Chapter 16

Rose somehow got back to her room. Numb from shock, she flung herself on the bed. She couldn't even cry, just lay there, trying, and failing, to understand why Deke had turned on her. He'd always been so friendly, so full of humor. But tonight? That stony expression on his face, those cold eyes… Why couldn't he see she wasn't at fault? That Mason had grabbed her?

She could hardly bear the thought of it.

And why did he tell her to speak to Jake?

After a time, she pulled herself together enough to get ready for bed. The simple task of removing the cream satin gown reminded her of how happy she'd been earlier in the evening, back when Deke had looked at her with love in his eyes. Now everything had gone wrong. What was left? Not only had she lost Lucy, she'd lost Deke, too. That night, she couldn't sleep, just tossed and turned. Maybe things would look brighter in the morning, but she highly doubted it.

She was right. The next day, a gloomy sky awaited when she got out of bed. A perfect match for her dark mood. She didn't even want to get dressed and leave her room, but life went on, she supposed, and the worst thing she could do was hide from the world and wallow in self-pity.

And besides, what had Deke meant? She very much wanted to speak to Jake Grunion.

Dressed in the brown wool bombazine—it suited her mood—she knocked on the door of Jake's office. He called to her to come in and broke into a gleeful smile when he saw who it was. "Have you seen the receipts from Gaston's last night? The Frenchie did all right. We made a small fortune."

Seating herself, she couldn't even pretend to smile. "That's not why I'm here."

Jake's smile faded. He couldn't miss the woeful state she was in. "So tell me."

She wouldn't hint around. A direct question would be best. "From what I understand, you were at the duel between my husband and Mason Talbot. Is that correct?"

Jake got a leery look in his eye. "I was there."

"You were Emmet's second."

"I was."

"I want you to tell me what happened. *Exactly* what happened."

"Be happy to, but it's nothing you don't already know." Jake accompanied his remark with an elaborate shrug.

"So tell me anyway."

"Well, it was like this..." In his harsh voice Jake told the same story she'd heard before. It had all started when Emmet—Mr. Peterson—figured he'd been insulted by Mason Talbot. Declared it an "affair of honor," and demanded satisfaction in a duel. Who fights duels anymore? Everyone thought he was crazy, tried to talk him out of it, but he got stubborn and wouldn't change his mind. "That's when he asked me to be his second. He'd asked Deke Fleming first, but Deke didn't want to get involved and had the guts to say so. Not me. I didn't want to lose my job, so I couldn't say no." Jake frowned in exasperation. "Are you sure you want me to go on with this? It ain't pleasant."

"Just tell me what happened."

"All right, if you're sure. Since I was Emmet's second, it was up to me to arrange everything, like finding a site for the duel. It couldn't be just anywhere. Being as dueling's illegal, it had to be a place where the sheriff couldn't find us. I discovered the perfect spot—two miles from town on the river, lots of trees, no farms around. The next day, shortly after dawn, that's where we met. I remember how cold and foggy it was—perfect weather for a duel, they said. Not many were there, only a few people from town who'd heard about it. Emmet's farmhand, Deke, was there. I'd found a doctor to be on hand, and of course Mason's second, Rudy Avery, was there, and that's all."

Jake opened a desk drawer and pulled out a flask. "Throat's scratchy." He took a swig and held out the flask to her.

She could tell how nervous he was. "Too early for me, Jake. Please go on."

He sighed and returned the flask to the drawer. "Mr. Talbot was the one who was challenged, so he got to choose the weapon. It's no surprise he chose pistols. Over in France, they fight their duels with swords, but I don't think either Emmet or Mr. Talbot ever owned a sword in their lives. When the time came, they stood back to back, each pointing their pistol up in the air. I'm the one who had to call 'Begin.' It was like some kind of bad dream, you know? I'd never seen a duel in my life, but here I was, about to see two people try to kill each other. They walked ten paces and turned. Each aimed at the other. Emmet fired and missed. Less than a second later, Mason fired and you know what happened."

"He was killed instantly?"

"Uh…yes."

Jake's hesitation told her a lot, but she ignored it. Hearing how Emmet had suffered would only add to her misery. "So that's all you know, Jake?"

"Uh…yes."

Why did he hesitate? Plain to see her shifty-eyed manager had either lied or left something unsaid. "You're not telling me everything. What did you leave out?"

Jake took his time answering, just sat frowning, rubbing his jaw. Finally he gave a firm nod, as if he'd come to a decision, and looked her in the eye. "You're right. I didn't tell you everything. Kept my mouth shut. Feared for my safety."

A chill gripped her heart. "Tell me now. I want to hear all of it."

"You've got to understand, Mason Talbot has a lot of power in this town."

"I'm well aware of that."

"He's got connections. He could do you serious harm."

"Just tell me. I'm ready for anything."

"All right, you asked for it, Mrs. Peterson, although I dunno what you can do when you find out." Jake shut his eyes a moment, as if to get his thoughts in order. "Like you already know, Mr. Talbot's second was Rudy Avery. The night before the duel, he came to my door and said he had to talk to me. Since one of my duties was to negotiate, see if I could keep 'em from actually dueling, I said sure and asked him in. So he comes in and…" Jake nervously ran his hand over his slicked back hair. "Damn, I don't like talking about it, but you say you've got to know?"

"I've got to know."

Jake took a deep breath. "Rudy had a message from Mr. Talbot that he wanted me to give to your husband. He said to tell him that when the duel started, and they'd walked their ten paces and turned, he would fire his pistol over Mr. Peterson's head. So, of course, he wanted Emmet to do the same."

"So in other words, they'd both aim high and neither would be harmed?"

"Yeah, that's it. I guess it's common to do that. After Rudy left, I rushed right over to the River Queen and told Mr. Peterson. You should have seen how relieved he looked. By then he'd calmed down a lot, got beyond all that rage and anger and how he'd been insulted. He knew he'd got carried away believing a duel was an 'affair of honor.' It had a romantic kind of sound to it. He'd be a hero like those fellows in *The Three Musketeers.* But by then he'd begun to realize his affair of honor was more like an affair of stupidity, and in the morning, he could be dead or badly injured."

"So he agreed?"

"He didn't hesitate. I got word to Rudy. The next morning, after we gathered for the duel, I checked with him to make sure Mr. Talbot got the message. When Rudy said he had, I was mighty relieved. We'd found the perfect solution. Mr. Talbot could keep his honor and no one would call him a coward. Emmet would still have his so-called satisfaction, for whatever that was worth, and he wouldn't be shot dead. He was a tough boss, but a good man, and I didn't want to see him killed for no good reason. The rest you pretty much know." Jake slumped back in his chair. "When they took their ten paces and turned, I wasn't worried. I knew what was going to happen, or thought I did. Like I expected, Emmet took aim and missed. Then Mr. Talbot aimed, fired, and my boss fell to the ground. I couldn't believe it."

At first, Rose's mind refused to register the significance of Jake's words. "So what you're saying is, Mason Talbot deliberately shot my husband?"

"He was supposed to aim way high, like your husband did. Well, he didn't. The plain truth is, Mason Talbot murdered your husband in cold blood."

His words were hard to accept. Several seconds went by before she trusted herself to speak again. "But why would he do such a terrible thing? I can understand Mason would be angry at being challenged to a duel, but was that reason enough to deliberately murder my husband?"

Jake sat straight and gave her a long, searching gaze. "You don't understand, do you?"

"I guess I don't."

"Then it's time you knew the truth. The River Queen sits on one of the most prime pieces of land in all Sacramento. Mason's been after it for years. The building itself is well built, of sound construction. He wanted to remodel and expand it, like you're doing now. The Egyptian looks good, but it's flimsily built and probably won't survive the next flood. It isn't enough for Mason Talbot. He wants the River Queen so bad he'd sell his own mother to get his hands on it."

She struggled to understand. "If that's the case, then how was my husband able to buy the River Queen when it was up for sale?"

"Mason's luck ran out. The day it went up for sale, he was in San Francisco. By the time he got back, it was already sold. He went wild—went to your husband and offered nearly twice the sale price, but Emmet refused to sell."

"I wish to God he had."

Jake shrugged. "So Mason was hung out to dry, and he's been mad ever since. He hasn't given up, though. I don't want to hurt your feelings, but I've seen how he sweet talks you. Maybe he means it, but maybe—I've gotta be honest here—he's more after your hotel than you."

"I see." She must stay calm and composed. It wouldn't do to break down in front of an employee, even though he'd totally shocked her. She'd asked for it, though. And easy to see he'd spoken the truth. Deke must have known. Now she understood why he got that cold, hard look in his eye when he talked about Mason. "Thank you, Jake. I appreciate your honesty." She stood to go.

"Any time, Mrs. Peterson." He stood, too. "I don't know what you plan to do, but one thing you'd better keep in mind."

"And what is that?"

"Mason Talbot is an evil man. He's got no conscience. If he wants something, he'll go after it, and he don't care who gets in his way. If I was you, I'd have nothing more to do with him." Jake gave a rueful smile. "It's not my business, but I'm just saying."

"I appreciate your honesty."

When she left Jake's office, all she wanted was to get upstairs and back to her room. She didn't throw herself on the bed this time. Enough of such a time-waster. But for a while, she sat on the side of the bed, willing her insides to stop shaking, struggling to understand the significance of Jake's shocking words. The worst of it was, she'd asked for it. Now that she knew the truth, that Mason Talbot had deliberately killed her husband, what should she do? She tried to think, but couldn't concentrate. So much had gone wrong. Her life was a disastrous mess. She needed help. Someone she could talk to. Someone calm and rational who had good sense.

* * * *

Dulcee Bidwell picked up her flowered porcelain teapot. "Would you like more tea, Rose? Looks to me like you could use a second cup."

"I would." Sitting in Dulcee's cozy kitchen, Rose felt more relaxed already. The warmth of the ginger peach tea had done a lot to calm her jangled nerves. Pouring her heart out had helped, too. She couldn't ask for a better listener than her elderly friend who'd sat nodding with genuine sympathy while Rose recounted the several causes of her misery. "So there you have it, Dulcee. I've lost my daughter. The man I love has rejected me, and I just found out my husband was deliberately murdered."

Dulcee pursed her lips. "Landsakes, you've got more problems than you can shake a stick at."

"You could say that, yes."

"You need to take them one at a time. Let's start with Lucy, shall we? Isn't getting her back most important of all?"

At the thought of her daughter, a pang of desperation welled within her. "Of course it is. I want my child back. I've gone about as far as I can go."

"I agree." Dulcee finished pouring the tea and set the pot down firmly. "From what I've heard, what you've done with the River Queen is amazing. But the problem is, you live there. That's fine for you, but you don't want Lucy living over a saloon, do you? You can't move back to the farm, so first off, you've got to find a decent place to live."

Dulcee was making a lot of sense. "I never thought of living by myself."

"What woman does? We're not supposed to be independent. We live under our parents' control until we marry." An ironic smile crossed Dulcee's face. "Then our husband takes over."

"I've been so dependent I never gave a thought to living by myself. The more I think about it, though, the more I realize I wouldn't want to go back, even if I could."

"Now you're getting some sense in your head. There's no reason you can't find a place of your own."

"Of course I can. A little house would be nice, if I could find one to rent or even have built. I could afford it."

Dulcee nodded approvingly. "And then you'd need someone to look after Lucy when you're at the hotel. I hear Sacramento's finally going to have a school. You could enroll her. She's old enough."

"Of course she is. That would be perfect."

"Problem solved." Dulcee flopped out her hands. "You see? All you need do is keep your head straight and think it through. Here's what else you should do. When you leave here, you should march right next door and have a talk with Ben and Coralee. Tell them what you plan. Give them a deadline. Not longer than a couple of weeks, I'd say, and then you're going to take Lucy and that's that. Meantime, you're looking for a house and enrolling Lucy in school."

"You make it all sound so easy. They might not let me in, though."

"You've got to try, that's all I can tell you." A corner of Dulcee's mouth pulled into a slight smile. "Now what's the next problem?"

Rose had to laugh. Dulcee might be old, but her mind hadn't lost a bit of its sharpness. "The next problem is Deke Fleming. I've fallen in love with him, but he doesn't love me anymore, if he ever did in the first place. Now he's very, very angry." She heaved a sigh. "Not much you can do about that, I'm afraid."

Dulcee cocked her head. "Now, hold on, missy. You told me Deke got mad because he saw you kissing Mason Talbot."

"*Thought* he saw me kissing Mason, but like I said, I wasn't."

"Doesn't matter. Either way, do you think he would've gotten this mad if he didn't care about you?"

"I suppose not."

"It's plain to see the man was jealous. That's why he acted that way. Of course, he loves you."

"So what do you think I should do?"

Dulcee sat back and rolled her eyes. "Goodness gracious, you don't have to do anything. Don't let this go to your head, but no wonder the men are after you. You're pretty and you're smart. You're witty and you've got a good sense of humor. And besides all that, you've got spirit and you stand up for yourself. That's what men truly admire in a woman, what they find irresistible. We're supposed to believe that to catch a husband a girl should be all mealy-mouthed and not a brain her head, but that's not so. Deke sees you for the special woman you are. Mark my words, he won't stay away for long, and you won't have to lift a finger."

"You think so? I'm not so sure I'm the independent woman you think I am, especially after last night."

"Don't underestimate yourself. No woman without spirit would have chosen to run that hotel. From what I've heard, you're making a big success of it. You took a chance, defied everyone to do it, and by golly you've come out on top."

Maybe Dulcee was wrong, but even if she was, Rose felt better. "You don't think I should go find Deke and apologize?"

"What for? Judging from what you've said, you didn't do anything wrong. If you ask me, it's all Mason Talbot's fault. He's an evil man. Bad enough he killed Emmet, but he did it on purpose? What a terrible thing."

"I know, and I'm trying to decide what to do about it."

"Oh, my dear!" Dulcee's eyelids lifted in alarm. "You can't do anything. It's not fair, and it's not right, but you're looking for trouble if you go after a man like Mason. I know you'd like to, but if you value your safety, you'd best leave it in God's hands."

"I'm listening." Rose took another sip of tea. "And I do believe you're right."

* * * *

At the end of her visit with Dulcee Bidwell, Rose climbed in her buggy and drove straight next door to the farmhouse. Walking to the front door, she recalled the last time she was here, that awful night they'd locked her out and thrown her clothes on the ground. What a wreck she'd been, her belief in herself in shreds. Today was different, though. This time she strode to the front door with head held high and knocked with a firm hand.

Coralee opened the door. To Rose's great surprise, she smiled. "Come in." She swung the door wide. "Ben's gone at the moment. Lucy's in the kitchen. She'll be so glad to see you."

In the kitchen Lucy was at the table eating her lunch. With a dimpled smile, she hopped off her chair and flung herself into Rose's arms. "Where have you been? I missed you."

Holding her daughter tight, Rose lost the last of her doubts that what she was doing was right. She held Lucy at arms' length and grinned. "It won't be long now, sweetheart. Everything's going to be fine, and we'll soon be together again."

Later, after Lucy had gone down for her nap, Rose had an honest talk with Coralee. "As soon as I can find a place to live, I'll be coming for Lucy. You can tell Ben she'll have a nice place to live, a nice school to attend, and she'll be with her mother, which is how it should be. Surely he'll have no objections."

Coralee nodded decisively. "You know how he is, Rose, hardheaded and stubborn, but he's beginning to waver. Deep in his heart he knows Lucy should be with her mother. I can't wait to tell him your plans. By the time you come back, I promise he'll be gentle as a lamb."

* * * *

Rose drove the buggy back to town with spirits high. No more muddled thinking. Now that she had a plan, she needn't spend another anguished minute worrying over Lucy. Tomorrow she'd start looking for a place for the two of them, and that would be pure pleasure.

As for Deke...

Dulcee had it right. Deke was jealous. Maybe that meant he loved her and would surely come back. If so, she wouldn't have to lift a finger.

As for Mason ...

For a brief moment, her mind clouded with worry. Mason Talbot had deliberately murdered her husband. Now that she knew, shouldn't she go to the sheriff? Surely that would be the just and proper thing to do, but like Dulcee said, she'd be looking for trouble if she went after him. No, she wouldn't do it. She was a mother with a child to raise, and that came first.

How wonderful that she'd finally made her decisions and knew exactly what she was going to do! She laughed aloud and burst into a chorus of "Oh! Susanna," perfectly timed to the clip-clop of the horse's hooves. The worst of her problems were behind her. Nothing more could go wrong.

Chapter 17

When Rose returned to the River Queen, she found Cherry waiting in her office. Rose had stopped by her second-floor room from time to time, always pleased to find the baby doing well and Cherry with a contented look about her, a far cry from that pale, desperate-looking young woman who had threatened to kill herself.

Cherry got up to greet her. "I hope you don't mind me waiting in your office, Mrs. Peterson. I had to talk to you."

"Of course, I don't mind." Rose seated herself at her desk and waved for Cherry to sit down. "Is the baby all right?"

"Oh, yes! My little James is a joy. When he smiles at me and waves his little fists, my heart melts. I can't imagine life without him, thanks to you."

Rose held up her hand to protest. "Compared to your benefactor, I haven't done much. He's the one you should thank, although, as I made clear, he doesn't want your gratitude."

"I wish I knew who he was. The thing is…" Cherry frowned and chewed on her lip, clearly struggling to find the right words. "I know how selfish this sounds, especially after all my benefactor has done for me, but I can't stay in that little room much longer. I feel trapped. There's hardly any sunshine. Did you know he sent me a baby carriage? I was ever so grateful, but I can hardly use it, being as every time I take the baby out, I have to bump the carriage all the way down the stairs and then past all those men acting like they never seen a baby before in their lives. And then when I get James and me out the door, there's men on the street gathering around, all ogling and poking their fingers at the baby. They mean well, but I can't get away from them. Besides that, the street's all muddy, and I have to push really hard to make the wheels turn, and that's why I don't want to stay." Cherry stopped to catch her breath. "I'm a terrible, ungrateful person, but that's how I feel, and I don't know what to do."

"You're not thinking of going back to what you were doing?"

"Never!" Cherry spiritedly shook her head. "I cringe when I think about it. I could never go back."

Rose took a moment to gather her thoughts. If she'd taken the time to think, she would have realized a hotel was a poor place to raise a baby, even on the second floor. Terrible, in fact. "I hear what you're saying, and of course, you're right. This is my fault. I've been so busy with other things I didn't take time to realize you can't stay in that room forever."

"I'm so sorry that I—"

"Don't you dare be sorry. I'm glad you came to me. Don't worry. I know exactly what's to be done, and I'm going to take care of it right now."

After Cherry left, Rose hastened to her room and went straight to the Bible that sat on the table beside her bed. She'd always held a great admiration for those virtuous souls who could instantly quote a suitable verse from the Bible for any and all occasions. Despite her many years of attendance at church and Sunday school, she couldn't come close to such piousness. She would do her best, though. Where to start? She opened the cover and racked her brain. Ah, yes, Mark 11:25 would be good. If that didn't work, Mathew 6:14-15 would surely do the job, or maybe something even better.

When she finally closed her Bible, she changed her dress to her favorite, the rose-colored cotton. She checked the mirror to make sure her hair was neat and the little tendrils around her face hadn't blown all over the place. She planned on seeing Mitch, who wouldn't have the least interest in how she looked. But what if Deke happened to be at the ice house? What would she say to him? More important, what would he say to her, or would he say anything at all?

Not that she cared. In fact, she hoped he wouldn't be there. Did she really? She laughed to herself. Whom was she trying to fool? Of course, she hoped she'd see Deke, but then what would she do? Dulcee had said she wouldn't have to lift her little finger to get him back, but she wasn't at all sure that was so.

When Rose parked her buggy beside Fleming & Carter's Ice House, she hid her disappointment that only Mitch was in sight, loading ice on a wagon in front. "Good afternoon, Mitch." Smiling, she climbed from the buggy. "You're just the person I wanted to see."

"Me?" Mitch asked in his usual modest fashion.

"Yes, you. Can you spare a minute? I want to talk to you."

They sat on the dock in front of the ice house. "It's about Cherry," Rose began. "She so appreciates all you've done for her, even though she doesn't know who you are. But now..."

She went on to explain why the difficulties of caring for a baby in a hotel like the River Queen had put Cherry in a dilemma. "She can't take it much longer, and I don't blame her. But the thing is, what will she do?"

Mitch had listened carefully to her every word. "You don't think she'd ever go back to...uh, her previous occupation?"

"She'll never go back. Of course, being as women are so outnumbered around here, she'll have no trouble finding a man to support her. But will he really love her? Or will he just want a woman to wash his clothes, cook his meals and...you know."

"I see." For a long moment, Mitch sat in silence, lips pursed in thought. "That night I met Cherry, when I helped bring her baby into this world—"

"You did more than help. Little James wouldn't be here if it weren't for you."

"You're very kind, but what I was saying was I felt something special for Cherry even then. I admired how brave she was, gritting her teeth to keep from screaming, and how she never lost her sense of humor even in all that pain. I think I loved her even then. But when I found out what she did for a living..." A grieved expression crossed his face. "Some things are hard to forgive."

Ah, the perfect opening. In her head Rose quickly ran through the verses she'd so carefully memorized. She hoped she wouldn't stumble, but it was worth a try. "Mitch, are you familiar with Colossians 3:13? 'Bear with each other and forgive one another if any of you has a grievance against someone. Forgive as the Lord forgave you.'"

Mitch nodded solemnly. "Ah, yes. The Lord has forgiven me many a time. But still—"

"Mark 11:25: 'And when you stand praying, if you hold anything against anyone, forgive them, so that your Father in heaven may forgive you your sins.'"

Mitch arched an eyebrow in surprise. "I didn't know you knew your Bible verses that well."

"I don't." Despite the seriousness of the subject, she couldn't help a playful grin. "I had to look them up before I came here."

Mitch sat a moment and then broke into hearty laughter. Such unrestrained behavior wasn't like him at all, but through his laughter, she'd detected a strain of relief, as if—could it be possible?—he might have got beyond certain narrow-minded beliefs he'd been raised with, and good riddance.

Cautiously, she inquired, "Have I made any sense?"

"You always make sense to me. I've heard every word you said, and I—" The sound of a horse's hooves diverted Mitch's attention. Deke came riding up on Sidney. Mitch stood up. "Guess I'd better get back to work. Nice talking to you, Rose. I'll think about what you said."

She had an urge to grab Mitch, tell him not to go, but with a wave to his friend, he ambled off before she could stop him. God help her, she was going to be alone with Deke. Her heart started pounding. Nothing she could do about it, though. Her mind went blank. All she could do was watch as Deke swung from his horse, graceful as always. His unreadable expression didn't change as he touched two fingers to his hat in a brief salute. "Good afternoon, Rose."

His greeting sounded so cool, so distant. Well, so would hers be. "Hello, Deke." Good. She'd sounded just as cool. She'd pretend she was far too busy to talk and must depart immediately. "I was leaving."

She turned her back on him and started walking toward her buggy. With each step she took, she hoped he'd speak. *Please let him speak.*

But he didn't.

He must be watching, though. She unhitched Star and climbed in the buggy with extra care. God forbid she should trip on the hem of her dress and go sprawling. With a smart snap of the reins, she guided the buggy to the street, looking straight ahead, her nose in the air. She'd been crazy to think he cared a fig about her in the first place. She would never make such a stupid mistake again.

* * * *

Deke blew out his breath as he stared after her. Why hadn't she said something? Why hadn't *he* said something? But if Mason Talbot was her choice, what was there to say? Deke had pictured the scene a million times. Rose in the arms of that scoundrel—kissing him—or was she? At the time, he hadn't questioned what he'd seen so clearly with his own eyes. Only later, when he got past his rage—a rare thing for him—had he begun to realize he may have been mistaken. The light was dim. From what he could see, Mason had wrapped his arms around Rose, but now that he looked back, her arms were not around him. He remembered what she'd said right before he drove away. *Didn't you see he was forcing me?*

The more he thought about it…

He hadn't realized it was possible to fall in love with someone so completely, and in such a short time. He had, though. Since that night, his gnawing ache for her hadn't ceased. Fool that he was, he may have lost her, but by God, he was going to get her back. He just had to figure out how to do it.

* * * *

When Rose got back to the hotel, she found Howie waiting for her. "Your solicitor came by and left a message. He wants to talk to you."

How strange. She couldn't imagine a situation urgent enough to bring the dignified Mr. Field to the River Queen. "I'll go see him right now."

A visit to the solicitor's office provided a sharp reminder of that momentous day she'd stood up for herself and refused to sign over the River Queen. It wasn't that long ago, but already she felt like a different woman. Back then, she'd been anxious and ill at ease. Today she leaned back in her chair with confidence and addressed Mr. Field. "I received your message. What's this about?"

The solicitor picked up a paper from his desk. "I'll get right to the point. I have in my hand an offer from Mr. Mason Talbot. I must say, it's quite extraordinary." He regarded the paper with near disbelief. "Most extraordinary indeed."

"Please do go on."

"I won't read all of it." Mr. Field returned the paper to his desk, rested his elbows on the desk, and laced his fingers. "In essence, Mr. Talbot wishes to purchase your hotel, the River Queen, including all furnishings and various appurtenances, for forty-two thousand dollars. That's twice what he offered the first time. Even taking into account the improvements you've made, such as the restaurant, that's more than a generous offer."

For only a fleeting moment did Rose consider what the magnificent sum of forty-two thousand could do. A fancy new wardrobe for herself and Lucy. A new carriage. A big house in the best part of town. But profits kept growing at the River Queen. Part of the fun was the challenge of making them increase even more. "You can tell Mr. Talbot thank you, but I'm not interested."

With a start, the solicitor sat back in his chair. "Are you sure you understand? Offers such as this are hard to come by. You'll never—"

"You heard me, Mr. Field. I will not sell the River Queen, no matter what the offer. Please convey my answer to Mr. Talbot, and you might add that if he thinks a higher offer will persuade me, he's wasting his time."

A long silence followed. The solicitor seemed to be frozen with astonishment. At last he spoke. "Well, I must say, you surprise me. Not that I mistrust your business acumen, but I hardly expected a refusal after such a magnanimous offer."

She gave him a playful smile. "Well, you know how we women are. So scatterbrained and unreliable. It's a wonder we're allowed out of the house." She picked up her reticle and rose to leave. "Thank you very much anyway."

To her surprise, Mr. Field returned her smile, seeming to appreciate her attempt at humor. Quickly he grew serious. "Please sit down. I'm not through yet."

"Something more?" She dropped into the chair again.

"Yes, something more." He spoke slowly, as if carefully arranging his thoughts. "As I'm sure you're aware, I've built a highly respectable reputation for myself in this town. My entire practice is built on my high regard for ethical behavior and lofty principles. Today, however, I shall make an exception."

"You will?" She had no idea what he was going to say.

"I will." Judging from the look on his face, he could be about to plunge from a high cliff into dangerous, deep waters below. "Mason Talbot is a spiteful man. He's my client, so I'm definitely speaking out of turn, but I'm warning you to be careful, and I mean very careful indeed."

"Why do you say that, Mr. Field?"

"Several reasons. From the beginning, I've considered Mr. Talbot's behavior to be outside normal bounds, shall we say. Too pretentious...too ambitious...too ruthless. In his business dealings, he's shown a decided penchant for getting what he wants, no matter whom he might hurt. That's why I'm stepping away from my duties to my client to warn you."

"You mean Mason might wish me harm?"

"This morning when he appeared in my office, he appeared calm but too calm, if you get my meaning. For appearance's sake, he was keeping a tight control of himself, but underneath, I sensed he was seething with rage. He wants the River Queen, and he's a man who doesn't like to be thwarted. Anyone who crosses him does so at their peril. That's why I'm warning you to watch out. Frankly, the best advice I can give you is to accept his offer and be done with it."

"I can't do that."

Mr. Field threw up his hands. "You've been warned. Nothing more I can do except wish you well and ask that in any future dealings with Talbot, you at least stay vigilant."

The stark intensity in the solicitor's voice caused her to question her resolve. Was she making a mistake? Maybe she should take his advice and sell. But no, she refused to allow Mason Talbot to get the better of her.

She'd come this far, and she would not turn back. "I truly appreciate your advice. I won't change my mind, but I promise I'll be careful."

To her surprise, Mr. Field came around his desk, took both her hands in his and held them tight. His eyes brimmed with concern. "You're a very special woman, Mrs. Peterson. Please take care."

"I will, and don't worry. I know how to take care of myself. After all, short of coming after me with a gun, what could he possibly do?"

Stepping out of Mr. Field's office, she found a wet street and light rain falling. *Not again.* A big storm had just passed through. Now here came another. It seemed Sacramento had had more than its share of rain, and she fervently hoped it would stop soon.

Chapter 18

Rose had been looking forward to finding a house, but for the next two days a steady rain prevented her from leaving the hotel. She had plenty to do. Unable to work in a downpour, miners had flocked to town, filling every hotel room, crowding two- and three-deep around the gambling tables. She welcomed the extra work. It helped keep her mind off Deke, but even so, she spent far too much time agonizing over questions she couldn't answer. Why hadn't she spoken up the last time she saw him? Why had she walked off like a ninny and left him standing there? But what if she had spoken and he looked at her with that flat, hard look in his eyes like he had the other night? Once was enough. She'd been wise to hurry off.

Or so she kept telling herself.

Should she really be concerned over Mason Talbot? Mr. Field seemed to think so and had taken the trouble to warn her. But why worry? There was nothing she could do about it, and besides, the thought that Mason could actually harm her seemed so outlandish she couldn't take the solicitor's warning seriously.

After two days, the rain stopped and a bright sun broke through the clouds. Late that morning, she was in the lobby talking to Howie when Mitch Carter walked in. Other than the night of the shipwreck, she'd never seen him in the hotel before. After a greeting, she had to add, "This is a surprise."

"I've come to see Cherry." He usually looked so serious, but today an easy smile played at the corners of his mouth. "Must have been those Bible verses you quoted."

How wonderful that her little ploy had worked! Or at least, she guessed it had. Mitch was a man who carefully guarded his emotions, though. He wouldn't appreciate the ecstatic hug she wanted to give him, so she settled on a casual shrug instead. "Whatever the reason, I'm glad you're here. Follow me up the stairs, and I'll show you her room."

Cherry was cradling the baby in her arms when she opened her door. Dressed in a plain muslin gown, she bore little resemblance to the brazen ladies with their garish feathers and spangles who lived on the third floor. Seeing Rose, she smiled. "Hello, Mrs. Peterson." Her gaze shifted to Mitch. After a long, silent, sizing-up moment, she cried, "It's you!"

Mitch spoke softly. "It's me."

Tears welled in her eyes "I wondered what happened to you. I've wanted to thank you for all you did that night."

"It wasn't anything."

"Yes, it was. I never met a man as kind and generous as you. You saved my life that night, me and"—she glanced down at James who lay asleep in her arms—"my precious baby. Where have you been? Why haven't you—?" Her eyes went wide, as if she'd been struck by a revelation. "It's you! *You're* my benefactor—the one who's kept me and James off the street." She looked at Rose. "Am I right?"

"Yes, you are." Cherry's joy was so contagious that Rose felt like crying, too. "I must go," she murmured. "A million things to do."

Neither one appeared to notice she was leaving, and she wasn't surprised. Mitch was peering at Cherry with a tender, heart-rending gaze. She was regarding him as if he were her handsome Prince Charming, not the ordinary-looking man Rose saw.

She returned to her office with an extra bounce in her step. Her own love life might be in a mess, but a wonderful new life had opened for Cherry and little James.

Later on, Jake came by and said he'd heard she was looking for a house to rent. She told him she was. "Then you'd better get over to M Street. One of my dealers is quitting and going back East. It's not a bad little house, if you're interested."

Indeed she was!

She hastened to find Drucilla who said she'd be delighted to come along. Because of the heavy rains, she'd been stuck in the hotel for days and hadn't gone anywhere, not even home to the farm. Now, with her sister-in-law by her side, Rose drove the buggy to see the house on M Street. Because they'd been extra busy, they hadn't had a chance to talk. As they drove along, Rose caught a lilt of happiness in Drucilla's voice she'd never heard before. "You sound in good spirits," she said.

"Oh, I am." Her sister-in-law brought up her hand to stifle a giggle.

She'd never heard a giggle from Drucilla's taciturn mouth in all her life. "May I ask what's going on?"

"Gaston has invited me to the American Theater tomorrow night to see *Othello*."

"Ah, Shakespeare. And you want to go?"

"Of course."

"Does this mean you have an interest in him?"

"It means I have an interest in *Othello*."

Drucilla had reverted to her usual cynical self. Obviously she didn't care to pursue the subject any further. She hadn't fooled Rose, though, not for a minute.

* * * *

The house on M Street sat behind neatly trimmed hedges in a front yard surrounded by a white picket fence. Lilac trees and rose bushes bloomed along a walkway. Two stories high, the house was completely furnished and contained two bedrooms, a big kitchen, dining room, and parlor. "What do you think?" Rose asked Drucilla after the owner had shown them through.

"I love it, and I think Lucy will love it, too."

That settled it. In a week she could move in. Sheer joy flooded through her. For the first time in her life she would have a home of her own. At long last, she would be mistress of her own kitchen without her mother, Coralee, or anyone else telling her what to do.

If only Deke could see it...

Days had gone by and she'd neither seen nor heard from him. Their romance was over, if indeed it was ever a romance in the first place. She must move on, find comfort in knowing she and Lucy would soon be together again. She would not waste her time looking back. For years she'd grieved over Anthony, only to finally realize he was nothing more than a young girl's stupid mistake. But Deke? She'd never get over him but she'd try.

On their way back to the River Queen, Drucilla asked, "When are you going to let Ma and Pa know you've found a place to live?"

Rose glanced at the sky. "What about right now before it starts raining again? I'm glad you thought of it. They'll have a week to adjust to not having Lucy around. As far as I'm concerned, bygones are bygones. They'll always be welcome to visit any time they want."

"That's awfully considerate, considering how they treated you."

"They're Lucy's grandparents. How could I hold a grudge? Do you want to come with me?"

"Of course, I need to get some more clothes."

As they traveled the two miles to the farm, Rose couldn't remember when she'd been in a better frame of mind. The miserable days of living without her daughter were almost at an end. Best of all, because she'd restrained herself and acted in a reasonable manner, she'd managed to get Lucy back without creating an ugly scene. Maybe even the thing with Deke didn't seem quite as hopeless as it had been. She'd just solved one difficult problem over Lucy. Why couldn't she do the same with Deke?

A mixture of hope and determination filled Rose's heart as she turned into the long driveway that led to the farm. They had to watch their step as they climbed from the buggy. The sky might now be clear, but the heavy rains of the past few days had left countless muddy puddles.

They hurried up the steps. Drucilla opened the front door, swinging it wide. "Ma? Pa? I'm here and so is Rose. She brought some good news." She muttered to Rose, "At least I hope they'll think so."

"We're in the kitchen," Coralee called.

When they entered the kitchen, they found her in-laws having a cup of coffee at the table. To her relief, Ben gave her a friendly nod. Coralee smiled. "Sit down and have some coffee with us, Rose. I trust all is going well?"

"Couldn't be better." Rose pulled out a chair. "I just rented a house on M Street. It's small but very nice and in a nice part of town. Lucy will have her own bedroom. I'm going to start looking for a good school to enroll her in. I can hardly wait to tell her." Her gaze swept the kitchen. "Where is she? I hope she's not outside playing in all this mud."

Ben frowned in puzzlement. "But doesn't she already know?"

"What do you mean? I'm here to tell her."

Coralee looked even more baffled than Ben. "But Lucy's not here, Rose. Surely you know that."

"What do you mean, she's not here?"

"Well, I guess there's been a mix-up." Coralee took a sip of coffee, not yet concerned. "Mason Talbot came by yesterday. He said you'd found a place and were too busy to pick her up yourself, so you asked him to do it."

Rose's breath caught in her lungs. She could hardly speak above a whisper. "So what you're saying is, Lucy's not here and Mason has her?"

"Of course, that's what I'm saying." Coralee's pleasant expression slowly faded. "Oh, dear, is something wrong?"

Ben spoke up. "I don't understand, Rose. You'd warned us you were about to take Lucy, so when Mason stopped by, we assumed you sent him. Never gave it a thought, otherwise. What's this all about?"

Rose pushed back from the table and stood, nearly knocking her chair over in the process. "I did not give Mason permission to take my child. He's kidnapped her!"

"What are you talking about? Mason Talbot is highly regarded in this town. Surely he wouldn't—"

"He would! You don't know him, Ben. Of course, he would." Rose turned to Drucilla, who'd been listening in stunned silence, coffee cup halfway to her mouth. "I must get back to town. Are you coming?"

Drucilla set down her coffee cup with a bang. "I'll get my clothes and meet you at the buggy." She practically ran from the kitchen.

Coralee pressed a hand to her heart. Finally she understood. "He seemed so sincere, like he was doing you a favor. We should have realized—"

"Not your fault." Rose headed out of the kitchen. Over her shoulder, she called, "Mason's totally to blame, but don't worry, I'll soon get her back."

But could she? Fear and anger knotted inside her as she climbed into the buggy. How could she deal with a man as evil and ruthless as Mason Talbot?

Clutching an armful of clothing, a harried-looking Drucilla climbed in beside her. "What will you do?"

Rose picked up the reins. "I don't know why he's done this, or what he wants, but I'll soon find out. I will do anything to get my child back, Drucilla. *Anything.*"

* * * *

Upon arriving at the River Queen, Rose hastened to Jake's office, where he sat working on the books. After a quick look, he asked, "What's wrong, Mrs. Peterson? You look upset."

She wasn't about to confide in Jake, but he could be helpful. "I need to know where I can find Mason Talbot, and I need to know right now."

"Well, let's see. He hasn't moved into that fancy mansion of his yet, so he must be still living at the Egyptian. That's my best guess, anyway. He lives in suite 310 on the third floor."

"Thanks, Jake." He might have his faults, but he knew when not to ask questions. She turned to leave.

"Can I help in any way?"

"No!" she called as she hurried out the door. "This is something I must do by myself." Next stop, the Egyptian. She took a deep breath against the panic. Not easy, considering never had she been so consumed with rage, as well as sheer terror, both at the same time.

Chapter 19

A sick fear coiled in the pit of Rose's stomach as she hastened along the third-floor hallway of the Egyptian Hotel and Saloon. She knocked on the door of suite 310, fighting the urge to ball her fists and pound. Mason opened the door. Dressed in a morning coat and silk cravat, he lifted his eyebrows in phony surprise. "Well, well, look who's here. Do come in, Rose. Is something wrong? You don't look your usual cheerful self."

She ignored his mockery and stepped inside. Her eyes darted around what she could see of his suite of rooms, but no sign of Lucy. "Where is she? What have you done with her?"

He remained unperturbed and smiled pleasantly, as if blind to her distress. He graciously waved toward a chair. "Do sit down. If you're looking for your daughter, don't bother. She's not here."

She remained standing. She'd heard the edge of hysteria in her voice and forced herself to speak calmly as she could. "Then where is she? I know you took her."

"You won't sit down? Are you sure? I could order tea and we could have a good chat."

He was toying with her, deliberately trying to enrage her, but she must keep her wits about her. "Just tell me where she is. I'll go get her right now, and nothing more need be said."

His excuse of a smile disappeared. "Let's get down to business, shall we? Lucy is in safe hands. She—"

"*Where?*" She could contain herself no longer. "What have you done with her? How do I know she's all right? How do I know—?"

"She's fine, Rose. No need for hysterics. I assume you want me to return her?"

What a cruel, spiteful question. How she'd love to lash back with a scathing reply, but for now she was in his hands and must listen to whatever rubbish he chose to say. "How could you even ask such a question?"

By now, he'd lost the last semblance of his feigned amiability and was gazing at her with cold, hard eyes. "Before we go any further, I want you to understand why by all rights the River Queen belongs to me."

"Do go on."

Mason's pent-up anger began to reveal itself as he started nervously pacing the floor. "I had my eye on the River Queen for years. Kept waiting for the owner to sell, and when he did"—he was spitting his words out—"*your husband* stole it out from under me."

"That's not what I heard. Emmet bought it fair and square. It wasn't his fault you were out of town."

Mason shrugged with indifference. "And then, when Emmet died—"

"When you deliberately murdered him in cold blood."

"So Jake's been talking?" With a sneer, he waved his hand in a gesture of dismissal. "Such an accusation will get you nowhere. When Emmet died and Ben was ready to sell, you had the gall to claim the River Queen was yours. You, a mere woman, thought you could thwart me. It was all I could do…"

He came close to choking on his words, as if the very thought of her owning his precious hotel was too much to abide. "Tomorrow at ten o'clock, we will meet in Mr. Field's office, where you will sign over the River Queen to me. You will be pleased and happy that I have agreed to buy the hotel. You did your best but found it a great burden, far too much for a woman, and will be greatly relieved to be rid of it. You can forget my offer of forty-two thousand. You'll be more than happy to receive what I offered the first time."

The gall of the man! "You've kidnapped my daughter, and that's against the law. I should go straight to the sheriff."

"Joe Clark? I played poker with him last night. If you go, give him my regards."

She frantically searched for a rational argument—a threat—anything to make Mason listen to reason, but nothing came to mind. He had the upper hand, and there was nothing she could do about it, not for now anyway. "If I sell you the River Queen, how do I know I'll get my daughter back?"

"You don't know, but what choice do you have?" He feigned a look of sympathy. "Poor Rose, it didn't have to be this way, you know. I wanted to marry you. You could have lived in luxury the rest of your life. Been the mistress of that fine mansion I'm building. Enjoyed the prestige of being the wife of one of Sacramento's esteemed civic leaders. But instead..." He shrugged sadly. "An Australian? I thought you had better taste than that."

She ignored his insult. Lucy was all that mattered. "Please don't hurt her."

"I'm not a cruel man and resent your implying that I am. I would never hurt Lucy. Actually, it's not necessary. All you need to know is she's not close by so don't waste your time searching. This is a big country. She could easily disappear and live the rest of her life in a place where you'd never find her."

She clenched her fists. "Lucy had better be all right. If you've hurt her, I'll...I'll..."

"You'll what?"

His mocking attitude made her humiliatingly conscious of how helpless she was. "All right, Mason, I'll be there. You give me no choice."

He smiled pleasantly. "Tomorrow. Ten o'clock sharp in Mr. Field's office. I trust you won't forget."

Words failed her. She could not remain in his presence another moment and fled from his room.

As she drove the buggy back to her hotel, she never felt so alone. She had no one to lean on, and it was all her own doing, the price she had to pay for being an independent woman. When she got back to the hotel, most likely she'd cry on Drucilla's shoulder and get lots of sympathy, but what could Drucilla do? She couldn't stand up to Mason Talbot. Neither could Ben. Neither could anyone except...

Deke.

The Australian was the only person in the world who would fight her battles, only she'd lost him. Now she had too much pride to ask, especially when he would probably wish her well but turn her down.

A raindrop fell on her forehead, then another. They'd had enough rain to last the whole season and then some. Surely it wouldn't last.

* * * *

The rain never stopped. Rose lay awake most of the night, listening to the pounding of a constant deluge. Where was Lucy? Who, if anyone, was taking care of her? Was she sheltered and warm? Was she cold, wet, and frightened? Despite her agonized questions, she must have finally drifted off to sleep because toward morning, she was jolted awake by a frantic pounding on her door. She sprang out of bed, threw on her robe, and opened the door to find Jake, wide-eyed with excitement, standing in the hallway. "Come quick," he said. "We're about to flood."

She threw on her clothes, ran a comb through her hair, and rushed downstairs to find the gambling tables deserted. No one stood at the bar. Through the swinging doors, she saw a crowd gathering along the boardwalk. When she joined them, an astounding sight awaited her. The street had transformed from a busy thoroughfare jammed with horses, mules, wagons, and carriages, to a slow-moving river occupied only by a few small boats. Jake came up beside her, dubiously shaking his head. "We're lucky we're up pretty high off the street, but I dunno, Mrs. Peterson. You can see the water's about to flood over the boardwalk. I've sent for sandbags. All we can do is stack 'em up and hope for the best. Trouble is, they won't work if the water keeps rising."

She fought off a momentary panic. She must remember she owned the place and couldn't be acting like some frightened female desperate for guidance. She was the one in charge, the one to make decisions. "You've lived around here for years, Jake. What do you think? Will the water keep rising?"

"Probably. You know how much rain we've had. The ground's soaked through. Every gulch, ravine, creek, and river is full to overflowing, and when that happens, the water has no place else to go but to flood the city. I've seen it happen before. A few years back, the American and Sacramento Rivers both overflowed their banks and pretty much wiped out the whole town."

"What about us?"

"Every hotel along the river could be flooded. Some are built so flimsy they'll likely collapse. Some will stand, and that includes the River Queen. She's built of brick, so it isn't likely the walls will cave in, but if that water gets through the door, it'll do a lot of damage." Jake's expression turned grim. "I'll get the men started on the sandbags."

Rose turned away and headed back inside, her mind spinning with all she had to do. The guests on the second floor needed to be warned. The restaurant! Where was Gaston? They could start stacking chairs on the tables, everything high up as it could go. She must find someone to take care of the bar. It had looked deserted. Not a good idea leaving all that expensive liquor lying about with no one to keep an eye on it.

Gaston raced by, Gus and Cecil the bartender close behind. He looked concerned but not panicked. "Don't worry, madame," he called. "If we can save the restaurant, we will."

Drucilla followed after. Seeing Rose, she slowed down. "I'm going to help Gaston. I'm worried about the family, but there's no way to get home."

"They'll be all right." She tried to sound optimistic. "Ben will know what to do." But would he? The farm lay close to the rising river. Here was a new concern, piled atop all the others. So much to worry about she hardly knew where to start.

She had reached the staircase when she came to a sudden stop and pressed her hand to her mouth. *Dear God.* In all the excitement, she hadn't forgotten Lucy for a moment. Flood or no flood, her little girl still came first, and at ten o'clock she was supposed to be in Mr. Field's office signing away the hotel. But what was she thinking? His office would be flooded, same as here. There wasn't a chance in the world the prudent solicitor would be sitting at his desk waiting for her to arrive. So what would Mason do now? Would he give her another chance, or was her little girl gone forever? What should she do? Her knees started to buckle. With a moan of distress, she tried to force herself to keep going but wasn't sure she could. No one to help her. Never had she felt so desolate and alone.

"Rose?"

His voice came from behind her. She turned and looked into the depths of two warm grey eyes. "Hello, Deke."

His mouth curved into that crooked little grin. "Looks like you could use some help."

Chapter 20

At another time, Rose would have handled those first moments with Deke far differently. In the most minuscule of details she'd have wanted to know why he finally came to her. In turn, she would have revealed the depth of her despair when she thought she'd lost him. They would have talked on and on, immersed in their feelings for one another, and then, all differences settled, they'd have blissfully fallen into each other's arms. But that was before the Sacramento River overflowed its banks. Now the water was rising, Lucy was missing, and time was a luxury she couldn't afford. "Do I need your help? Oh, Deke, I'm so glad you came."

"I'll help all I can, but I don't know if we can stop the water—"

"It's not that. Mason has kidnapped my little girl." Standing at the bottom of the staircase, oblivious to chaos all around, she told him how Mason had taken her daughter, that she'd agreed to sell him the River Queen because if she didn't, she might never see Lucy again. She could hardly keep the hysteria from her voice. "What can I do? Mr. Field won't be there in this flood and…" The words stuck in her throat. "I…I…"

"Don't worry. I'll take care of it."

"How?"

"Guess I'd better have a talk with Mason."

He was going to help. If there'd been time, she would have thrown her arms around him in gratitude, but every minute counted. "I'll come with you."

"No, Rose. You're needed here. And besides, it's best you don't."

"What will you say? I spoke with Jake, so now I know the truth about how dangerous he is. He won't stop at anything to get what he wants."

Deke reached for her hands and held them tight. "Go see to your hotel and let me worry about the rest."

How could she not believe him after hearing the strength and resolve in his voice? "If you're sure?"

"I'm sure."

If Deke couldn't help her, no one could. "I'll wait to hear from you."

"I give you my word I'll find her or know the reason why." He gave her a quick salute and turned away. She watched until he was out of sight. Her heart a little lighter, she started up the stairs to warn the guests on the second floor.

* * * *

Deke Fleming was a careful man. He seldom, if ever, acted rashly, and never promised anything he wasn't sure he could deliver. Until today. As he walked toward the entrance of the River Queen, he had no regrets concerning his promise to Rose. The trouble was, at the moment, he hadn't the faintest idea how he could rescue little Lucy Peterson from that lowlife, coldblooded murderer, Mason Talbot. He had almost reached the front doors of the River Queen when Mitch hurried in, his usual placid face twisted with worry. Seeing Deke, he declared, "The water's still rising. We've lost all our ice, and we'll be lucky if we don't lose the ice house."

"We can always get more ice. Right now I've got a problem..."

Deke told his friend what Mason had done. By the time he finished, Mitch was staring at him in shocked alarm. "You mean, he actually kidnapped that little girl?"

"That he did, mate. I gave Rose my word I'd get her back."

"How?"

"I haven't figured that out yet."

"Blimey." Mitch pondered a moment. "I don't hold with violence, but—"

"You're thinking I should go over to the Egyptian and beat the hell out of him until he talks?"

"You don't want to do that."

"As a last resort, maybe. It wouldn't take much. I'd wager beneath those fancy clothes, he's a coward and a weakling."

"But you've got another plan?"

"Not yet, but I'm working on it."

Mitch clasped his shoulder. "Whatever you decide to do, I'm with you."

"I figure I might need you." Deke looked out the door. A trickle of water had begun to seep across the boardwalk. "Have you come to see if Cherry and the baby are all right?"

"I'm worried, but I think the safest place for them is here."

"Go see them. I got hold of a dinghy. I don't know what I'm going to do, but soon as you get back, we're going to pay a visit to Mason Talbot."

* * * *

Not in Deke's wildest imagination had he ever pictured Mitch and himself rowing along Front Street, but with the river rising ever higher, their dinghy was the only way to reach the Egyptian Hotel. At least three feet of water surrounded every hotel and saloon they passed. Those establishments housed in tents were already done for, a sorry sight with their collapsed canvas walls lying atop ruined gaming tables. On lower ground than the River Queen, Fanny Wentworth's Silver Star Hotel had not fared well. As they passed, desperate-looking guests were hanging out the second-story windows. Out front, Fanny herself sat in a rowboat holding a bulging valise on her lap. "Ah, the ice men," she called. "The cellar's long gone, boys, and so's the beer."

"That's the least of our worries," Deke hollered back.

"Everything's gone. All you can do is save yourselves."

"Good luck, Fanny." No time for conversation. Deke pulled harder on his oar.

They had almost reached the Egyptian Hotel when Mitch asked, "What are you going to do when we get there?"

Mitch's question gnawed at his faltering confidence. He must get Rose's daughter back, but how was he going to do it? A couple of punches in the nose and Mason would talk? Fine, if it worked, but Deke wasn't sure it would. "I don't know what I'm going to do yet, Mitch. Just keep rowing."

Of all the hotels, the Egyptian sat closest to the river. Even so, Deke had assumed the large, three-story building would survive the flood, but when they drew close, Mitch pointed at the north wall. "See there! It's sagging."

Several feet of swift, churning water surrounded the building, the main flow striking hard against the north wall, which looked as if it might collapse at any moment. The Egyptian appeared big and pretentious, but it was constructed of wood, probably cheap, flimsy wood that couldn't withstand the powerful force of water. In front of the hotel, a disorderly collection of dinghies and row boats was hauling disheveled-looking guests away. A couple of large, flat-bottomed barges were tethered close to the entrance. Two men waded toward one of them, each clutching a large picture. Deke recognized Rudy Avery, Mason's employee, who'd been his second at the duel. "Hey, Rudy," he called. "Isn't it time to save yourself? Looks like this place will float away any second."

Rudy caught sight of Deke and Mitch. "For God's sake, come help. All Mr. Talbot cares about is his fancy art collection. If I don't save his priceless paintings, he'll blame me, not the flood."

By God, that's it!

Under less dire circumstances, Deke might have given a whoop and thrown his hat in the air. Instead, he turned to Mitch. "Looks like I won't have to punch Talbot in the nose after all." Maybe God had a hand in it. Certainly Mitch would think so. All Deke knew was, he had his answer. "Sure, Rudy!" He reached for a rope to tie the dinghy. "Come on, Mitch, let's lend our friend a hand."

* * * *

Only minutes later, the north wall of the Egyptian had completely collapsed and the west wall was beginning to sag. When Deke waded through the main entrance, he expected to find the place abandoned. Instead, men Deke recognized as Mason's employees had formed a chain from the restaurant to the entrance and were frantically passing chairs, linen, china, all manner of valuable items from Mason's beloved Le Chantecler, to be loaded onto the second barge. Mason himself stood halfway up the main staircase, shouting directions, urging his men to move faster.

Deke reached the bottom of the staircase and peered up at him. "Why haven't you left? Your whole hotel is about to collapse and you're standing there?"

When Talbot looked down and saw Deke, his expression turned ugly. "You think I have time to talk to the likes of you? Can't you see I'm busy here? Get out of my sight, you ice peddler."

Deke sprang up the stairs to where he was standing. "What have you done with Lucy Peterson?"

Mason gritted his teeth. He looked as if he might explode. "I don't have time to talk."

"Then make the time. If you don't, you'll lose all those precious pictures of yours."

Mason's eyes went wide with alarm. "What do you mean?"

"I have your art collection. All of it."

The color started draining from his face. "You have my Rafael?"

"Yep."

"My Donatello?"

"Whatever it's called, I've got it. Every painting in that fancy collection of yours is sitting on a boat you'll never find. You want it back? Then give me answers. If you lie, the fish on the bottom of Suisun Bay will soon be nibbling at your Rafael, your Donatello, and all those other fancy pictures of yours."

"So what do you want?"

Deke told him exactly what he wanted. "And one more thing. Rudy got tricked. It wasn't his fault, and I don't want you blaming him."

"How do I know you're telling the truth?"

From below, a voice called, "Mr. Talbot?" Rudy Avery stood in three feet of water, hat in hand.

Mason peered down at him. "What's going on, Rudy?"

"They stole the boat right out from under me. Took your whole collection."

Mason gasped, grabbed the railing, and turned to Deke. "So it's true?"

"Yep."

"Why, you…you…!" For once, glib-tongued Mason Talbot found himself at a loss for words.

Deke looked upward. "For God's sake, give me an answer before the roof caves in."

Mason's mouth worked. His eyes kept shifting as if he was desperately searching for a way out of his dilemma. Finally his shoulders sagged in defeat. "I'll tell you everything," he said in a sick whisper. "Here's where you'll find Lucy…"

After Deke got all the information he needed, he peered down at the remains of the first floor. The fast-rising, muddy, debris-filled water had ruined everything, and that included Mason's priceless mahogany bar, his fancy gaming tables, and his beloved French restaurant. An odd cracking sound came from the back wall, as if giving a warning it, too, was about to go. The men in the chain started scattering, suddenly beyond caring what the boss would say.

Deke started down the stairs. He turned in time to see the owner of the Egyptian climbing the staircase. "What are you doing?"

Mason stopped and turned. "Get out of my hotel." His eyes seemed remote, as if he wasn't really there.

"Time to get out, Talbot. Your hotel's about to fall around your ears."

Mason continued up the staircase. The back wall groaned again.

Deke got out of there fast.

* * * *

Where was Deke? Had he found Lucy? In an agony of suspense, Rose fought to keep her fragile control as she worked with the others to save what they could. So far the sandbags had held, but for how much longer? The water continued to flow through the street. When she found a moment to look outside, she could hardly believe some of the items that were beginning to float past: large logs, furniture, what looked like a chicken coop. A kind of controlled panic prevailed inside the hotel. Tim, Jake, Cecil, Gus, Gaston, Drucilla, the third-floor girls—everyone pitched in to help. Nothing could be done about the heavy wood gambling tables, but lighter items were removed to the second floor. Along with Gaston and Gus, Rose worked nonstop in the restaurant, piling chairs and tables high as they could. "There's not much we can do about your beautiful carpet," she lamented to Gaston. "What a shame if we lose it."

"Don't give it a thought, madame. Lives come first. Anything else can be replaced."

Gaston's reply surprised her, but as the day went by, she'd found him to be a tower of strength. She had supposed her temperamental chef would fall apart at the thought his beautiful new restaurant was about to be inundated and ruined. Instead, in a calm, capable manner he'd led them in their efforts to rescue what they could. Eventually Drucilla joined Rose, helping to clear the kitchen cabinets of pots and pans. "Do you think they'll be all right?" she asked.

"I'm not sure." Aside from Rose's concern over Lucy, let alone the River Queen, she worried over the fate of her in-laws. Coralee was capable of taking care of herself, but she wasn't sure about Ben anymore. Since Emmet died, he'd aged a lot and didn't have the strength he used to have. And Raymond was Raymond. Anything could happen. "They're so close to the river. I can only hope they haven't been flooded out."

Gaston overheard. "I'll take care of it."

He meant what he said. As soon as they'd done all they could do in the dining room, he found a small boat and recruited Gus to help him row. Out front, from behind the sandbags, Rose and Drucilla saw them off.

Jake was standing nearby. "Better get upstairs," he said. "Looks like we're losing the battle."

Despite frantic efforts, a steady stream of water began to seep through the sandbags. With a heavy heart, Rose joined the others headed for the second floor. Where was Deke? These past hours, she'd done all she could to save the River Queen, but not for a moment had she forgotten Lucy. Her hotel might be flooding, and everything ruined, but all she really cared about was finding her little girl.

Deke arrived just as the water had begun to flow freely through the double doors and spread throughout the main saloon. Rose had been sitting at the top of the staircase helplessly watching. "Deke!" she called when she saw him.

She held her breath as he came up the stairs and sank down beside her. "I know where Lucy is. Mason said she's all right and I believe him. We've got a problem, though."

Chapter 21

Deke didn't bother to tell Rose how he got Mason to talk. She wouldn't be interested and would only want to know if her daughter was all right and where to find her. "If Mason told the truth, he had Lucy taken to his gold mine, the Majestic. It's above Hangtown. The family that lives there is taking care of her."

Rose slammed her hand to her heart. "She's in the mountains?"

"Yes, but that's the problem. It's stopped raining around Sacramento, but higher up they're saying it's been raining steadily. It fell eighty hours straight at Hangtown. Around Downieville, the north fork of the Yuba River has carried away most of the bridges."

"But we can get up there, can't we?"

He could hardly look into her pleading eyes. Hated to say what he had to say. "The trails are impassable. Nobody can get up there right now."

"But soon?" she asked in an agonized whisper.

"The minute I can." He wasn't telling her all of it. Far from it. He hadn't told her what he'd heard about the calamitous storms that had struck the entire mountain area. Many homes had been destroyed, bridges gone, roads washed away. No supplies had gotten through for days, and people were starving. He wouldn't tell Rose that, although she'd probably find out soon enough. "They're getting together a rescue party that'll leave as soon as it can. I'll be part of it."

"So will I."

"You? I know how worried you are about Lucy, but it's not a good idea. Judging from what they tell me, it'll be tough getting up there. I hate to say it, you being such an independent woman, but there are some things a man can do that a woman can't."

"This woman can."

"Stubborn, aren't you?"

"I want my daughter back." She cut him a sharp look that dared him to argue.

If he didn't take her, he wouldn't be surprised if she tried to get up there by herself. "I'll see what I can do." Something else weighed on his mind. "That's not all you should know."

She managed a wry smile. "More bad news? Haven't I had enough for one day?"

"The Egyptian Hotel is gone. Collapsed and carried away by the flood."

"That beautiful hotel? What a shame."

"That's not the half of it. Looks like Mason Talbot's gone, too." He described the last time he'd seen Mason, heading up the stairway to the second floor, not seeming to care his hotel was about to collapse on his head. Only a minute after Deke had made his way outside, the walls of the Egyptian had caved in. The building had broken apart and portions of it swept downstream. "I didn't see Mason Talbot get out, and I don't think he did."

Her reaction was what he expected. Not wasting time on false sentiments of regret, she whispered, "Oh, my God," and stared at him in alarm. "How will we know where Lucy is if he was lying?"

He couldn't find a good answer. "I don't know, Rose. There must be others who know where she is. We'd have to find them."

He thought she might start to cry, but she didn't. With a deep, shuddering breath she declared, "I can only pray the rain stops soon. Oh, Deke, what if we never find her?"

* * * *

When Gaston and Gus rowed back to the River Queen, they weren't alone. Ben, Coralee, and Raymond huddled wet, cold, and miserable in the back of the boat. After an ecstatic greeting from Rose and Drucilla, the three refugees were made comfortable on the second floor. Coralee explained what happened. "Landsakes, we could all have drowned! The water came up so fast we had to run to the second floor. For two days we were trapped up there, cold and nothing to eat. If it wasn't for Mr. Bernier, we would be there still." She cast a meaningful glance at her daughter. "He's a fine man, Drucilla."

"Yes he is, Ma," she said quietly. "He's not as tall as I am, but I'm finding there's more than one way to look up to a man."

Coralee described how Gaston had insisted they check the family next door and found Tom Murphy and his mother had also been trapped on the second floor. "That Dulcee! Everyone tried to get her to leave but she refused to budge. That was her home, and she saw no reason to leave even though the water was creeping up the stairs to the second floor. Mr. Bernier made sure Dulcee and Tom had plenty of food, so they should be all right."

Rose laughed to herself when she pictured that stubborn old lady refusing to go. She hoped she could be that independent when she reached Dulcee's age. Relieved though she was that her in-laws had survived, as each hour passed, her anxiety grew. Nothing mattered more than getting to Hangtown to rescue her little girl.

* * * *

By the end of the second day, the water began to recede. "We'll be forming the rescue train," Deke said. "Are you sure you want to go, Rose?"

"You can't stop me."

"It'll be cold up there. Better wear your warmest clothes."

She found one of the old wool dresses she'd worn on the wagon train along with gloves, boots, and a heavy wool scarf to cover her head. She'd ignored the newest of fashions, but when Tillie offered to loan her a pair of white flannel bloomers, she gave it some thought. "But, Tillie, wouldn't I look ridiculous?"

"Yes, you would, but if you want to keep your you-know-what warm, you'll wear them."

Rose took the bloomers.

Deke and a big Swede named Axel Johansson had joined together to form the pack train. Axel lived in Hangtown with his wife and children but had been trapped in Sacramento when the flood came. He was as anxious to get up there as Rose was. He'd been a reluctant guest at the River Queen where he spent his days loudly railing at God, Mother Nature, and whoever else he could think of who was keeping him from getting home. He and Deke easily recruited three more men who also lived high in the mountains and were anxious to get back to their families.

Most of the livestock had been moved to higher ground, but Deke managed to find fifteen mules to form the train. Not only did local stores volunteer food and supplies, as word of the devastating flood spread, donations were arriving from as far as San Francisco and all over the state.

At dawn, the day after the water receded, Rose left Sacramento with the pack train. At first, all the men except Deke regarded her with barely contained amusement. Who was this woman wearing those strange-looking bloomers under her dress? She'd never survive such a hard journey and would soon turn back. She was so set on getting to Hangtown, so relieved to be doing something other than sitting around imagining the worst, she didn't care what they thought. Riding Star, she kept close to Deke, who maintained a steady pace on Sidney. Since the rain had melted all the snow on the lower slopes, the first day's journey was easy. On the first night, everyone wrapped themselves in blankets and slept around the campfire. Rose had assumed she'd sleep alone, for propriety's sake, if nothing else, but she got so cold she couldn't sleep. Shivering, she slipped under Deke's covers. Without saying a word, he arranged the blankets over them both and pulled her tight against him. Sinking into the warmth and security of his arms, she fell asleep in no time and hadn't a care what the others might think. They had never discussed that terrible scene when he found her in the arms of Mason Talbot. What with everything else, they had yet to find the time. Sooner or later they would, though. Deke wasn't much on talking about himself and his feelings, but she would insist.

The trip took four days. Easy at first, the higher they climbed into the soaked and muddy Sierra Nevada Mountains, the more obstacles they encountered. Roads washed out. Bridges gone. Two of the men wanted to turn back, but Deke and Axel persisted, and on the fourth day the train entered the storm-devastated town of Hangtown. The starving citizens gave them an ecstatic reception. Rose would have enjoyed the outpouring of praise and gratitude, but only two questions occupied her mind: where was the Majestic Mine and how could they get there?

While Deke helped unload the mules, Rose paid a visit to the general store, where she found an elderly male clerk eager to talk. Who hadn't heard of the Majestic, one of the biggest, most profitable mines around Hangtown? It was owned by a man named Talbot who'd made his fortune off the Majestic. He gave Rose directions. "You can safely go up there during the day, but better not go at night."

When she asked why, he explained, "Because of the high-graders. Talbot's got an armed guard who lives up there with his family. From what I hear, he's got instructions to shoot first and asks questions later."

When she asked what a high-grader was, the clerk shook his head in disgust. "High-graders are lowlife thieves who sneak to the mines at night and steal the rich pieces of ore already mined. They're a big problem around here. Hang 'em all, I say."

Rose had just spent four days traveling on a journey that couldn't have been more exhausting. Her body ached with fatigue, cried out for a good night's sleep. But none of that mattered, and when she left the general store to go find Deke, she had to keep herself from running.

* * * *

Tom Watkins, his wife, and two children lived in a log cabin overlooking the entrance of the Majestic Mine. As Rose and Deke rode up and dismounted, her heart pounded in her chest. As they walked to the door, from inside she could hear children laughing. The door opened before Deke had a chance to knock, and a short, plump woman with a kindly face peered out. "Yes? You wanted something?"

Rose could hardly get the words out. "I'm looking for my daughter. Her name is Lucy. Is she here?"

After the two longest seconds of Rose's life, Mrs. Watkins beamed. "Why yes, dear, she is. What a lovely little girl. Tom and I have so enjoyed having her."

* * * *

When Rose, followed by Deke, stepped inside, she found her daughter playing with dolls on the floor with another little girl. When Lucy looked up and laid eyes on her mother, she stared with disbelief and burst into tears. "Mommy! I thought I'd never see you again."

Rose swept Lucy into her arms. "Never mind, I'm here now. From this day on we'll be together, and I mean that with all my heart."

"You promise?" Lucy asked through her tears.

"I promise."

"Is Grandpa still mad at you?"

"No, and neither is Grandma. Everything's fine now." She held her daughter at arms' length. "Your cheeks are a bit thin, but otherwise you look fine."

Lucy broke into a smile. "You look fine too. I had fun playing with Luke and Sally."

"She's talking about my two children," Mrs. Watkins said. "They got along well together." She shook her head regretfully. "I'm afraid we're all a bit thinner. Like everyone else who lives up here, our pantry's nearly bare. For the past few days we've existed mainly on watery porridge and the last of my peach preserves."

Deke turned toward the door. "We'll soon take care of that. I packed enough for a good meal tonight, and then some."

That night, they all sat down to a dinner Mary Watkins called "the best meal we've had in weeks, maybe ever." Later, after the children had been put to bed, Rose and Deke sat before a fire blazing in the huge stone fireplace and listened as their hosts expressed their shock. "I can't believe

Mr. Talbot would do such a thing," Tom said. "One of his employees brought
her up here. Said Lucy was an orphan. Mr. Talbot wanted us to keep her
until he could find her a new home."

"Good heavens, I never dreamed," Mary Watkins declared. "Tom and
I had no idea Lucy was stolen."

Rose kept trying to reassure them that they weren't to blame. "I'm so
happy to have her back, I wouldn't hold a grudge against anyone." Except
for Mason Talbot, she thought, but he was likely dead and not worth
thinking about. "I'm so very grateful to you both. You took good care of
Lucy, and that's all that counts."

Rose had been living with the darkest of fears, that she would never see
her daughter again. Now she had to keep telling herself this moment was
real. The nightmare was past. How incredibly lucky she was. Whatever
the future might hold, she knew beyond doubt this day was the best, most
wonderful day of her life.

* * * *

When they returned to Sacramento, they found the entire riverfront
area in a disastrous tangle of collapsed buildings and heaps of debris. But
despite the devastation, Rose took heart at the manner in which business
owners, from the smallest shops to the largest hotels, were out on the streets,
feverishly clearing the muddy mess. Not once did she hear anyone say they
were pulling up stakes and leaving. All the talk was of rebuilding, and fast.

At the River Queen, Rose found everyone had pitched in to clear the
floors of the residue of mud that had seeped in and covered most of the
first floor. Some of the gambling tables were ruined but most had been
saved. The restaurant suffered the worst damage, but Gaston seemed not
the least distressed. "*Mon Dieu, quel foutoir!* Even though the carpet's
gone, we'll be up and running in a week, madame."

That night, Rose luxuriated in a hot bath and delighted in crawling
into her snug, warm bed. As she fell asleep, Lucy curled beside her, she
couldn't have been more content.

Except for one thing.

She and Deke had spent the last ten days together, hardly apart for
a moment, yet they still hadn't had that talk. Maybe they never would.
Maybe he didn't love her after all, and had been helping her for no other
reason than out of the goodness of his heart.

* * * *

After Deke escorted Rose and Lucy to the River Queen, he hastened to Fleming & Carter's Ice House. Or what was left of it. When he got there, he found Mitch, hands on hips, surveying the wreckage. Deke burst into a joyful yell. "Hey there, mate! So you didn't drown in Suisun Bay after all."

Mitch filled him in on what had happened after he made off with Mason's art collection. "I took that barge clear to San Francisco. Stored the paintings in a warehouse."

When Deke told him Mason had likely drowned in the flood, he wasted no time on sympathy. "So now we've got us a warehouse full of fancy artwork. Did he have any relatives?"

Deke had no idea, and right now it didn't matter. They turned their attention to what was left of the ice house, deciding it wasn't worth saving. "We'll start all over again," Deke said. "From what I've seen, the saloons will be up and running again in no time, and they're still going to want ice."

For now, only one subject took up most of Deke's thoughts, and that was Rose. She'd been so worried over Lucy that he kept putting off that talk he planned. Long speeches made him uncomfortable, but he would wait no longer. For better or for worse, he'd talk to her tomorrow.

* * * *

The next morning, Deke found Rose alone in the still-closed saloon with a mop in her hand. She was wearing the blue dress he liked. She smiled when she saw him and stopped mopping. "Hello, Deke. What brings you here so early?"

He peered down at the hem of her dress. "What happened to the bloomers?"

"Do you miss them?"

He kept his face straight. "They drove me wild."

"Oh, did they now?" She started laughing.

"I've been wanting to talk to you."

She got serious. A kind of knowing look crept into her eyes. "And I've been wanting to talk to you, Deke."

He took a deep breath. Now was the time for the speech he'd practiced. "It's about that night that I—"

"Stop." She let the mop fall to the floor. "You're going to tell me you made a mistake that awful night when you thought I was kissing Mason. Well, I know that already, so why should we discuss it?" She stepped closer, reached out, and gently clasped his arms. "Is there anything else?"

The tenderness of her touch told him all he needed to know. No long speech necessary, thank God. He knew what he was going to say and would have no trouble saying it. "I love you, Rose, and can't think of living my life without you. Will you marry me?"

Her lips curved into a delighted smile. "Now that you mention it, I do believe I will."

Epilogue

Rose Fleming stood on the dock, waiting for the steamboat that would bring Deke home to her. Six long, lonely months he'd been gone. She'd kept herself busy, easy to do, what with two lively sons to take care of. Lucy had just turned a beautiful, bright fifteen and was no trouble at all. These days, the River Queen didn't take much of her time. Tim Delahunty was such a competent manager she left almost everything in his hands. She'd been luckier than she deserved when Jake Grunion ran off with a week's receipts, and Tim took over.

She heard the blast of a boat whistle and looked down the river. At last! Here came the side-wheeler, *Senator*, direct from San Francisco. After his long journey from Australia, Deke would be elated to be back.

Or would he?

During the years they'd been married, he never complained, and no wonder. The ice house was just the beginning. Every business he touched was successful. The River Queen continued to flourish, even though she'd got rid of the gambling years ago. The third-floor girls were long gone, too. Not long after the flood, Tillie chose to follow her profession at a new hotel and had taken most of the girls with her. The rest stayed as maids, all of them long since married. Now the River Queen was best known for its fabulous French restaurant and priceless Renaissance art collection, although she'd still give it up if ever a relative of Mason's was found.

What more could they ask for in life than three healthy children, family, friends, and their beautiful home overlooking the river?

And yet...

On the night of their tenth anniversary, she'd caught a wistful gleam in his eye and knew what it was. "You miss Amalie Station, don't you?"

He took a long time to answer. "You know how happy I am with you, but sometimes..."

"You wish you could see it again."

His silent nod told her all she needed to know. "Then you should go for a visit. What better time than right now when your business is booming, the children are doing well, and so am I."

On the day he left, she smiled and waved as the steamboat pulled away from the dock. He needn't know the tiny fear that kept gnawing at her. All these years, whenever he talked of Amalie Station, the undercurrent of yearning in his voice revealed how much he longed to return. Now that he'd seen it, did he really want to come home? She loved him completely, but if in his heart he longed to return to Amalie Station, their marriage would never be the same.

As the *Senator* glided to the landing, Rose scanned the cheering passengers standing on the deck. Her heart leaped when she saw him, her beloved Deke, looking much the same as when she married him, only with a bit more grey in his hair. He broke into a grin when he saw her. She'd like to think she hadn't changed much either. No grey in her hair, and she'd kept her figure.

One of the first down the gangplank, he hugged her tight. "I missed you, Rose. It's good to be home."

Was it? She still wasn't sure.

On the way home they caught each other up on all the news. "Ben and Coralee are doing fine," she said, "and of course, Raymond is Raymond. Gaston and Drucilla just left for another trip to France. This time they took the children along. I've never seen Drucilla so happy. And Gaston, too. Such a happy couple. He absolutely adores her and she adores him."

"The same with Mitch and Cherry," he replied. "I paid them a visit while I was there. They're up to six kids now, and not done yet, I think. Cherry loves Australia. She's beginning to sound like a native."

When Deke brought the carriage to a stop in front of their riverfront home, Rose started to get out, but Deke said, "Wait. I have something to tell you."

That he wanted to go back to Australia? She tried to keep the alarm from her voice as she asked, "And what is that?"

He got that crooked little smile on his face, the one that could still send a tingle through her veins. "You know how much Amalie Station has meant to me, and how much I needed to go back and see it. I'm glad I did, but that's the end of it. Before I left, I put Amalie Station up for sale."

"You mean you don't ever want to go back?" She held her breath, waiting for his answer.

"Why should I?" He took her hands in his. "You are my life, Rose. I never want to leave you again. My place is here with you, now and forever."

Wagon Train Cinderella

If you enjoyed *River Queen Rose*, be sure not to miss Shirley Kennedy's
Women of the West series, including

1851, Overland Trail to California. As a baby, Callie was left on the doorstep
of an isolated farmhouse in Tennessee. The Whitaker family took her in,
but have always considered her more a servant than a daughter. Scorned
by her two stepsisters, Callie is forced to work long hours and denied an
education. But a new world opens to her when the Whitakers join a wagon
train to California—guided by rugged trapper, Luke McGraw . . .

A loner haunted by a painful past, Luke plans to return to the wilderness
once his work is done. But he can't help noticing how poorly Callie is
treated—or how unaware she is of her beauty and intelligence. As the two
become closer over the long trek west, Callie's confidence grows. And
when disaster strikes, Callie emerges as the strong one—and the woman
Luke may find the courage to love at last . . .

Keep reading for a special look!

A Lyrical e-book on sale now.

Chapter 1

Along the Overland Trail, 1851

Walking through the woods, Callie Whitaker was drawn to the sound of a waterfall. When a snake slithered across her path, she dropped her bucket and stopped in her tracks. It disappeared into the dense undergrowth. *What brought me here? I cannot believe this is happening to me.* Only a month ago, she was leading a dull but safe existence in the Tennessee farmhouse where she'd lived her entire life and rarely left. Now here she was in the middle of a wilderness she never knew existed, heading to California, a place she'd never heard of. Bone-tired from the endless work, she was sleeping on the ground under a wagon instead of her tiny bed under the eaves. The farm wasn't much, but she'd give anything if she could return to Tennessee, where she didn't have to worry about Indians, snakes, and who-knew-what-would-happen-next?

A lump formed in her throat. *Silly girl, you have no time for feeling sorry for yourself.* Darkness was about to fall. She must get to the stream, scoop a bucketful of water, and hurry back to the wagon where everyone expected their supper. She picked up her bucket and trudged on. Through tall trees, the flowing water came into view. Ah, there it was. She drew close. How beautiful. Cascading water falling over moss-covered boulders, gorgeous ferns in every shade of green, clumps of tiny violets growing around the pool beneath and standing in the pool, the water up to his knees... Oh, my stars. She froze in her tracks, backed a few steps away, and peered over the top of a red hawthorn bush. It was a man—tall, lean, sinewy, with long, dark hair—and completely naked. He appeared to be bathing, bending to scoop water into his palms, then bringing it up over his head with a giant splash. The water cascaded over a powerful set of shoulders, down over the rippling muscles of his stomach to his sturdy thighs, to his...

Why was she gawking like a schoolgirl? Shameful. She'd seen her little stepbrother's thing many a time. She'd never forget when crazy Grandpa Pearson from the next farm escaped and ran naked down the road. So, of course, she knew what a man looked like, but still...oh, my. Neither her brother's tiny thing, nor that of Grandpa Pearson's, all shriveled, looked anything like this...so big, so very, very...

He looked up. She ought to run before he spied her, but she couldn't move a muscle. His gaze caught hers and his eyebrows lifted ever so slightly. He'd spied her! Oh, she should run, but her feet refused to move, and her eyes refused to turn away from the fascinating sight before her. Taking his time, he casually looked to the left, then the right, as if he might find some kind of cover, which, of course, he could not. He shrugged, as if admitting defeat. With a mischievous smile, he spread his arms wide and bowed toward her. "Good afternoon, madam. Taking in the sights?"

Oh, Lord. His laughter brought her back to her senses. Her cheeks heating, she clutched her pail and started to back away from the hawthorn bush, intent on running off as fast as she could. But wait a minute. Why should she make a fool of herself and bolt and skitter off like a panicky calf? He was the one at fault, the one who should have done his bathing farther upstream. She didn't back off. Instead, gripping her faded skirt, she held it out and dipped a deep curtsey, boldly returning his grin as she did. Only after she'd risen, forcing herself to take her time, did she turn and head downstream at a dignified pace.

She hadn't recognized him. He must be from the large wagon train that had camped close by. In the morning, it would be gone, thank goodness, and she need never lay eyes on him again.

* * * *

"Callie!" Hester Whitaker glared at her stepdaughter. "It's about time you got back. Where were you? Did you expect me to fix supper by myself?"

"Sorry, ma'am." Callie stepped to the campfire and set down the heavy pail of water. She didn't attempt any excuses. Ma wouldn't listen anyway. Nor would it do any good to point out that never in Callie's memory had her stepmother fixed supper by herself. "I boiled a mess of beans this morning and baked some bread. It'll be ready in no time."

Lydia, Callie's older stepsister, tossed her blond curls and pouted. "I'm getting awfully tired of beans."

"So am I." Nellie, her other stepsister, loved to complain.

"Sorry, girls. We'll just have to bear it until we reach California." Ma settled herself on a log next to their wagon and frowned at her stepdaughter. "Did you bake a pie today, or anything?"

"No, ma'am, I did not." Long ago Callie had given up making excuses that always fell on deaf ears. Nor did she question why Nellie and Lydia, both older than she, were required to do only the lightest of chores. According to Ma, they were both much too frail and delicate for heavy work. Ma often said so, whereas she, the lowly stepsister, was as strong as an ox and should labor to pay for her keep and be grateful she had a roof over her head. That was the way of it, all she could remember since she was born. Not that she minded, or ever questioned her fate. Ma often pointed out how lucky she was the Whitakers had found her abandoned on their doorstep all those many years ago and, out of the kindness of their hearts, taken her in.

A ripple of laughter floated across their campsite. Pa, who'd been working on one of the wagon wheels, rose up and cast a look of disgust at the source of the sound, a large company of wagons, at least fifty, that had camped in a circle on the other side of the meadow. "We were here first," he muttered. "The damn fools should find their own place." He addressed his wife and daughters. "You're to stay away from them. Is that understood?"

"Yes, Pa," came quick answers. Caleb Whitaker ruled with an iron hand.

Ma gazed across the meadow. "Do you think I'd have anything to do with that trash? A while ago I saw one of the women wearing the most outlandish outfits I ever saw."

Lydia giggled. "Those are bloomers, Ma. They're like a man's pants only baggier and gathered on the bottom."

"Disgraceful." Ma's face took on its usual look of disapproval. "It'll be a cold day in hell before I, or any of my family, are caught in such an outfit." She addressed Callie. "Are you going to just stand there?"

"No, ma'am."

Callie went about fixing hot biscuits with fresh butter, salted meat, beans, and green peas gathered from vines along the trail. When supper was ready, she banged the bottom of a pan with a spoon. Tommy, the baby of the family at seven, came running. He was the only young'un left. Ma had birthed eight children altogether. The two older boys were grown and gone on their own. On the day the family left for California, Callie had paid her last sorrowful visit to the three tiny graves under the big oak tree. Far as Callie knew, Ma never went there. She had never mentioned the babies she'd lost at birth or soon after. As it was, she paid little attention to Tommy, whom she considered, "not right in the head." No one knew exactly what was the matter with the boy, except he seemed to live in a world of his own, never played with other children, and didn't like to be touched or held. Sometimes Callie wondered what would happen to Tommy if she weren't around to take care of him. The rest of the family had long since given up and considered him nothing but a burden.

Their two hired men joined them for supper around the cook fire. Andy and Len, both in their early twenties, helped drive the family's two wagons and cared for the hundred head of cattle they'd brought along. They were working their way west so they could get to the gold fields and make their fortune. Callie didn't much like Len, who had a sly way about him. She didn't trust him, either. Andy, the tall, awkward one, was "dumb as a stump," she'd heard Pa say, but at least he was always pleasant and did his work well. Lately, he'd been casting longing glances at Lydia. It was clear he was smitten. Sensing his feelings, Lydia had begun to make fun of him behind his back, calling him her little puppy dog, laughing at his "moonstruck gazes."

Callie felt sorry for Andy. He might not be very bright, but at least he gave Callie a sincere "thank you" after every meal, which was more than anyone else did. Tonight was no exception.

"Those beans was mighty good, Miss Callie," he remarked in his shy way.

"Why, thank you, Andy."

He was just being kind. They had been on the road for two weeks, eating beans every day. There was nothing special about them.

After supper, when Ma and her two stepsisters sat around the cook fire, and Callie had just finished washing up the dishes, someone approached from the wagon train across the meadow. Lydia pointed. "Looks like we've got company."

Ma looked toward the lone figure and frowned. "I do believe it's one of those women wearing pants."

"Bloomers, Ma," said Lydia.

Ma's lips tightened. "I don't want to talk to such a woman. I'm going in the wagon."

She half rose, but before she could retreat, the woman waved and cried a friendly, "Woo-hoo, everyone!" from halfway across the field. "Are you going or coming?"

"Too late now," said Lydia. "We're going to California," she yelled back.

"Now you've done it." Ma sat back down, brow furrowed in a frown.

The visitor approached. She appeared to be in her thirties, a big, full-bosomed woman with a round, smiling face, wearing a small white cap.

Two young children clung to her short, full skirt that fell to her knees. Below the skirt, a pair of bloomers extended to her ankles. How strange. Never had Callie seen such an outfit.

The woman reached their campfire. "We're going to California too. Hello, I'm Florida Sawyer, and these here are two of my young'uns, Augie and Isaac. There's more where they came from." Without waiting for an invitation, she seated herself on a log by the campfire and thrust her pantalooned legs before her. "Lordy me, it feels good to get the load off." She turned to Ma. "And who might you be?"

Ma's lips pursed, as if she'd bit into a persimmon. Would she be nice? Callie held her breath. Ma could be the soul of politeness when she wanted. She could also get downright nasty with someone she even faintly disliked.

"We are the Whitaker family, Mrs. Sawyer. As my daughter said, we're traveling west to California."

Callie let out her breath. Ma's reply was decidedly cool but at least civil.

If Florida Sawyer noticed Ma's less-than-friendly attitude, she didn't let on. Seeing Ma's gaze travel to her bloomers, she laughed. "I know they look strange, but they're the perfect thing for a woman to wear when she's got to walk clear across the country. You'd be surprised how comfortable they are compared to a long, heavy skirt. You ought to try them sometime."

"That's not likely to happen, Mrs. Sawyer."

Undaunted, Florida continued. "I'm a widow traveling with my brother, two hired hands, and my seven children. My husband, God rest his soul, passed on a short time ago—mind you, after we'd already sold the farm and bought the wagons. He was dead set on moving to Oregon. Then, all of a sudden, he was gone. His heart. One minute we were nearly ready to leave, and the next, there was Henry slumped over the milk pail, stone cold dead. Can you imagine? Left me and the young'uns to fend for ourselves. I didn't know what I was going to do until Luke, that's my brother, stepped in and saved the day. He's a trapper and mountain man, the perfect guide for our wagon train. I don't know what we would have done without him, bless his heart."

"How fortunate for you."

Callie inwardly winced over Ma's abrupt answer to their friendly visitor. How could she be so rude? To cause a distraction, she got to her feet and indicated a pot of coffee next to the campfire. "I believe the coffee's still hot, Mrs. Sawyer. Would you like a cup?"

"Well, I don't mind if I do."

Callie had scarcely picked up the pot when a horseman approached. A man on a horse was one of the most common sights imaginable, yet the graceful, easy manner in which he sat in the saddle held her spellbound. He drew close. He was casually dressed in buckskin. Closer still, he was somewhere in his early thirties with long, dark hair and... Oh, no, the naked man in the river. *It's him.*

He reined to a stop.

"Here's my brother now." Florida's voice filled with pride. "Luke McGraw. Ain't he something? Luke, say hello to the Whitaker family. They're traveling by themselves."

In acknowledgement, Luke briefly touched a finger to the brim of his hat and returned the briefest of smiles. He addressed his sister, "Better come along. Hetty needs you."

Florida threw back her head and laughed. "Hetty always needs me. Luke, you come down here and be nice to these people. Hetty can wait."

Luke gave her a reluctant nod and swung from his horse, performing a graceful dismount that revealed his lean and sinewy body, muscular legs, and broad shoulders.

Lydia stepped forward, cocked her head, fluttered her eyelashes, and thrust out her ample bosom. "So, you're going west, Mister McGraw? Are you going to hunt for gold or go into farming?"

"Don't I wish!" Florida gave her brother a rueful glance. "Luke's a trapper. His idea of a wonderful winter is to live in a lonely log cabin high in the mountains by himself. Can you imagine? Nobody to talk to for months and months, which I'll never understand. Now, out of the kindness of his heart, he's guiding the Ferguson wagon train west. I keep hoping when we get there he'll decide to stay, but he says no, he'd rather be fighting Indians and chasing grizzly bears."

Luke flashed a wry glance at Florida and seated himself beside her. "My sister exaggerates. She's right, though. I've got wandering feet. I wasn't meant to be a farmer or a gold seeker either." One corner of his mouth pulled into a faint smile. "I do better when I'm off by myself."

Lydia came up with her best, most flirty giggle. "Perhaps you should try it. Don't you want to settle down someday and raise a family?"

Don't be so obvious, Lydia. Callie hid her amusement with her stepsister, a silly girl to begin with, vain and rather shallow. Actually, she had every reason to be conceited, with her curly blond locks, blue eyes with long, fringed lashes, and tiny waist.

Luke, apparently realizing he couldn't make a quick getaway, turned his attention to Lydia. "The day I settle down is the day I'm dead."

The arrival of a handsome young man had dispelled Ma's hostile mood. She gave Luke a friendly smile. "This is my oldest daughter, Lydia, Mister

McGraw." She nodded toward her second oldest. "This is my second daughter, Nellie."

Nellie remained seated and managed a barely acceptable greeting. A sullen girl, she contrasted with her flighty sister in temperament as well as looks. She tended to sulk a lot when she didn't get her way.

Luke gave the barest of nods to the sisters. His gaze shifted to Callie as she stood by the fire, coffeepot still in hand. She froze. If he said anything about their meeting by the stream, she'd die of embarrassment.

He didn't. Instead, with an interested nod of his head, he asked, "And you are...?"

Callie opened her mouth to speak, but before she could, Ma replied in an offhand way, "That's Callie. She's my stepdaughter."

If Luke noticed the contrast in introductions, he didn't let on. Solemn-faced, with only the slightest hint of a twinkle in his eyes, he looked at Callie. "Haven't we met before?"

"I don't believe so." Warmth crept over her cheeks and she wanted nothing more than to run and hide.

"Callie, if you're going to pour the coffee, then pour it. And offer Mister McGraw a cup."

Grateful for the diversion, Callie busied herself serving coffee to their guests. She hardly noticed Ma's pointed reference to her being a stepdaughter, not a daughter. Long ago she'd learned her place in the Whitaker household, which was somewhere between unwanted stepchild and lowly servant. She should be grateful just to have a roof over her head and three meals a day. Grateful forever, she supposed, although every once in a while she gave some thought to the fact she was now twenty-two, old enough to have a family of her own. Not often, though. Working from dawn to dusk on the Whitaker farm hadn't left much time for contemplation.

Night had fallen. Florida pointed across the meadow, where the glow from a large campfire cut through the darkness. "See our campfire? We have one every night when the day has gone well and the weather's good. We sing, dance, play games, tell jokes and stories. Oh, we have grand time! One of the reasons I came over here was to invite you over to join us."

Lydia clapped her hands. "We'd love to come!"

Callie was about to echo her words when Pa, quiet until now, stepped forward.

A tall man with big square hands and massive shoulders, he gave the appearance of strength and rigidity, a man not likely to change his opinion. Like most older men in the train, he wore a bushy beard, which he seldom trimmed, wool pants held up by suspenders, a cotton shirt, and a wide-brimmed, round-crowned hat. The stiff way he held himself said it all. "This family doesn't hold with such frivolities, Mrs. Sawyer."

Ma nodded. "My husband's absolutely right. We keep to ourselves, so thank you, but we can't accept your invitation."

Callie wasn't surprised Lydia made no attempt to appeal her father's decision. She knew better. In the Whitaker family, Pa's word was law. None of them would dare disobey, although Callie was tempted to speak up. For once, it would have been nice to sit with people who were laughing and having a good time. The farmhouse where they'd lived in Tennessee had been isolated with only a few neighbors, none of them close by. She suspected Pa had wanted it that way. Aside from a monthly shopping trip, they had gone into town only on Sunday to attend church. Afterward, they had returned straight home, never joining any of the social activities. No picnics or parties, and certainly not the dances.

Another ripple of laughter filtered from across the field, causing Callie an odd twinge of disappointment. Yes, it would have been very nice indeed.

Soon after, Florida and her brother Luke bid them good-bye. The jovial woman left with a friendly wave of her hand. "If you folks change your minds, come on over."

Luke mounted his horse and followed, touching his hand to the brim of his hat. His eyes didn't seek Callie's. Why should they when Lydia was around? She was the beauty of the family. Nellie's dark looks weren't nearly as attractive, marred by a figure like Ma's, short-waisted and on the heavy side. Callie had no way to compare herself to her stepsisters. Pa didn't believe in the vanity of a full-length mirror, so she'd never seen her whole self reflected. Judging from Lydia's tiny, hidden scrap of a mirror, she had brown hair, maybe with a touch of red, which she pulled straight back into a bun and paid little attention to. Her face didn't seem remarkable in any way with its straight little nose and brown, wide-set eyes. Maybe not so bad—a face neither startlingly beautiful nor horribly ugly. *I wish Luke had at least glanced at me again.* She pictured how he had looked, standing in the creek in the altogether, an image that sent an unfamiliar tingle down her spine. Am I crazy? No man would look at her once, let alone twice. She wasn't much better than a servant girl and should be grateful for her keep. It wouldn't be fitting for her to forget her place and start getting grand ideas.

Gold Rush Bride

Letitia Tinsley's well-ordered spinster life is thrown into chaos when she learns her beloved brother has mysteriously disappeared from his gold mining claim in California. Determined to discover the truth, Letty sets out on the treacherous journey west. But there's only one thing more perilous than a single lady traveling alone into the rugged frontier—and that is sharing the passage with Garth Morgan. The wealthy bachelor is astoundingly arrogant—and dangerously handsome. Worse, Letty is forced to lean on his strong shoulders, again and again . . .

Humbled by the harrowing expedition, Garth resolves to keep Letty safe—though the courageous beauty is unwilling to give an inch when it comes to trusting him. Still, despite her defiant resistance, he's ready to stand with her as she faces the truth about her missing sibling. And by the time they reach California, Garth is determined to stake his own claim on the lovely Miss Letty—if only she will let him . . .

Wagon Train Sisters

After the death of her abusive husband, Sarah Gregg is free to join her family along with thousands of others in the nation's westward march for gold. But in the middle of the hard journey, Sarah's younger sister, Florrie, disappears. Devastated by the family's failed attempts to find her missing sister, Sarah now wants only to settle into a quiet, uneventful life when she reaches California . . .

But Jack McCoy, a drifter and one-time gambler riding along their wagon train, sees so much more for Sarah. In the roaring mining town of Gold Creek his attentive persistence points Sarah toward new vistas. Then unexpected news of Florrie arrives—and it's worse than anyone expected. But driven by a new hopefulness, Sarah seeks help from Jack, despite his troubled past. The two have traveled a rough road together, and only their hearts can tell them where they are headed . . .

Meet the Author

Shirley Kennedy was born and raised in Fresno, California. She lived in Canada for many years and graduated from the University of Calgary, Alberta, Canada, with a B.S. in computer science. She has published novels with Ballantine, Signet, and several smaller presses. She writes in several different genres including Regency romance, western romance, and contemporary fiction. She lives in Las Vegas, Nevada, and is an active member of the Romance Writers of America, Las Vegas chapter.

Please visit Shirley at www.shirleykennedy.com,
or follow her Twitter account @ladyk360, or on Facebook at
https://www.facebook.com/shirley.kennedy.52.